THE LONDON SEASON WAS AT ITS HEIGHT

and Ian Carmichael, Duke of Portmaine, was frantically casting about for any excuse to escape the onerous task of escorting his betrothed, the lovely Miss Felicity Trammerley, to every boring fête the town had to offer. To Felicity's anger and dismay, Ian found the answer in a sudden Scottish inheritance and departed posthaste to claim his earldom.

Felicity, not to be robbed of her pleasure, was soon chasing after Ian, determined to lure him back to London to play his proper role. But she hadn't counted on the presence of Ian's new ward, Brandy Robertson. Brandy was everything Felicity was not—charmingly straightforward, innocent, and captivated by Ian's personality rather than his position. And when the spoiled London lady met the untamed Scottish beauty, sparks were bound to fly. . . .

The Generous Earl

The Generous Earl

by
Catherine Coulter

Ⓢ
A SIGNET BOOK
NEW AMERICAN LIBRARY
TIMES MIRROR

Copyright © 1981 by Catherine Coulter

SIGNET, SIGNET CLASSICS, MENTOR, PLUME, MERIDIAN and NAL
BOOKS are published by The New American Library, Inc.,
1633 Broadway, New York, New York 10019

First Printing, July, 1981

1 2 3 4 5 6 7 8 9

PRINTED IN THE UNITED STATES OF AMERICA

Publisher's Note

TO GEZA

ᔥ 1 ᔥ

The Honorable Miss Felicity Trammerley, eldest daughter of the Earl of Braecourt, had long ago determined in her own mind exactly what was due to her, particularly from her betrothed, the Duke of Portmaine. That he believed her a docile, rather malleable young lady, was an impression that it had taken her no little pains to achieve, but it was a part she found at times trying. Particularly at the moment, after the duke had explained the purpose of his visit to her. Although she had succeeded in bringing him to the mark, their engagement having only the previous week been formally announced in the *Gazette*, she sensed that she must still tread lightly in reacting to his most recent display of selfish, and in her view, freakish behavior.

"My dear Ian," she began, "to be sure I am much delighted about the inheritance, even though it is but a Scottish title and estate. But I fail to understand any urgency in your traveling now, in the midst of the season, to inspect some moldering old castle that has probably been close to ruin for the past hundred years! Surely, the turrets will not crumble if you postpone your trip until the summer. No one could expect you to forego your more pleasurable pursuits for such an absurd reason."

She did not add that her own pleasurable pursuits were very much intertwined with his, for the umbrella of his consequence as a wealthy and powerful peer had made her a very sought after young lady, now that they were affianced and she was the accepted future Duchess of Portmaine.

Ian Charles Curlew Carmichael, 5th Duke of Portmaine, regarded the frail, altogether delightful specimen of womanhood seated before him with an indulgent look in his dark eyes. "No, you are quite correct, Felicity, no one would expect such an excess of landlordly zeal—no one save myself. If I take my leave from London within the week, I should not be gone above a month. I trust that you will understand, my dear. I cannot simply turn my back on my obligations, no matter if they must intrude upon other, more interesting pursuits." Actually, he thought, it was more to the point that he would willingly escape for an even lesser motive, as the prospect of having to attend the endless round of assemblies and routs during the season was distasteful to him.

Miss Trammerley felt herself go quite stiff at his concise and autocratic dismissal of her concerns. She carefully swallowed her acid words and said, with reasonable good humor, "But, Ian, you have told me yourself that you do not even know these people. And you know the Scots—hateful barbarians! I cannot imagine that they would welcome an Englishman. Can you not dispatch Jerkin, your solicitor, to handle your affairs?"

The duke gazed into the soft leaf-green eyes, slightly slanted at the corners, eyes that reminded him so much of his first wife's. "It is likely that you are quite correct in your opinion, my dear. But I feel it is my duty to at least visit Penderleigh Castle and determine what must be done with the place. After all, these hateful barbarians, as you call them, are related to me, albeit somewhat removed in blood lines. The title comes to me through my great aunt, whom, I understand, still lives at Penderleigh. I regret to leave you alone during the height of the social whirl—" he had the grace to avoid looking at her directly as he spoke this blatant untruth—"but you can trust Giles to take you about wherever you wish. Such a gay fellow he is, as you well know, and you do not even seem to mind in the least that he is in grave danger of becoming a pluming peacock of a macaroni!"

Miss Trammerley held Mr. Giles Braidston, the duke's cousin, in fashionable esteem and believed his mode of dress far more elegant than the overly simple styles affected by the duke. And Giles, with his slender, far more slight frame, seemed less overpowering than the duke. She felt a sudden flush burn her cheeks, recalling her brother, Lord Sayer's, coarse teasing about the duke when he was informed of her betrothal. He had tweaked her chin in that hearty, loathsome way of his, all the while allowing his laughing gaze to flit over her petite figure. "Well, little puss," he had said, " 'tis a man mountain who will be your husband! I bravely took him on in the ring the other day, saw him stripped, you know. All hard muscle, my dear, not a patch of fat on him! Most *noble* proportions. I vow you'll have a lusty wedding night with him!"

Felicity quickly averted her eyes, realizing that she had been gazing at Ian with embarrassed trepidation. She repeated to herself stoutly that Ian was, after all, a duke. Being a duchess would certainly have its compensations. She managed to regard him with complaisance, knowing well enough that she would not be wise to protest his decision further. She had seen often enough how he would withdraw from her at any hint of opposition to his opinions. She drew herself up confidently. When she became the Duchess of Portmaine, her influence could not help but curb the duke's more undesirable inclinations. She forced a trembling smile to her curved lips. "You know that I shall miss you dreadfully, Ian."

The duke rose from the rose brocade settee and clasped Miss Trammerley's slender fingers. "I shall miss you too, my dear. I am delighted that you understand my reasons. I shall not be gone long, you will see."

Miss Trammerley had actually not understood his reasons at all, but forebore to say more on the topic. She allowed the duke to plant a light kiss upon her proffered cheek. As he prepared to take his leave, she said in a wistful voice, "August seems an eternity away, Ian. A full six months until our wedding."

A vivid image of his first wife, Marianne, rose uninvited to his mind. That lady was indeed an eternity away from him. He looked down at Felicity, in whose company he had rediscovered pleasures that had long since been missing from his life. She bore a striking resemblance to Marianne, and as he had come to know her better, he had seen more and more the same gentleness and modesty. He could not deny that it was time for him to marry again; it was expected, and he was in need of an heir. He reminded himself how lucky he was to have a Marianne and a Felicity come into his life. He gazed at her a moment longer, then took his leave.

Later that day, in the drawing room of the Portmaine townhouse, Mr. Giles Braidston twirled the delicate stem of his sherry glass between his slender fingers, remarking as he did so to his cousin, the Duke of Portmaine, "Felicity informs me that you've determined to travel to Scotland. Rather a trying adventure, I should say. Of course, you realize that she is, shall we say, rather perturbed about your decision."

Ian was leaning over a large oak desk, scrutinizing a map of Scotland. "Bedamned, Giles, as far as I can tell, I must allow a full five days to reach Penderleigh Castle. And from what I understand, the roads are rutted paths, more suited for sheep than for carriages. It's near to Berwick on Tweed, on the eastern coast. I'm sorry, old fellow, what did you say?"

"Your betrothed, Ian, and her crochets."

Ian turned a jaundiced eye toward his cousin. "If she has sent you to add your five pence worth of argument against the trip, I beg you to refrain."

"I wouldn't dream of it, Ian! You shall go to that mucking, squalid country and I . . . well, I shall enjoy the fruits of your absent consequence. Being your nominal heir has its benefits, you know."

The duke thought of the pile of bills he had instructed Pabbson, his secretary, to pay for Giles not above a month ago. He was fond of his fashionable cousin, and did not begrudge Giles's occasional dipping into his much larger till. Thank God Giles wasn't addicted to the gaming tables, but only to silver buttons and outlandish waistcoats. He said aloud, "Do just as you please with my consequence, Giles. The only favor I ask of you is to see to Felicity. Since you are my cousin, the gossiping tabbies cannot find fault with you as her escort. She dearly loves town life, just as did Mari—" The duke quickly averted his gaze from his cousin's alert eyes and finished hastily, "If she wishes her routs and balls, I do not want her to be disappointed."

Giles said shrewdly, "It seems to me, Ian, that your trip to Scotland is exquisitely timed. A rather drastic measure, I should say, to avoid the season and all its flittering about."

The duke looked thoughtful for a moment. He carefully

rolled up his map of Scotland and fastened it with a short length of ribbon. "Methinks, Giles, that you sometimes see too much. If you would know the truth of the matter, I should have to admit that my motives for traveling to Penderleigh are not quite as laudable as I made them seem to Felicity. True, it is my duty to see to the place, and I do have some curiosity about my Robertson relatives, but if you would know, the thought of squiring another betrothed about for the length of the season leaves me quite cold. Indeed, if I were never again in London for the season, I would by no means be cast down!"

"How wise of you, cousin, not to tell Felicity as much. Lord, would that put a flea in her ear."

"I warrant you that she would be disappointed, Giles, but her natural amiability and modesty would prevent her from flying into the boughs."

Giles could not repress an incredulous look. "Good God, Ian, I grant you that Felicity bears a striking physical resemblance to Marianne, but all similarity ends there. Incidently, Felicity has told me that you resolutely refuse to speak with her about your first wife. It is natural, I think, for her to have some curiosity about Marianne."

The duke stiffened and his voice sounded more harsh than he intended. "Felicity will know exactly what I wish to tell her, Giles, and I have told her that I have a great fondness for girls of her general coloring."

"Lord, Ian, isn't it enough that most of your mistresses over the last seven years have been endowed with black hair and green eyes? If Felicity ever discovers that fact, you will soon learn the extent of her gentle nature." He threw up his hands as Ian's eyes darkened. "Acquit me of mischief, Ian, I will say no more on the matter. If you wish to marry Felicity, for whatever reason, who am I to gainsay you?"

"I thank you, Giles," the duke said sarcastically, "for your concise opinions. As for Felicity's character, I daresay that she will become whatever I wish her to be, if, that is, she is not already exactly what I require in a wife." No sooner were the rather pompous, arrogant words out of his mouth than he regretted them. He abruptly changed the subject.

"You must know, Giles, that poor old Mabley has not ceased in his predictions of doom. I told him that if he did not wish to accompany me, being an older man and perhaps not quite up to it, I would take Japper. That quite set him on his ear! Told me I'd like as not forget my waistcoat and cravat if he wasn't there to remind me. He still cannot think of me as a man grown despite my thirty years."

Mr. Braidston unconsciously fingered his own flawlessly displayed cravat. Although nature had not seen fit to endow him with his cousin's grand height or broad shoulders, he believed that he presented a far more elegant picture. In his view, Ian was a dull dog, much too serious by half, and his attire illuminated the fact.

"Mabley is an old man, Ian. Valet to your father, wasn't he? Time to put him out to pasture, I'd say."

How very like Giles, the duke thought, to think only of the benefits of a title and wealth, without any concern for its responsibilities. He said only, "No, I think not, Giles. I daresay that I should be as lost without him as he would be without innumerable pairs of hessians to polish. But enough of my time honored valet. Did Felicity tell you of the roundabout manner in which I have succeeded the Earl of Penderleigh?"

"She mentioned something of a great aunt, an Englishwoman. I am loathe to say that she quite lost interest in the subject when a new ball gown arrived from Madame Flauquet. She wanted my opinion of the gown, of course."

A slight grimace pulled at the corners of the duke's mouth. "Well, I have no waistcoats that require your opinion, so you have no choice but to attend me. Not, of course, that I know all that much."

Mr. Braidston waved his monocle and settled back against the settee, a look of gentle suffering setting comically on his face. "I await with heart apounding," he said languidly.

Ian had no time to continue, for at that moment James, his butler, gently opened the double doors. "Excuse me, your grace. A Dr. Edward Mulhouse is here to see you."

"Edward! Good God, it's been months! Show him in, James."

"You remember Edward Mulhouse, don't you, Giles? I fancy that with him I'll have a more attentive audience."

Edward Mulhouse strode into the drawing room, his tanned, lean face alight with pleasure. He was nattily dressed, though not as elegantly as Mr. Braidston, a fact that Giles quickly noted.

"Edward, how delightful, old fellow!" The two gentlemen shook hands and Ian clapped his friend's slender shoulders. "However did all your patients allow you to escape from Suffolk?"

"There was naught but one lame horse when I left, Ian. I'm here visiting my father and thought I would drop by to see you."

"Excellent. Edward, you remember, of course, my cousin, Giles Braidston?

"Indeed I do. A pleasure to see you again."

Giles suffered having his hand gripped in a manful clasp and said with a sigh, "Do sit down, Edward. There are now two of us that Ian can bore to flinders!"

"Dog," Ian said amiably. "If you must know, Edward, I have just come into an earldom in Scotland and was in the process of telling Giles here how it all came about." He handed Edward a glass of sherry. "But first, my friend, does all go well at Carmichael Hall? Is Davers still his same stiff, crotchety old self?"

Without a trace of envy, Edward pictured the duke's Suffolk estate, Carmichael Hall, and its many inhabitants. "Davers is just as you describe him. I swear, Ian, your butler many times makes me feel as though he's the master. His dignity tends to be overwhelming!"

"Ian keeps him on to bolster his consequence."

"Untrue, Giles, 'tis you who does all the necessary bolstering."

Conversation continued in this vein for some minutes before Edward cocked his head to one side and said, "Enough of Carmichael Hall, London, the king, and everyone's consequence! What is all of this about a Scottish earldom, Ian?"

"Oh," moaned Giles, "I had thought he would forget."

"Narry a chance, Giles. 'Tis a pity that I have so few facts, for I would like to string out the telling for your benefit."

Giles rolled his eyes heavenward, but the duke ignored him, and for a moment, he appeared lost in his thoughts, his long fingers stroking the firm line of his jaw.

"It's curious, really," he said finally. "I come to the estate and title through my great aunt, my grandmother's only sister, who, as I understand it, married Angus Robertson soon after Bonnie Prince Charlie's final and last bid for the throne." He paused a moment and cast a twinkling eye toward his cousin. "The lowland Robertsons are not, of course, to be confused with the highland Robertsons."

"Indeed not," Giles said dryly. "Never would I have put the two together."

"All that I know from my English solicitor is that there are no Scottish male relatives to inherit, the only son remaining to the earl having died in seventeen-ninety-five, leaving three daughters."

Mr. Braidston yawned delicately. "Ancient history is such a bore, do you not agree, Edward?" At Edward's rueful grin, Giles added, "Thank God, Ian, that you have brought us quickly to the present. I do not suppose that you informed Felicity about this multitude of females. That would make her less complacent, I vow."

"As to Felicity's complacency, Giles, from my understanding, all the females in question are children, at least that is what I inferred from my great aunt's letter."

Edward Mulhouse looked startled. "What? The old woman is still alive?"

"Very much so. She must be at least seventy years old now, I would venture."

Mr. Braidston rose, and allowed a look of commiseration to darken his face. "Poor Ian! Playing nursemaid to an old harridan and guardian to a gaggle of brats! Well, I must be off, old fellow. I'll leave poor Edward here as you contemplate your fate!"

"A new waistcoat awaits your inspection, Giles?"

"Indeed it does," Mr. Braidston responded in all seriousness. "I must decide if the yellow stripes will be best complemented by gold or silver buttons." Giles turned to Edward. "Do call on me in Brook Street. Ian, here, is journeying to Scotland before the end of the week."

"Off with you, fop! Hopefully, I shall see you again within the month."

"I do hope that your reception in Scotland will not be unpleasant," Edward said after Giles had been shown from the drawing room by James. "Even though it's been fifty years or so since Culloden, I understand that the Scots do not in general look favorably upon their English neighbors."

The duke said quietly, "I have thought about that, Edward. I have decided to take only Mabley with me. Whatever their attitudes toward the English, I have no wish to be taken into immediate dislike with any display of unnecessary consequence. Damn Giles anyway! Trust him to ring a peal over me with an old harridan and a gaggle of girls! Now, enough of my affairs, Edward. Tell me, which of London's more infamous fleshpots would you like to frequent during your visit?"

Actually, Edward had composed a quite impressive list, as his visits to London were few and far between.

"Good God, Edward," the duke said when his friend had finished, "you'll have me quitting London with a head so dizzy with brandy that it will take me the entire journey to recover!"

~ 2 ~

Lady Adella Wycliff Robertson, Dowager Countess of Penderleigh, lifted her worn ebony cane and waved its blunted tip toward her granddaughter. "Come, child, I won't have ye slouching about in that hoydenish way! Though ye bear the Robertson name, there's still English blood in yer veins and that makes ye a lady. Ladies don't slouch, do ye hear?"

"Aye, Grandmama," Brandy said, and perfunctorily squared her shoulders. The dowager's large, circular sitting room admitted chilling drafts that made her want to huddle into a round ball for warmth. Even though the stone walls were covered with ancient thick wool tapestries, they had long ago been permeated to their fiber by the damp cold from the sea. Occasionally, Brandy saw the frayed edges of the tapestries billow forward as the harsh sea winds whistled through the cragged castle stones. She inched closer to the fire in the age-blackened hearth.

"Is the new earl really an English duke, Grandmama?"

"That he is, child. As I've told ye, his grandmother was my only sister." She snorted. "She was weak, had pap for blood and water for spirit! Lord, what separate paths we traveled. . . ."

Lady Adella's voice trailed off and Brandy realized that her grandmother was far away from her, many misty years in the past. She waited patiently for a few moments, then leaned forward and shook her grandmother's billowy black sleeve. "Grandmama, do ye think he will come to Penderleigh?"

"He?" Lady Adella straightened and focused her faded blue eyes upon her granddaughter. "Och, the duke. Come here, ye say?" She curled her lips. " 'Tis not likely, child. I

10

would imagine, if anything, he will send one of those horse-faced men of business in their shiny black suits to poke about. An absent English master is what we'll have, Brandy, who will care only to increase our rents."

Brandy's expressive face turned stormy. "But, 'tis ridiculous! We have no rents! Why, our crofters would starve were it not for the fishing. Grandmama, ye must be wrong—the blood in my veins that makes me a lady, it can't be English."

Lady Adella sat back and drummed her arthritic fingers on the curved handle of her cane. She could not hate the English, for she was one of them. Still, she could not forget Culloden, and the years of vicious English reprisals, the devastation of crofts and manors alike, the destruction of the once proud clans. She had managed to save the Robertsons, not the highland branch, to be sure, for the Duke of Cumberland had sworn to crush them beneath the heel of his boot. Until nearly ten years ago, even the innocent bagpipes were forbidden, the English masters reasoning that the sad, harsh sounds might reunite the clans, calling forth their now far distant glory. Yes, she thought, she was still English to her bones, despite the more than fifty years spent in this isolated, forbidding castle on the eastern sea. She drew a deep sigh and said slowly, "Nay, child, I was wrong to castigate the English duke. He is of my blood and thus also of yours. Time will show what kind of man he is."

She watched Brandy's amber-hued eyes narrow and her slender nostrils flare in disdain. At least the girl had pride, not from the weak, willful Robertsons, but from her. If only she had been born a boy, how very different everything would be now. There would be no Englishman to lay claim to a Scottish title and estate.

Brandy suddenly uncoiled her arms and legs and came up to rest upon her knees, never losing her balance on the small square pillow at her grandmother's feet. She stretched languidly, pulled her arms above her head, and arched her back.

Lady Adella blinked, seeing her with new eyes. Although she could not be certain, it seemed that the girl's breasts were straining against the bodice of her old blue muslin gown, the slender line of her waist unmistakable against the arch of her back. Somehow the years had escaped her. Brandy must have

11

long since begun her monthly cycle. Lady Adella frowned. "How old are ye, child?"

Brandy swung around at her grandmother's words, the two heavy blond braids falling forward to touch the faded carpet. "Why, Grandmama, I am turned seventeen—last Michaelmas, do ye not remember?"

"Of course I remember," Lady Adella snapped. "Do ye think me a senile old woman?"

"Nay, Grandmama. Stubborn and imperious, but never senile."

"See that ye don't, miss!" Lady Adella said obscurely. She closed her eyes and settled back into the soft cushions of her favorite chair. Seventeen . . . eighteen next Michaelmas. Marriageable age, she was. And there was Constance. Lord, she must be all of fifteen now. And little Fiona, not so very small now. Lady Adella ticked off years in her mind. Sniveling little Emily, dying in childbed with Fiona . . . why that was all of six years ago, the same year the ridiculous French were busily slaughtering each other. Amiable and weak Clive, her second son, left to himself with three daughters. How disconsolate he had been, before he, too, had died.

Brandy pulled her tartan shawl again over her slender shoulders and tied it with her usual sturdy knot. It would be her constant companion until the end of April, when the heather burst into purple bloom. She smiled in anticipation of the warm, breezy spring weather, though even then the sea currents sometimes chilled the winds as they swept across the rocky cliffs. Perhaps she would be lucky enough to find a patch of white heather this year—'twas said to bring one good fortune. She wriggled her cramped toes and shifted her position. She knew not to interrupt Grandmama whilst she was in one of her reminiscing moods. She thought of her grandfather, and felt a twinge of sadness that he was gone, yet, she was forced to admit to herself, she hadn't been particularly fond of him. He was even crustier and bawdier than the rest of the family, delighting, she sometimes thought, at making her blush scarlet at his coarse jests. What a pity it was that he had died resolutely refusing to reconsider Uncle Claude's disinheritance. If only Uncle Claude could have been the next Earl of Penderleigh, there would be no English stranger coming to take their lands.

Brandy glanced up at the ancient clock that sat precariously on the mantlepiece. Nearly four o'clock and time for tea, a tradition that Lady Adella had firmly established over her husband's grumbling some fifty years ago. She tuned her ears to Crabbe's familiar heavy wooden step.

A knock sounded on the oaken door.

"Grandmama."

The glazed look fell slowly from Lady Adella's eyes. "Och, tea time, is it?" She raised her voice. "Well, come in, Crabbe!"

The tall, stout Crabbe, a silver tea service held gently in his hands, strode into the sitting room. Cousin Percival stood behind him.

"Master Percival be here to see yer ladyship," Crabbe said, quite unnecessarily.

Brandy watched with a sinking heart as Lady Adella's parchment features cracked into a wide smile. 'Twas always so. Brandy shivered and rose slowly to her feet, retreating to stand behind her grandmother's high-backed chair. She disliked Percy intensely, not only because he cozened Lady Adella so shamelessly but also because she had begun to fear him. Last Michaelmas, at her birthday, he had begun to stare at her oddly, his hooded green eyes stangely intense.

Lady Adella said, "Come, Crabbe, don't stand there like a dolt! The tea tray sets on the table as it has for the past fifty years. That's right. Now ye may take yerself off . . . and tell Cook that I have no wish to see another tureen of lentil and rice soup this evening!"

Having thus disposed of Crabbe, Lady Adella turned to Percival and waved her cane in the direction of a faded green velvet settee opposite her.

"Well, my boy, 'tis about time ye present yerself. Sit down, sit down. Brandy, child, pour the tea. My fingers are stiff as my cane today."

Brandy slithered self-consciously from behind her grandmother's chair. She reached down to clutch the silver handle of the teapot when Percy's hand covered her wrist.

"Good day to ye, little cousin. You are looking . . . well." His hand tightened about her wrist and she felt his fingers gently stroke the palm of her hand.

"Good day to ye too, cousin," she said sharply, and jerked her hand free of his hold.

He laughed softly and tweaked her chin. She felt angry color suffuse her face and turned abruptly away.

"My dear Grandmother, how do ye contrive to grow more fair by the year?" He bowed low and planted a light kiss atop her blue-veined hand.

"Ye are a dog, Percy, my boy." The pleasure in her voice belied the sharpness of her words. "Ye didn't come when I bid ye. Three months late to offer yer condolences. Were the truth to be told, it surprises me even now that ye would forego all yer dissipations in Edinburgh!"

" 'Tis in a most unkind light ye cast me, lady! Ye must know that the passing of Lord Angus must bring all his saddened relations sooner or later back to this heap of damp stone to pay their respects."

"Ye talk fustian, young jackanapes!"

"Yer tea, Cousin Percy."

"Ah, a bright light amid the dismal shadows! My thanks, little cousin. Ye grow more and more like the fair anemones waiting to be plucked."

"Yer attempt at simile sets wrong with the child, Percy," Lady Adella said sharply, realizing with a sour start that Percy's practiced masculine eye had observed the womanly changes in Brandy before she had.

"Grandmama, may I be excused now? I promised to go for a walk with Constance and Fiona."

"Aye, child, ye may, but mind ye not to be late."

Brandy dipped an awkward curtsy toward her cousin, picked up her skirts, and fled. She thought she heard a chuckle as she slipped from the room.

"Not so much a child anymore, lady," Percy said with sufficient loudness that Brandy caught his words from the corridor.

"Don't flirt with the girl, Percy! She's far too young yet and inexperienced to glean yer meaning." She locked her stiff fingers about the cup handle and took a noisy sip of the scalding tea. She saw his hooded green eyes narrow, as if in a challenge, and smiled to herself. Aye, all Robertson males were the same!

"To yer continued immortality, lady," Percy said, raising his cup.

Lady Adella gave a parchment laugh. "Aye, indeed! I swore that I would cleave to this world longer than Angus. He was exceedingly furious when the doctor told him that he was dying. If there had been any money left, I swear he would have burned it rather than leave it in my hands!"

"Poor old Grandfather! I do wonder how he feels now, roasting in Hades!" Percy smoothed the bitter sarcasm from his voice. "At least now I can visit Penderleigh at my leisure."

"That ye can, Percy." Lady Adella paused for a long moment, eyeing him speculatively. "What would ye say, my boy, if I were to make ye legitimate?"

Percy felt his blood suddenly pounding at his temples, but there was wariness in his voice. "Ye think to make up for years upon years of slights, lady? Old Angus must assuredly curse ye from his grave!"

"A fond thought, I can't deny. But ye can't be blind to the advantages it would bring ye."

"Advantages?" Percy sneered. "Mayhap it would bring me a better chance of wedding an heiress, but 'twould gain me naught here. The English duke would still have claim to Penderleigh and the title, would he not?"

"Perhaps, my boy, but ye then would also have full claim to the Robertson name. I have not liked Davonan's son called the Robertson bastard. Come, Percy, don't glare at me. Ye know that I've never been one to mince matters or deny a truth! Who can know what may happen if ye become legitimized? Well, do ye want it or not?"

Percy thought of the rather squat, myopic Joanna MacDonald, daughter and heiress of a wealthy merchant in Edinburgh. Unless his instincts had grossly misled him, she was much enamored with him. Her stiff-lipped father would not be able to deny him. He smiled at Lady Adella, his full, sensuous lips curving into a boyish grin. "Aye, Grandmama, I should like much to be legitimate. I suspect even my creditors would be properly impressed." He added thoughtfully, "I do wonder what would happen to my claim to Penderleigh if my name were secured."

"Mayhap ye should wonder what would happen were the English duke not to produce an heir?"

"Or if the English duke were to fall ill, say . . . and not survive."

Lady Adella regarded her grandson with a malicious eye. "Och, my boy, the English duke is, I believe, rather young-ish—too young to depart this world without some outside assistance. As to heirs, the duke may already be wed and have a nursery full of hopeful brats!'

Percy gave a flippant wave of his shapely hand. "Acquit me of murderous designs, lady! I have raised a question of speculative interest."

Lady Adella snorted in disgust. "Aye, and a question our dear Claude's son, Bertrand, would ask, were he not so lily-livered! One illegitimate grandson and one disinherited grand nephew! Angus bedamned! He was always a fool and stub-born as a donkey in a hay field. I will tell ye, Percy, if I make ye legitimate and reinherit Claude and Bertrand, the English duke might very well find his soup poisoned even if he doesn't budge from London!"

"Ye speak nonsense, Grandmama. Angus would never have reinherited Claude and Bertrand. Ye make me legiti-mate, and 'tis I who will have claim, after the English duke."

"Aye, it disgruntles ye to think about Claude and Bertrand, eh, lad? 'Tis like dust in the wind yer claim would be were I to reinherit Douglass's son." She shrugged her thin shoulders, all the while watching him closely. "Time will tell, Percy, about yer claim—time and me, of course."

For a moment, Percy gazed at Lady Adella in dumb sur-prise. Why the old woman is like a great bloated spider, he thought, weaving her web and taunting me to come into it. Does she want all of us at each other's throats? Rather, he quickly corrected himself, does she want me at their throats? He consciously pulled himself away. For the moment, he hoped that she would make him legitimate. He rose and clasped Lady Adella's hand.

"I will stay, if ye do not mind, until all this business is straightened out. When I return to Edinburgh, I have a fancy to carry my legitimate name with me."

"As ye will, Percy," Lady Adella said, seeming to lose in-terest in the matter. "Tell Crabbe to have MacPherson fetched here on the morrow and I shall tell the old crow what to do."

"Aye, Grandmama," Percy said, and turned to take his leave.

"Percy."

He turned. "Aye?"

"Brandy will have naught to do with ye. She's much too much the child yet and doesn't know what use to make of men." She saw the suppressed gleam in his eyes as she nodded dismissal, and wondered if he knew how much like he was to the grandfather he hated so much.

Alone, Lady Adella parted her lips in a smug grin, revealing most of her remaining teeth. She knew something of the law, and now that Angus had finally left the world to take up residence with the devil, she fully intended to stir the legal pot to boiling. Old MacPherson would do her bidding, no fear about that. She would legitimize Percy and aye, perhaps even reinherit Claude and Bertrand. As to what the English duke would think about her machinations, she shrugged her scrappy shoulders. He was, after all, safely stored away in faraway London.

She gazed down at the small square pillow at her feet, Brandy's pillow. Her granddaughter, with the curves and hollows of a woman's body. Lady Adella thwacked her cane in annoyance. Three granddaughters, none of them with any prospects and even less dowry! Absurd thought to believe that the unknown English duke, although now the girls' nominal guardian, would freely part with some of his guineas for some unknown Scottish relatives. Even though she admitted to herself that it was an outlandish idea, she did not relinquish it. Time would tell, and she would be there to help in the telling.

At least Percy would be able to fend for himself, once she had seen to legitimizing him. Handsome and carefree he was—exactly as she had been once, many a long year ago. Drat Davonan anyway for not at least giving Percy's mother his name! But then Davonan had always been odd. She remembered how delighted she had been to hear that Davonan had even lain with a woman. But it hadn't lasted, of course. Not a year later, he'd gone off with a brawny Irishman, leaving her to care for his small, helpless son. She won-

17

dered idly, with no pain now, if Davonan had really gone willingly to the guillotine with his French lover, a dissolute comte who had deserved to have his worthless head severed from his decadent body. At least Percy had not inherited *that* tendency from his father!

Lady Adella slewed her head about toward the clock. Time to call Old Marta to assist her to dress for dinner. She gave a sudden cackle of laughter. Old Marta indeed! A saucy piece that one had been! Thank the lord Angus had never gotten *her* with child.

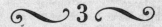

3

Bertrand Robertson hunched over a ledger and moodily chewed on the end of his quill. His only servant, the sharp-eared Fraser, had just told him that Percy had returned. Damned blighter! Well, there was no money for him, so let him cut a wheedle around Lady Adella, he growled to himself.

He forced his eyes back to the stark column of numbers, neatly entered row upon row in the account book. Penderleigh had lost ground this year, what with Angus dying and certain of his creditors demanding payment, and the black-faced sheep's wool bringing only a modicum at market. The English duke was sure to be disgruntled.

He ran ink-stained fingers through the shock of bright red hair that fell habitually over his forehead. A disinherited grand nephew he might be, but old Angus had known his worth and trusted him to eke out every possible groat from the estate. His eyes burned as he gazed down at the scraggly numbers, and he felt a sudden stab of fear. Angus was dead and now he might very well find both himself and his gouty father tossed unceremoniously off Penderleigh land. How would he be able to convince the man of business the English was sure to send that he had tried to force economies, indeed, that the castle and dower house were in a fair way of crumbling about their ears because there were no funds to make repairs?

He glanced up, abstracted, as Fraser, his step soundless despite his rotund body, poked his round face into the small, airless room.

"Master Bertrand, yer father's just heard tell of Master

19

Percival's acomin' to the castle. He be in a tither, if ye ken me meanin'."

"Aye, Fraser. Tell him I shall join him presently."

"Och, 'tis a bad time, wi' Master Percival bein' aboot." Fraser shook his grizzled head, his perennial smile fading a bit.

Bertrand said grimly, "Percival is naught but a buzzing, bothersome fly, Fraser. 'Tis the English duke, our new master, who will tighten the collars about our necks!"

"Be the dook like the Black Cumberland, think ye, master?"

Bertrand laughed humorlessly and rose from his chair. "This isn't seventeen-forty-six, Fraser, and the English duke wasn't born yet! Doubtless though, he's a proud man and, like all the English, disdainful of the Scots. Ye know, of course, 'tis likely he'll dispatch one of his London men here to grub about for more rents."

Fraser's close-set brown eyes, as round as his face, narrowed, but he remained silent. He said finally, "Ye'd best go to yer father's room now, master. I canna be sure, but my ears tell me he's apokin' his stick on the floor. I'll hae some tea brewin' fer ye an' bring it."

"All right, Fraser." Bertrand left the bookroom with a lagging step. As he mounted the rickety stairs to the upper floor of the dower house and his father's dank stuffy bedchamber, he continued to ponder his problems, and with each step he became more depressed.

"Well, don't just stand there, Bertie, come in, come in! By the time it takes Fraser to fetch ye, I am near to forgetting what I wanted!"

"How are ye feeling, Father?" Bertrand asked calmly as he crossed the bare floor to Claude, who sat wrapped from head to toe in a heavy tartan blanket next to a roaring peat fire.

"Ye have eyes in yer head, Bertie," the old man snapped crossly. "My foot's the size of a bloated, rotting dung heap, no thanks to ye!"

Bertand sighed and waited patiently for his father to get to his point.

"Don't stand there blocking out my only sunlight! Sit here, Bertie."

Bertrand obligingly sat himself in a cracked leather winged

chair across from his father. He ran his hand over his forehead, for the blast of heat from the fireplace was making him sweat.

Claude said without preamble, "Ye know, of course, that Percy is come back. The vulture swooping to gnaw the bones afore old Angus is worm-picked in his grave!"

Bertrand sighed. "Father, it makes no difference what Percy does. There's naught but bones for him to gnaw, so much the worse for us. Ye may believe me that Percy is the least of our worries."

Claude raised blazing eyes to his son. "Don't ye treat me like a dim-witted chirper, my fine young man!" The blazing eyes suddenly grew crafty and the wizened cheeks more sunken. "Did ye know that Adella plans to legitimize yer fine bastard cousin?"

"That's ridiculous, Father! Whoever told ye such a buffoonish story?" Bertrand's hands tightened convulsively around the arms of the chair even as he spoke.

The old man cackled and hunched himself forward. A momentary spasm of pain deepened the myriad wrinkles in his cheeks.

"Crabbe told me, Master Prim an' Prissy!" he said roughly, enjoying the whitening of his son's already fair face. "Crabbe is a good man—minds others' business and keeps his ears open! Ye know what that means, don't ye, lad?"

Bertrand shrugged and forced indifference into his voice. "It means that my esteemed great aunt is growing more eccentric."

"Young fool! Take off yer blinders, Bertie! Yer cousin will now be next in line to Penderleigh, if the English duke doesn't yet have heirs."

Claude achieved the result he perversely desired. Bertrand said between gritted teeth, his voice heavy with bitterness, "That bloody bastard! He's taken so much money already from Penderleigh for his own frivolous amusements in Edinburgh. Damn him and damn Lady Adella, 'tis not just!"

Claude seemed to pay no attention to his son's outburst. He leaned back with a crooked grin on his lips and tapped his fingertips together. "And just what would ye say if I told ye Lady Adella also intends to reverse my father's disinheritance?"

For an instant, Bertrand's eyes blazed as brightly as his father's. Penderleigh. How he loved every stone, every crumbling, damp turret! If his father would be reinherited, perhaps some day, he would be Bertrand Douglass Robertson, Earl of Penderleigh . . . he would be the master. Painfully, he brought himself back to a grim present, to hear his father say, "Nay, Lady Adella is a deep 'un, and takes her time. I think it highly likely, though, that she will do it. If she lifts dishonor off one Robertson head, she might as well lift it from ours as well."

"One can't make plans with suppositions, Father. Even if she were to reinherit us, 'twould probably gain us naught. The English duke is bound to have heirs."

"Ye talk like a clothhead, Bertie! First we must lift the curse of our disinheritance, then we shall see."

"She's naught but a senile, old witch who loves to make mischief!"

"Mayhap ye're right, and it is foolish to trust her. But there is heavy guilt upon her soul. Methinks she must make amends afore she dies. I would not doubt that she helped Old Angus to his eternal reward, for she could do naught about either us or Percy as long as the old lout lived."

"*Her* guilt, ye say, Father? Will ye not tell me now why our line was severed? Why did great grandfather disinherit Grandfather Douglass?"

Claude stared for a long moment into the roaring fire. "Nay, boy, I can't tell ye. Mayhap afore I die ye will know the truth of the matter."

"I asked her once, ye know," Bertrand said.

"Ye surprise me, Bertie! What did Adella say to that?"

"She screamed for me to get out. She was quite livid with rage."

"Perhaps ye haven't yer mother's spun-cotton brain. Ye've shown spirit, Bertie. Now, fetch me that damned smiling Fraser. I believe we shall dine tonight at the castle."

"Cousin Percy is so very handsome, do ye not agree, Brandy?"

"Nay, I do not, Constance!" Brandy eyed her younger sister apprehensively. "Connie, please, promise me ye'll not make yerself—forward with Percy." She tried to speak calmly, to control the irritation she felt at both her sister and Percy. Why couldn't Connie see that Percy wasn't to be trusted, that he was a ne'er-do-well and most likely a scoundrel where the ladies were concerned?

Constance fluttered thick dark lashes. "Why, Brandy? Do ye want him for yerself?"

"Connie, for God's sake, don't be such a fool! Of course I don't want him!" She saw that her words made no visible impression and changed her tactics. "Percy is really quite old, ye know. Why he must be nearly thirty!" She shuddered convincingly. "And he drinks so much—'tis likely he'll have gout just like Uncle Claude."

Constance's green eyes widened in patent disbelief and she screwed her full lips into a pout. "Pooh, dear sister! Those long braids ye persist in wearing have addled yer brain. Percy old, indeed!"

Brandy was silent for a long moment. She walked to the edge of the grassy cliff and gazed out to sea. The size of the white tops on the waves, the tide level, and the darkening horizon surely portended a violent early spring storm. She tried to remember if she had tied her small boat firmly to its moorings, for the storm that was brewing would send crashing waves even into the small inlet. " 'Twill blow up strong tonight," she said more to herself than to her sister. She kicked a small pebble off the edge of the cliff and watched it bounce down the narrow rocky path and land in the sand on the beach below. She turned back toward her sister and sank slowly to her knees amid the thick carpet of bluebells and wild anemones that grew in great profusion nearly to the cliff edge. She breathed in the sweet fragrance of the purple-blue flowers and for a moment forgot Percy and her too-grown-up little sister.

"Brandy, do come along! Ye'll get yer skirt stained and Old Marta will complain to Grandmama."

Brandy sighed and slowly rose to her feet. The wind was rising, whipping her skirt about her ankles. She tightened her thick tartan shawl about her shoulders. "Aye, ye're right, Connie. I suppose that since Percy is here, we must change for dinner."

She wished she hadn't mentioned Percy's name, for Constance's pert, oval eyes became instantly sultry, and narrowed in a provocative way.

"Connie, please, ye must not behave so! He is' but our cousin and not at all proper. Besides, ye are but fifteen years old . . . a mere child to him."

She could have cut out her tongue at her unguarded comment. Constance took instant exception, her green eyes flashing. "How dare ye, my *ancient* sister, to call *me* a child! It is ye who wear a child's braids and that disgusting old tartan shawl! No one would ever think of ye as a woman grown, and ye are seventeen! Ye're a jealous cat, Brandy, I know it. Well, I have no intention of shriveling into an old spinster, alone and poor in this beastly place! Stay if ye wish among all the crumbling stone and pick yer stupid wild flowers. I, for one, am going to be a rich and fine lady!"

Constance whipped about, her dark hair swirling about her shoulders, and flounced away from the promontory back toward the castle.

"Connie, wait! I didn't mean what I said!" Brandy waved her hand toward her sister's retreating back, but Constance only tossed her head and continued on her way.

Brandy called out again, over the rising wind, "Connie, wait for me on the path. I must find Fiona." She saw her sister pause and turn about, impatience turning down the corners of her mouth.

Brandy hurried to the edge of the cliff and started down the winding rocky path, careful to watch her footing on the treacherous rocks and pebbles. "Fiona!" she called down, cupping her hands around her mouth. She scanned the desolate beach below, searching for the bright red thatch of hair that topped Fiona's head. There was no movement among the coarse marram grass that grew thick and sturdy amongst the rocks on the beach, and the only sound above the waves was the hoarse squawking of the seabirds, intent upon finding their dinner. Her attention was caught a moment by a large bobbing porpoise, alternately skimming and floating on the white-tipped waves.

"Brandy! Brandy, here I am!"

She turned about, a scold upon her lips at the sight of Fiona scurrying toward her up the path, her once neat braids hanging about her small shoulders in fiery, wet disarray. Her woolen gown clung damply to her skinny legs and Brandy suspected that the hem was thick with gritty sand.

Her scolding words were forgotten when Fiona grabbed her arm and cried, "Did ye see him, Brandy? He's been lying on his back ever so long. I called to him and I promise that he twitched his nose at me."

"Yes, love, I saw him. But he is gone now, searching for some abalone for his dinner. And that, little poppet, is what we must do. It grows late." She ruffled the flying red hair and resolutely turned the child about.

Brandy espied Constance standing in the protection of a beech hedge, combing her black tresses with her fingers. She gave an ugh of distaste at Fiona's fly-away appearance. "Really, Fiona, ye look like a crofter's child! And ye needn't look at me like that, for I have no intention of brushing the tangles out of that rat's nest!"

Untroubled by this stricture, Fiona gave a secret smile to Brandy, a smile filled with wonder at the gray porpoise.

"Ye won't have to, Connie. I shall make her presentable. Come, it grows late."

They rounded a curve in the path that led onto the rhododendron-lined avenue. Penderleigh Castle rose before them like a giant gray monolith, its ancient stone gleaming in the dull gold of the setting sun. Constance paused and picked a soft magenta blossom and tucked it over her left ear. "I would offer ye one, Brandy, but I do not think that such a *womanly* ornament would enhance yer braids."

Brandy did not reply, for her attention was on the fluted turret, once the housing for the now rusted cannons that lay in a heap, forgotten, in the grass-filled moat. She fancied she could hear the strident call of the bagpipes, daring the enemy to approach. She remembered the oft-repeated ballad of the Earl of Huntly, whispered by Marta in her blurred singsong voice:

> Wae be tae ye, Huntly
> And whaur hae ye been?
> They hae slain the Earl o'Moray
> And laid him on the green.

She found herself humming softly, lost in a strangely romantic past. But it was, she thought, a past plundered and lost forever after Bonnie Prince Charlie's bloody defeat. She remembered tales of the hated Duke of Cumberland, the Englishman's avenging devil. She stared hard at the proud old castle and a knot of anger grew in her stomach. Penderleigh Castle, her birthplace, her home, now belonged to another duke, another Englishman.

"I am sorry, Connie, what did ye say?" she asked, suddenly aware of her sister's voice. She pulled her eyes unwillingly from the turrets and momentarily closed her ears to the roaring sounds of the sea battering the rocks just behind the castle.

"I said that I saw Bertrand and Uncle Claude crossing from the dower house to the castle. Bertrand is such an old stick! Odd that he is so prissy prim, when Uncle Claude is reputed to have tumbled many a young maid when he was young!"

"Connie, wherever did ye hear such nonsense! I do wish ye wouldn't talk like that—it's so loose."

"Och, ye're as prissy prim as Bertrand! What a perfect match ye two would make—both old stuffy sticks!"

"Bertrand old? He is younger than Percy, ye know, Connie."

"Old is as old does," Constance replied somewhat obscurely and tossed her long black hair.

Brandy sighed to herself. It seemed lately that she and Constance were scarce five minutes in each other's company without one of them twitting the other. She struggled to understand her sister. It was as if Constance wanted to hurl herself into womanhood, to scoff at all the pursuits Brandy still held pleasurable and dear. She refused to go out in Brandy's small boat to fish, turning up her nose at the strong fishy smell and deploring the sticky damp sea spray on her gown. If attaining womanhood meant spending all one's time on how one looked and openly flirting with the likes of Percy, she wanted none of it. She had no intention of aping her younger sister's ways.

She hunched her shoulders forward, pulling her shawl more closely about her. At least Constance didn't have to worry about going through life with the deformity Brandy had to endure. She couldn't even take deep breaths, for fear of popping the buttons on her gowns. What a dreadful jest nature had played upon her—a slight frame supporting a cowlike bosom!

She thought again of Percy, and found herself wondering why he looked at her with that disgusting, knowing look in his hooded eyes. There was certainly nothing about her appearance or her behavior to give him any encouragement. He was probably just bored here, and could find naught else to do but tease her in that loathsome way of his.

Brandy looked up to see Fiona astride one of the old cannons, crying delightedly, "Giddyup, ye old nag, giddyup!"

"Oh, Fiona, but look at yer gown!" Brandy rushed forward, saw the rust flecks on the child's face and hands, and lifted her bodily from the cannon. "If Old Marta sees ye like that, she'll tell Grandmama for certain! Hold still, little wriggler, let me clean ye off!"

"Brandy, look, someone is coming up the drive. It looks like one of those gentleman's sporting vehicles." Constance shaded her eyes from the dying sun, still bright through the gathering storm clouds.

Brandy straightened, holding Fiona's grubby hand, her own face now covered with copper flecks of rust. She gazed at the on-coming curricle with only mild curiosity. Surely the man was driving too fast, for great whirls of dust whipped around the wheels.

"Great horses!" Fiona cried, jumping with excitement.

"Aye, that they are, poppet."

"They're much better than these stupid old cannons!"

Brandy felt a sudden tug. Fiona broke free of her hold and ran as fast as her stubby legs would carry her toward the curricle.

"Dear God! Fiona, come back!" Brandy yanked her skirts to her knees and dashed after the child. "Fiona!" she screamed, fear suddenly clogging her throat. She saw the steaming stallions, their eyes flaming with surprise, rearing and plunging, and heard the blurred shout of a man's voice. With a hoarse cry, Brandy leaped forward, grabbed at Fiona's arm and, with all her strength, hurled the child backward. She heard the fightened whinnying and snorting of the stallions as she rolled upon her back beside Fiona in a tuft of

27

yellow anenomes. She gulped down two heaving breaths and turned frantic eyes to her sister.

"Poppet, poppet, are ye all right?"

"Of course, Brandy, but ye hurt my arm. Big horses!"

Brandy growled to herself, half in relief and half in anger at Fiona's stupidity.

She saw Constance standing but a few feet away from them, her eyes widened upon a gentleman who was jumping gracefully down from the curricle.

"Pull yer skirt down, Brandy," Constance hissed, her eyes never wavering from the man's face.

Brandy jerked her skirt over her old woolen stockings and bounded to her feet. The gentleman was striding toward them, his dark eyes narrowed and his swarthy face suffused with anger. He was wearing the most elegant driving coat she had ever seen.

She forgot his elegance when his voice, cold as ice crackling in a glass bowl, cut through the air. "Just what the devil do you mean letting that child run in front of my horses!"

Fiona stared up at the huge gentleman, her eyes wide with excitement. "They are so grand! I just wanted to see them up close!"

"So close that they could have broken every bone in your body! And you," he scowled, turning a dark eye upon Brandy, "your bravery was quite unnecessary! I always have quite good control over my cattle! You could have killed yourself!"

"Nay, sir, ye must forgive my sister," Constance interposed, curtsying formally. "She did not think."

Scalded by Constance's defection, Brandy rounded on her sister. "We seek no forgiveness from this—person who must needs drive like a madman! As for ye, sir, I doubt very much that ye had much control at all over those horses! No thanks to ye that we are still alive!"

A very clipped English voice snapped back, "Now that I see that you are unhurt, I have no desire to cross swords with a rowdy, thoughtless pack of children. I suggest that you remove yourselves quickly before I am sorely tempted to take my hand to your backsides!"

Brandy gasped. It was obvious that the stranger believed them to be peasants' brats, beneath his exalted notice.

"And I suggest to ye, ye arrogant cur, that ye remove yerself from Penderleigh land!"

The Duke of Portmaine, his nerves frayed and his temper already sorely tried from his long journey, took an unmeasured step toward the abominable brat who dared rant at him. He stared hard into great amber eyes and halted in his tracks. Damnation, the girl did not even flinch. He drew a tired breath and said with finality. "I am sorry that I frightened you, children." He gazed at the two grubby faces, purposefully ignoring the other young girl, who appeared openly enthralled with his presence, and thought to himself that he could make them as well as their probably very poor parents quite satisfied. He quickly drew several guineas from his waistcoat pocket and tossed them to the youngest child. "Here, this should cleanse your wounds and salve your feelings."

Brandy was so stunned that she stood stock still, staring at him with mouth agape. In the next instant, he had turned and climbed into the curricle.

"How dare ye!" Brandy cried. But he had already whipped up the horses and was bowling away from them.

"Look, Brandy, they're gold. Big gold pieces!" Fiona held out the two guineas in her grubby hand and proudly displayed her fortune.

"Give me those," Brandy snapped, and grabbed the coins. Fiona began to sob.

Constance pinched Brandy's arm. "How could ye be so nasty to that gentleman! I was never so mortified in all my life!" She added her Parthian shot as she flounced away, "And don't expect me to take any of the blame when Grandmama finds out! If Papa were alive or Grandpapa Angus, ye'd get the whip."

Brandy ignored her sister. "Oh, do quit yer sniffling, Fiona," she snapped. "The man gave us the guineas because he thought we were poor crofters' children. It would be wrong for us to keep them, don't ye see?"

Fiona sobbed all the harder, and Brandy, at the end of her patience, grabbed her sister's arm and hauled her none too gently toward the small wooden door at the side of the castle. She put the odious gentleman out of her mind, and concerned herself with how to escape Old Marta's sharp eyes.

"Please hush, poppet," she whispered, her voice gentle. "I will scrub ye down myself and no one need know."

Fiona settled into erratic hiccups and scampered ahead of her sister toward the winding back stairs to the nursery wing.

It was close to an hour later before a well-scrubbed Fiona was tucked into her bed, her small stomach filled with cold chicken and buttered scones. Luckily, Morag had brought up Fiona's dinner.

"I canna stay, lassie," Morag said. "Cook be all aflutter wi' so many mouths to feed." She cast a disinterested rheumy eye over Brandy. "Ye best to ready yerself, lassie. Yer lady grandmother be already wi' the family downstairs."

"Thank ye, Morag, I shall hurry. Good night, poppet," she whispered softly to Fiona. "I shall visit ye before I go to bed."

Brandy carried a candle across the hall to her own small bedchamber. No fire burned in her room this time of year. She thought angrily that *dear* Cousin Percival in all likelihood had a roaring fire in *his* room. The way he cozened and flattered Old Marta—he probably had buckets of hot water for his bath.

She stripped off her filthy gown and shift, and with cold fingers pulled away the tight lacings of her chemise. She gritted her teeth and splashed cold water over her body. The myriad flecks of rust clung stubbornly and she was covered with gooseflesh before the harsh lye soap had done its job.

She toweled herself dry and grabbed for a clean shift and chemise. She thought of Percy and that odious way he had stared at her this afternoon. She looked down at her excessive bosom, and wondered if he had been staring at that part of her. She jerked the strings painfully tight over her breasts. She gazed into her mirror and saw that the effect was not as flattening as she had hoped. Well, there was nothing more she could do about it, she thought with a grimace. She chose a pale blue muslin gown, a young girl's dress, high-necked and sashed at the waist. The buttons over her bosom gaped apart and in desperation, Brandy unearthed from her mother's chest a dark blue shawl. She quickly brushed out her long thick tresses, the habitual braids causing deep ripples that fell to her waist. Her hair, she thought, was her only fine feature, and remembering Percy's roving eyes, rebraided her hair more tightly than usual and wound the long rope into a tight bun at the nape of her neck.

She did not bother to look again in the mirror. Pulling the shawl tightly about her, she blew out her candle and slipped from her room.

One smoky flambeau lit the long expanse of corridor, its acrid smell making Brandy's nostrils quiver. She gingerly made her way down the wide oak staircase, for the carpet was threadbare on several of the steps, making the descent rather perilous.

Crabbe was nowhere to be seen and Brandy thought again of Percy and how his presence had placed an undue burden on the servants. She heard voices coming from the drawing room, and mindful that she was late, hurried across the worn flagstone entrance hall and, with the greatest care, eased open the drawing room door.

A rush of warm air enveloped her from the great roaring fire at the opposite side of the room. She saw her grandmother dominating the family, holding court from her faded, high-backed chair, smoke-blackened from its years of proximity to the fireplace. Scores of candle branches illuminated the cozy scene. She heard a rich, deep laugh. In an instant, her eyes sought out the owner and she found herself staring, mouth agape, at the gentleman from the curricle. She felt color rush to her cheeks, and stood rooted to the spot, held by mortified anger.

He laughed again at something Grandmama said. Even though she was across the room from him, she saw his strong white teeth flashing in his humor. She realized that he was even larger than she remembered, his swarthy countenance heightened by the snowy white ruffled shirt that reminded her of a pure expanse of clean snow. In the glowing candlelight, his eyes seemed as dark as his black satin evening coat. A very elegant gentleman he appeared, and certainly many pegs above any of Grandmama's friends from Edinburgh.

"Brandy! There ye are, child! Come here at once and make yer curtsy."

Brandy's eyes flew to her grandmama's face, and with the hesitance of a naughty child called forward to receive a well-deserved trimming, she bowed her head and followed her lagging feet.

"Ye're quite late, miss, but no matter! His grace has just been telling us of yer interesting meeting."

Brandy fully expected to be raked down in front of the gentleman, for Grandmama was never one to moderate her fits of ire, regardless of the company. She forced her eyes to her grandmama's face and saw amusement written there, not the anger she expected. *His grace!* The truth of the matter struck her with such force that she gasped aloud. He was the English duke—their new master!

"Miss Brandella," came a rich, lazy voice. Without thought, she said, "Brandy, my name is Brandy."

"Very well, Miss Brandy."

"Make yer curtsy, child!"

Awkwardly, Brandy bent her knee, her eyes still refusing to rise to his face.

Lady Adella snapped, "I've never seen ye tongue-tied before, miss! Stop yer nonsense and bid hello to our kinsman, the Duke of Portmaine."

"Good evening, sir," she mumbled. "I—I mean *yer grace.*"

"Ian, my name is Ian." He strode to her and with the grace of long practice, detached her hand from the folds of her skirt and planted a light kiss on her palm. "I am most delighted to see you again, cousin. Your older sister, Constance, has already regaled your family with our small . . . contretemps of this afternoon. You appear none the worse for it, my child. I trust that now you will most sincerely accept my apology."

"I am never the worse for anything, yer grace," Brandy muttered in a tight voice, wondering if he mocked her.

Percy chuckled from his place beside Lady Adella's chair. "Yer grace mistakes the matter. 'Tis Brandy who is the eldest. Appearances are sometimes deceptive, do ye not agree, Brandy?"

"No, Percy, I do not agree," Brandy snapped, her amber eyes darting daggers.

"Do leave the girl alone, Percy," Lady Adella chided, tapping his arm with her fan.

"Well, I for one do agree with Percy," Constance said, drawing attention to herself. "Most gentlemen do think I am the eldest." She patted several soft black tendrils into place and gazed at the duke with the melting look she had been practicing in front of her mirror.

"Perhaps that is so, Constance," the duke agreed easily.

"Where could that old sot, Crabbe, be," Lady Adella wondered aloud. "I swear we would all starve to death if he had his way in the matter."

Brandy took the opportunity to move away from the duke, uncomfortable at the scrutiny of his dark eyes.

"Good evening, Brandy," said Bertrand in his quiet voice.

"Good evening, Cousin Bertrand, Uncle Claude. How are ye feeling, sir?"

"As fit as can be expected with this damned gout!" He gazed over at the duke, who stood in conversation with Lady Adella, and added with barely veiled malice, "Much more the thing than poor Bertrand here, I vow. Of course, Bertie here is much too timid a fellow to tell us how he feels."

"Father," Bertrand said in a low voice.

"Look ye at Percy," Claude continued, disregarding. " 'Tis an oily viper's tongue he has, but at least he doesn't chew his cud in silence like a stupid cow."

Seeing an angry flush mount Bertrand's cheeks, Brandy quickly interposed. "Uncle Claude, why did the duke come here? Grandmama said he would have no interest in us."

"I can't say, lassie. Mayhap he was visiting in Scotland and thought to deign to visit his poor relations."

Brandy frowned, thinking of their crofters. Her jaw tightened. The English were always taking. He was here to see for himself how much he could squeeze from the land.

Crabbe flung open the doors and announced in his wheezy voice, "Dinner be ready!"

Brandy felt a tug of embarrassment. The duke would think them terribly backward. Why could Crabbe not say that dinner was served, like a well-trained English servant?

" 'Tis about time, ye old sot," said Lady Adella, planting her cane and rising slowly. Percy slipped his hand under her arm, all solicitude.

"Brandy, ye're the oldest. Let his grace lead ye to dinner, child."

"But Grandmama," Constance protested. She encountered a quelling frown and shrugged her shoulders. "Come, Bertrand," she said, rising.

Brandy stood awkwardly, unconsciously pulling her shawl more closely over the gaping buttons. Without turning, she reached out her arm. She felt soft satin beneath her fingers and sent a fleeting glance up at the duke.

He was smiling down at her kindly, the kind of look, she thought sourly, that a tolerant adult bestows upon a skittish child. As she walked beside him through the entrance hall and across to the dining room, she felt the two guineas click together in her pocket. She had thought to give them to Lady Adella. Now she wasn't quite certain what to do with them.

"The past seems most disturbingly alive," the duke said, eyeing the rows of bagpipes strung from nails about the walls. Indeed, he thought he had entered another world in another century. A huge battle ax hung from the mailed hand of an empty suit of armor. What he assumed was the Robertson colors, a plaid of red, yellow, and green, were draped about a red coat of arms in the shape of a shield above an empty cavernous fireplace.

Brandy followed his eyes. "Yes," she said softly, "particularly during a winter storm blowing from the sea. The winds whistle down the chimney and make the tartans quiver, as if they were alive." She stiffened, rather put out with herself that she had answered him in such a friendly manner, as if he were one of them.

Ian looked down at the girl beside him and saw that her arched brows had drawn together in a frown. He said gently, "If you are remembering my shocking behavior of this afternoon, Brandy, I would again pray that you forgive me. I was out of reason cross, primarily because you and Fiona could have been seriously hurt. Will you contrive to forgive me?"

She looked up at him, startled, for he had misread her thoughts. She felt churlish. "Of course, 'tis forgotten, yer grace," she said, hoping he would not probe further.

He smiled and directed her attention to the fireplace. "The three wolves' heads in your coat of arms—do they snarl in fury at invaders?"

"Nay, but I sometimes fancy that they were once proud and fiercely alive, defending the castle. It's as though they are under some sort of evil spell, holding them lifeless for all time."

The duke had meant a jest, but at the glow of Scotland's

rich, fanciful past in her amber eyes, he asked seriously, "And those are the Robertson colors?"

"Aye. Once they were a rich bright crimson, and yellow, and green. Old Marta takes no care of them now."

"Old Marta?"

"Grandmama's maid. I think she must be as old as the castle and just as durable."

The duke suddenly realized that the others had passed into the dining room. "Come, Brandy, we do not wish the others to wait."

"I wondered why I had no hot water for my bath. I blamed it on Percy's being here."

Ian blinked at this change of topic and raised a black brow.

"Oh, 'tis not yer fault, yer grace! Strange, though, that Morag did not tell me of yer being here."

"The rather slovenly woman who keeps scratching her head?"

Brandy stiffened. "She doesn't scratch her head *all* the time!"

"Very well, then, she scratches only in my presence."

He gazed down again at Brandy, at the proud straight nose, and the firm chin, a stubborn chin. A precocious child, he thought, and not without intelligence and charm. Perhaps someday, with proper nurturing, she would become a lovely woman. He realized with something of a start that he was now her nominal guardian.

"Come, yer grace," Lady Adella called, " 'tis the earl's chair for ye. Brandy, ye will be seated in yer usual place."

The duke looked about the long rectangular dining room. How very medieval it looked, with the long table flanked by rigid lines of carved chairs. The high wainscotting was as dark as the heavy furniture, and the firelight and the branches of candles could not permeate into the corners. All that was needed to complete the scene, he thought, was a rush-strewn floor and giant mastiffs gnawing at discarded bones on the hearth. He helped Brandy into her seat and crossed to the head of the table. The ornately carved earl's chair stood nearly as tall as his shoulders, exuding a kind of crude power. The three Robertson wolves' heads were carved into its back and pressed against his shoulder blades when he seated himself. He thought of the quiet elegance of Carmichael Hall and shifted his position.

"Ye old sot, pour the wine," Lady Adella's strident voice reached him from the other end of the table, and he winced, wondering if all Penderleigh servants were meted out similar insults. The impassive Crabbe filled his goblet.

Lady Adella thwacked her glass upon the wooden table. "All of ye, let us toast the new earl of Penderleigh!" There was mockery in her voice and Ian saw that she raised her glass first to Percival, then to Claude and Bertrand, before turning to him.

So much for a friendly welcome, he thought. "I thank you all," he said quietly, and sipped at the heavy, fruity wine.

Morag set a steaming bowl in front of him. He assumed it was soup but was at a loss to determine its origins.

Claude cackled. " 'Tis in Scotland ye be now, yer grace. Partan bree it is and not yer usual English fare!"

" 'Tis a crab soup," Bertrand added in a friendly voice. "Quite tasty I think ye'll find."

"It is a lucky happenstance that we poor Scots still have the sea," Percy said. "Even the English could not destroy that."

"Nor the Danes or Vikings or other unfriendly Scottish clans either, I suspect," Ian said quickly.

"Percy, mind yer tongue," Lady Adella snapped, "or it appears that Ian may very well nip it off."

Ian lowered his head to look more closely at the partan bree. Percy had been introduced to him as Lady Adella's grandson. Why the devil wasn't the fellow the heir to the earldom? Perhaps that fact went a good distance in explaining his snide comments on the English in general, and himself in particular. He lifted a spoonful of the crab soup to his mouth and found the meat smooth and rich, the cream tangy. At least as yet he hadn't any complaint to make of Scottish food.

"Cousin Ian," Constance said in a soft woman's voice, "where are yer servants? I always thought that English gentlemen had simply hundreds of servants."

"Not hundreds, I assure you, Constance," the duke replied with a smile. "I had the misfortune of breaking an axle on the carriage. My valet, Mabley, is, I pray, successfully negotiating with a blacksmith in Galashiels. I came alone in my curricle, as you know."

"Ye brought only one servant?" Constance asked, clearly disappointed.

"I am but one man, not an entire household." He thought of his gently sighing valet and grinned to himself. Whatever would Mabley think of the scratchy Morag!

"Ye came from London, yer grace?" Brandy asked.

"Yes. 'Tis a long journey, you know. Nearly six days."

"But why?" Brandy asked, without thinking.

Ian paused with his last spoonful of the crab soup suspended over the bowl, and cocked his head to one side. "Why did I come?"

"Aye, yer grace. We did not believe ye would ever come to Penderleigh, being an English duke and all."

"Ye pry into matters none of yer concern, child," Lady Adella said, but Ian saw that the old lady's faded eyes were filled with curiosity.

"I suppose it is a natural question. But did you really believe that I would ignore my Scottish kinsmen?"

"What my little cousin means, yer grace, is that we did not mind at all being ignored. It is the land and rents we feared would gain yer attention."

"Percy, that is not at all what I meant!" Brandy snapped. "I will thank ye to let me put my own words in my own mouth!"

"From outward appearances, I would venture to say that the lands are much in need of my attention," Ian said dryly.

Lady Adella said, "Ye are my sister's grandson, Ian, and part of my blood. I am heartened that ye visit yer holdings."

The duke would have been pleased by Lady Adella's placating words had he not seen the taunting look she threw toward Percival.

Bertrand interposed quietly, "I have seen to the estate for many years now, yer grace. I, myself, am much concerned. At yer leisure, I will show ye the accounting books."

"I thank you, Bertrand." The duke gazed up as Morag removed his empty soup bowl and placed a large platter before him, containing something he could not identify.

"Haggis," Claude announced.

"Haggis?" the duke repeated dubiously.

Constance leaned forward toward the duke and said brightly, "A mixture of oatmeal, liver, beef suet and the like. Cook always serves it with potatoes and rutabagas."

Still looking mystified, Ian raised a tentative forkful to his mouth.

Percy tossed in, "The whole mess is boiled in a sheep stomach."

The duke swallowed convulsively and sternly repressed the image of the stomach. He gingerly forked another bite into his mouth. There was a strong taste of black pepper and he downed more wine to avoid sneezing.

Following several more ventures into the haggis with his fork, the duke decided the dish was not at all to be despised. He looked up to see various pairs of eyes gazing at him expectantly.

"A most unusual and delicious dish. My compliments to Cook and to the sheep."

Brandy found herself grinning at Percy's crestfallen look.

Ian allowed his gaze to wander about the table. Lady Adella, his great aunt, sat like royalty born at the foot of the table, gustily attacking the haggis. She must be at least seventy, he thought, trying to remember his grandmother, her sister. All he could recall was a vague, wispy wraith of a stooped lady who seemed to have spent most of her remaining days reclining on a comfortable sofa with his own mother in constant attendance. Surely, she could not have had the iron personality Lady Adella appeared to enjoy in abundance. She had welcomed him graciously enough, yet had seemed to derive pleasure in pitting him against Percy and Bertrand. He glanced at Claude, who sat on Lady Adella's left, seemingly quite content to noisily chew his dinner. He had been introduced as a nephew, and Bertrand, his son, as a grandnephew. Why the devil had not one of these men inherited Penderleigh? He disliked mysteries and vowed to himself to unravel these confusing relationships on the morrow.

His gaze passed to Constance, then quickly to Brandy, and back again to Constance. He found it difficult to believe that the two girls were sisters. The one with the unattractive braided hair, and the other with lush, thick black tresses that curled provocatively over her rounded shoulders. Brandy wore a shapeless muslin gown, far outdated, and topped with a faded blue shawl, and Constance a daringly low-cut violet silk gown that showed the promise of a maturing bosom. And Fiona, the redheaded little urchin who had almost dashed herself under his horses' hooves, in coloring at least was very different from both of her sisters. He looked back down the long expanse of table toward Lady Adella and decided that he had never before seen such a rag-tag collection of gentry.

Lady Adella met his eyes and said, "No string of endless courses here, yer grace! When ye are finished with the haggis, we'll have the trifle served up."

The duke smiled easily. "Trifle, my lady, I have enjoyed many times."

"Not the way Cook prepares it, ye haven't!" Claude cackled.

"At least it is not made in a sheep stomach, I trust," Ian said. He was beginning to find Claude's cackle grating on his nerves.

Unfortunately, he discovered after several mouthfuls what Claude meant. The sherry was sour and the cake soggy. Civility required him to finish the bulk of the noble portion that Morag had accorded him. He downed a large draught of wine to soothe his offended palate. He gazed toward Lady Adella after some moments, wondering if in Scotland the ladies retired to the drawing room and left the gentlemen to their port, as was the custom in England.

"We'll take our port in the drawing room," she said presently, as if reading his silent thoughts. He raised his eyebrow fleetingly and rose with the rest of the company.

As he passed Brandy, she whispered, "Ye are most polite, yer grace. The trifle was terrible, but Cook was only trying to impress ye."

He grinned ruefully and shook his head. "It was a noble effort. I could do naught else." He lowered his voice. "Does not poor Crabbe resent being called an old sot?"

Brandy bit her lower lip. "Nay, yer grace, I assure ye, 'tis one of her more gentle ways of addressing him. I had hoped that she would refrain from being so . . . colorful in yer presence." She added under her breath, "Ye mustn't pay any attention to Percy. He is ever hateful and, I think, most jealous of yer position as new master here."

Lady Adella's omnipresent eye prevented him from questioning Brandy further.

"Come, Brandy, Constance. We must show the duke that Scotland is not an uncivilized land. His grace is in need of entertainment."

She turned to the duke, who at the moment wanted nothing more than his bed and a long night's sleep. "Ye'll find the girls not without ladies' accomplishments. Constance, since ye're the younger and it is growing late, ye may perform for his grace first."

Although Constance presented a quite attractive picture seated at the old pianoforte, her rendition of a French ballad in a small wooden voice made the duke pray that the song had not many verses. When she rose from the pianoforte and curtsied demurely, he forced himself to hearty applause.

"Ye still sound like a rusty wood pipe, girl," Lady Adella said.

"Oh, Grandmama!" Constance wailed.

The duke felt compelled to say, "I enjoyed your performance much, Constance. I look forward to hearing you again."

The petulant child's look vanished to be replaced by a sultry smile. Her eyes darted to Percy in search of a similar accolade. To her disgruntlement, Percy was staring hard at Brandy.

"The duke is kind, child. Now 'tis off to bed with ye. Say yer good nights and then 'tis yer sister's turn."

Constance saw there was no hope for it, and with as much good grace as she could muster, swept a curtsy and left the drawing room with a lagging step.

"Grandmama," Brandy said, "it is rather late and the duke must be tired from his long journey. Perhaps he would prefer not to hear—"

"Hush, child. If ye do not begin, ye'll not finish."

"I should enjoy hearing your performance," Ian added gallantly, wishing for the moment at least that he were back in London, in his own home, doing precisely what he pleased.

"I will turn the pages for ye, Brandy."

Percy rose and drew close to her. Brandy quickly revised her selection. "Ye need not bother, Percy, I have no pages to turn."

"Then I will stand next to the pianoforte and ye may sing to me."

"Please Cousin Percy, I would that ye did not," Brandy said between gritted teeth.

He gave her a caressing, mocking smile, sketched a slight bow, and turned to seat himself next to Lady Adella.

Ian watched this exchange with some perturbation. He heard Lady Adella hiss to Percy in a low voice, "I told ye to leave the child alone, Percy. She doesn't ken yer meaning."

In a pig's eye, she doesn't, the duke thought. He did not hear Percival's reply, for Brandy touched her fingers to the keyboard. Three soft, sad chords filled the room and in a low, rich voice, she sang,

> "Oh my luve is like a red, red rose,
> That's newly sprung in June:
> Oh, my luve is like the melodie,
> That's sweetly play'd in tune.
>
> Till a' the seas gang dry, my dear,
> And the rocks melt wi' the sun;
> And I will luve thee still, my dear,
> While the sands o' life shall run.
>
> And fare thee weel, my only luve!
> And fare thee weel a while!
> And I will come again, my luve,
> Tho' it were ten thousand mile!"

The duke was held in silence for a moment by the haunting words and the deep minor chords that added to their beauty. He had not understood all of them, for she had sung with a lilting Scottish brogue. He heard Lady Adella snort in what he assumed was her form of applause. He said, " 'Tis a lovely ballad, Brandy. Who is the writer?"

She turned on the stool and said softly, as if still enthralled by the music, "Robert Burns—Rabbie Burns, as we call him. He died but four years ago, quite near to here, in Dumfries."

"Ye might add, my dear," Percy said with a marked sneer, "that yer beloved Rabbie was a drunk and a womanizer. Peopled these parts with brats, ye know, yer grace."

The duke saw a dull flush of anger creep into Brandy's cheeks. He said quickly, "If all of his music is as stirring as this ballad, I do not think he will be remembered for any of his lesser qualities."

Lady Adella said with a lewd twinkle in her eyes, "I for one wish that our dear Rabbie had been born some forty years earlier. I wouldn't have minded atakin' a tumble with that one! I ask ye, Percy, 'how can ye doe ocht when ye've nocht tae dae ocht wi'?' Aye, that makes ye lose yer wig!"

The duke understood none of Lady Adella's lapse into the vernacular, but he saw Percival's face redden. Evidently she had insulted his manhood.

"I will go to bed now, Grandmama, if ye don't mind," Brandy said, stiff with embarrassment.

Lady Adella had lost interest and waved her hand in dismissal. "Off with ye, child."

Brandy kept her head down and walked quickly from the room. Why, in heaven's name, was Grandmama speaking in such an outrageous manner? It was as if she was being purposefully vulgar and crass in the duke's presence.

The duke rose slowly. "I have much enjoyed my dinner and the entertainment, Lady Adella. But I fear that I am much in need of my bed. If you will all excuse me, I bid you good night."

Lady Adella said, "If all is not to yer liking, yer grace, lay yer hand across Morag's back. She's a lazy trollop, that one!"

"I am certain that nothing left undone could warrant such an excess of feeling, Lady Adella." The duke nodded and left the room. He heard Claude's cackle sound behind him.

Crabbe awaited him outside to escort him to his bedchamber. "I was afeared that ye might 'ae lost yer way, yer grace," he explained, allowing himself to unbend a bit.

It was scarce likely that the duke would have lost his way, as he had been accorded the old earl's bedchamber. It lay at the end of the long drafty west corridor, in splendid isolation.

The furnishings were as dark and cumbersome as the pieces in the dining room, and the corners of the room just as gloomy. He wished he had more than one branch of candles to make the room less forbidding.

Crabbe gazed impassively at the pitiful fire that lay smoldering in the grate. "Morag laid the peat fer ye. I took the liberty to lay oot yer things, yer grace."

The duke nodded wearily. "Thank you, Crabbe. That will be all for this evening."

The old man essayed a shallow bow and left the room.

Mayhap Morag did need a violent excess of feeling, the duke thought wryly as he bent down to build up the fire. Some of the peat clumps were damp to the touch, in all likelihood brought in from outside at the height of the storm this evening. No wonder the result was wispy fingers of gray smoke.

He hurriedly undressed and eased his large frame between the cold sheets. The covers smelled faintly musty. He fell asleep to the sound of pattering rain against the window panes and the roar of the waves breaking against the rocks at the foot of the cliff behind the castle.

4

"Hie ye, Brandy, tell me more about the new earl."

"Fiona, the porridge is dripping off the end of yer spoon!"

The child hastily slurped in the porridge, her great blue eyes never leaving her sister's face.

"Very well, poppet, but I know little more than do ye. First of all, he is a duke, which is far more important than an earl."

"Ye mean he is not the Earl of Penderleigh?"

"Aye, certainly, but he's a 'yer grace,' not a 'yer lordship.' I suppose even though he's English, he is rather kind, but ye must promise me that ye will not make a nuisance of yerself, poppet. He probably hates to be teased by children. I imagine that he will be leaving us soon enough, for we cannot be at all what he is used to."

"Why did he come if he only wants to leave us?" Fiona pursued, her child's logic discomfitted.

"I don't know, Fiona," Brandy said frankly. "Come, poppet, finish yer breakfast. It grows late." Brandy knew it was only just past eight o'clock, not late at all. Percy, as a rule, was not an early riser, but she wanted to avoid his company as much as possible, and she intended to take no chances. She sipped at her tea and gazed out onto the overgrown moat. The storm of the night before had blown itself out, and it promised to be a glorious spring day, with just a nip of chill in the air and a light wind to ruffle the bluebells.

"This is a pleasant surprise."

Brandy jerked about in her chair, expecting to see Percy's unwelcome face. "Yer grace!" Relief so flooded her voice that the duke cocked a black brow, puzzled.

"Ye're the man with the grand horses," Fiona exclaimed and slipped from her chair. She raised great candid eyes upward. "Are ye really a grace and not just a lordship like Grandpapa Angus?"

Ian surveyed the sturdy little girl, standing arms akimbo before him. Her hair was thick and bright as crimson velvet. "Yes," he said solemnly, "I am indeed a grace."

"Fiona!" Brandy rose from her chair and hurried to her sister's side. "I beg ye, don't tease his grace! Please forgive her, she means no harm."

"So you are Fiona," he said, gazing down from his great height.

"Aye, but Brandy calls me poppet. Do I have to call ye grace? That's funny, like a lady's name."

The duke smiled broadly and touched the riot of red curls. "You may call me Ian, 'tis much less of a mouthful."

"Ian," Fiona repeated, savoring the name. "I like that. Would ye like some porridge? It's not nearly as watery as usual."

"A remarkable recommendation," the duke said, his eyes twinkling. He managed to quell uncharitable thoughts about the porridge. "Come, girls, back to the table. I am sorry to have interrupted your breakfast. You slept well, Brandy?"

"Aye, yer grace."

"Did ye sleep in Grandpapa Angus's bed, Ian?" Fiona asked as she climbed back into her chair. "He died in that bed, ye know," she added with ghoulish relish.

"Fiona, every Penderleigh earl has died in that bed!"

"There was not one vision from the past to disturb me," the duke said. He warily took his first bite of porridge and was surprised at its tastiness. He looked up to see Fiona frowning at him.

"Whatever is the matter, Fiona? Is there porridge dripping from my chin?"

Fiona giggled. "Oh nay, Ian. I asked Brandy why ye came here if ye only wanted to leave us."

Brandy hung her head in an agony of embarrassment. If only Fiona were close enough so she could give her a sharp kick in the shin!

"And what did Brandy reply?" the duke asked, his dark eyes resting for a moment on Brandy's averted face.

"She said she didn't know. Will ye tell me?"

He thought of all the selfish reasons that had motivated his departure from London, discarded them without a thought to his perjured soul, and said, "I came because you are my cousins and I wanted to meet you."

Brandy's eyes flew to his face, patent disbelief etched in every contour of her own. He arched an elegant black brow and gave her the blandest of looks.

"When may I see the grand horses, Ian?"

"When you give me your solemn promise that you will not go dashing in front of them."

"I promise!" Fiona agreed, much too rapidly for the duke's adult ears.

"Poppet, ye must realize that his grace has much to do. We must not tease him for attention."

He smiled at the stern eye Brandy was bending on her little sister. She is behaving just like the child's mother, he thought to himself, and a very ineffectual one at that. He felt a curious tug of liking for her.

"Would ye care for more tea, sir?"

"Brandy, if Fiona can call me Ian, surely you can bring yourself to do the same. Yes, I would like more tea, thank you."

Brandy did not realize that he had given her a very mild setdown. Indeed, she found herself beginning to question exactly what it was she thought about him. Of course, it was not *his* fault that he had inherited the earldom and Penderleigh, anymore, she pursued, than it was his fault for being English. As she poured his tea, she gazed at him from beneath her lashes, comparing his appearance with the other gentlemen she knew. Although she had not had much experience in the realm of fashion, she felt that his immaculate buff breeches, exquisitely molded to his muscular thighs, and the matching buff jacket were simply, yet artfully styled. She had the fleeting urge to touch the snow white ruffles on his shirt. Everything about him was elegant, even the shining black hessians. She tugged at her skirt, and thought of herself as gauche and awkward in comparison.

The duke watched the changing emotions cross the girl's face, though he could not guess their meaning. She seemed to him to be suddenly ill at ease, mayhap embarrassed. He said with a smile, "What I would like most on my first day here is a tour. The storm has blown itself out, and I would much like to see the sea."

"That is just what Brandy and I were going to do!" Fiona exclaimed, casting him a look of staunch approval. "Do ye like to build things in the sand?"

Ian thought of his buff riding habit, the last item of clean apparel in his portmanteau. He could not take the chance that Mabley would arrive today with the rest of his trunks. "What I would most prefer, that is if you would not mind, Fiona, is to walk along the cliffs."

How superbly polite he is, Brandy thought, applauding him with warm eyes. "Poppet, go fetch yer shawl."

Fiona obligingly slipped from her chair and scampered from the room. "I'll be back afore the mouse gets caught in the trap!"

The duke laughed and settled himself back in his chair. He saw that Brandy already wore her shawl, tightly knotted about her shoulders.

"Are you not warm, wearing that shawl all the time?" he asked, nothing particular in his mind save the urge to make conversation.

To his dismay, she flushed scarlet and said in a strangled voice, "Nay, indeed, I am always . . . cold." She hunched her shoulders forward. One long braid fell over her shoulder, dipping its tip into the warm cream at the bottom of her porridge bowl.

"Your braid, Brandy," Ian said, and leaning over, grasped the long rope of hair.

Startled, she jerked away from him so quickly that he did not have time to release her hair. She gritted her teeth at the stab of pain in her scalp.

He managed to hide his surprise and handed her a glass of water. "Here, dip the braid in the water. I did not mean to hurt or frighten you."

"I know," she said, flushing anew. She swished the cream from the braid and dried it on a napkin. "I—I hear Fiona. Are ye ready, Ian?"

"Aye," he replied, savoring the lilting Scottish form.

She looked at him askance and, seeing no mockery in his dark eyes, returned his smile and rose.

The three of them walked out of the castle, across the graveled path that cut over the grassy moat, and along the rhododendron-lined walk that led to the cliff and the sea.

They soon gained the edge of the grassy cliff and Ian gazed out to sea, now placid and calm. Close to shore, the shallowness of the water made it appear a translucent turquoise. Farther out, the water shimmered with varying hues of darker blue. He gazed up at the serene sky, fancying that the fluffy white clouds took on distinct forms and shapes. He felt the fresh breeze ruffle his hair and drew a long breath.

"Be careful, poppet, and don't get too dirty!" he heard Brandy call after Fiona, who was fast disappearing down a well-worn path to the beach below.

He turned to her. "You've a magnificent home, Brandy."

" 'Tis yer home now as well, Ian," she said, shading her eyes after Fiona until she was certain the child had gained the safety of the beach.

"Do you mind?' he asked quietly.

She was silent for a moment. She said finally, a touch of sadness in her voice, "Nay, it is not for me to mind. Many years have passed, and although many Scots mislike to admit it, change must come. Ye cannot help the fact that ye are English. Ye must remember that I am but a female, and thus of very little worth. My opinion cannot much influence how ye'll be treated or accepted here."

"Regardless, I find that I am much concerned with your opinion."

She shrugged her shoulders. "I cannot see why. I mind not that ye inherited, not really. Some male relative had to, else our line would die out."

He was not certain that he was comfortable with such plain speaking from a young girl, and forced light dismissal into his voice.

"Well, I see that it is my duty to marry soon and father a brood of future heirs. If I did not, then the Earl of Penderleigh would be my cousin, Giles, of no blood tie whatsoever to you."

"Oh, I had thought ye married with many children!" Seeing a black brow arch up, she instantly said in a contrite voice, "Do pardon my impertinence. It is just that I believed that ye would be terribly old."

He grimaced slightly. "I suppose that thirty would seem ancient to one of your youth."

"Not at all. Ye see, I am seventeen so ye are not at all old."

Ian smiled and let his attention be drawn to sea birds squawking shrilly overhead. He thought of Felicity, only nineteen, and yet so very different from this girl. And Marianne. He welcomed the familiar deep ache, for it nourished her fading image in his mind. She would be twenty-six now and very likely the mother of a numerous brood. He wondered yet again what her children would have looked like. Certainly her daughters would have been delicate and frail like her, their large eyes a luminous green. And her sons, *his* sons, proud and strong.

He heard Brandy say, "Ye see, Ian, Fiona is forever trying to build a sand castle just like Penderleigh. Poor child, the fluted turrets are always collapsing on her."

He pulled his thoughts to the present and gazed down at Fiona. He imagined that her fiery hair must already be gritty with wet sand. "None of you appear to resemble each other. Who does Fiona take after, Brandy?"

"From what Grandmama says, Fiona is the only one of us who really looks like anybody. Her hair and eyes are the exact color of my mother's sister, Aunt Antonia. As for Constance, she has somewhat the look of our mother. And I, well, Grandmama calls me her changeling."

"Just as long as she does not call you an old sot!"

Brandy blinked several times and laughed. "Poor Crabbe! She used to do horrid things with his *real* name, very fishy things! Thank God he is not related, else she would show him no mercy!"

"Speaking of relations, who exactly is Percival?"

"He's a bastard."

"I did not refer to his character, rather his relationship to us."

"He's a bastard."

He saw that she was perfectly serious, though her amber eyes twinkled at her own jest. He said carefully, "For a bastard, he certainly seems to have the run of the castle."

"Aye, Grandmama is very fond of him, more's the pity."

He gave her a sharp look that she did not see, for she had

slipped down to her knees and was busily gathering yellow anemones on her spread skirt.

He dropped to his knees, forgetful of his immaculate buff riding breeches, and began absently to pluck the flowers with her. "Just what exactly are his antecedents?"

She raised her eyes to his face and said matter-of-factly, "His father, Davonan, was my uncle, one of Grandmama's sons. When Uncle Davonan was quite young, he seduced a young merchant's daughter in Edinburgh. When he discovered she was pregnant, he refused to marry her. From what I have been able to glean from Old Marta's gossiping and Grandmama's occasional spurts of anger, Uncle Davonan left Penderleigh and went to Paris. He died there some ten years ago, with one of his . . . lovers."

"Lovers?"

"Aye, Uncle Davonan did not prefer woman, ye see. Although I must say," she continued with ill-concealed bitterness, "that Percy is continually endeavoring to make amends for that fact."

"To the point of making himself a nuisance where you are concerned, Brandy?"

"Aye," she said shortly.

He thought about her calm acceptance of her Uncle Davonan's preference for men, the mention of which would undoubtedly cause a young English lady to turn red to the roots of her hair, and found her straight speaking refreshing. He decided though, after eyeing the tightly woven blond braids, the faded old shawl, and the plaid woolen gown, that her openness reflected a childlike candor. He said, "Methinks that Percy should direct his attention to women and not children. Perhaps he is unnatural in his own way."

She turned on him angrily. "I told ye, yer grace, that I was seventeen! Hardly a child!"

"Pardon me, Brandy, a gross mispronouncement on my part!" Seeing that her feathers were still ruffled, he added hastily, "Tell me why Percy seems to resent my presence so very much. Of course, I can understand that he would take exception to my being English, but after all, he is a bastard, and would thus never hold claim to either the earldom or Penderleigh Castle."

Brandy was silent for several moments, struggling with the

fact that although Percy was, in her opinion, a rotter, he was nonetheless a Scot whereas the duke was English. The tug of liking and trust she was beginning to feel for Ian won the day. "There is more to it than that, ye see. Constance overheard Grandmama tell Percy that she planned to legitimize him. She wants him to marry an heiress and repair his fortunes."

"Ah."

Worry lines puckered Brandy's forehead. "I must own, though, that Percy is not precisely stupid. I fear that once he is legitimized, he may try to overturn yer claim."

"Most interesting," the duke said, more to himself than to Brandy. Now, what could Lady Adella be up to, he wondered silently. He looked at Brandy, delighted that upon his second day at Penderleigh he had found such a wealth of gratis information. "And just how do Claude and Bertrand stand in all this? You see, my solicitors really knew nothing about the more interesting relationships that seem to abound here."

"Ye did not know that Uncle Claude as well as Bertrand are disinherited?"

"Good Lord! This grows more a tangle with each passing minute!"

"Actually, I do not know the real reason why my Great Uncle Douglass was disinherited. He was Grandpapa Angus's older brother and heir to the title. From what Old Marta says, Grandpapa Angus's father, the old earl, literally threw him off the estate and made Angus his heir. After Douglass died, Grandpapa Angus allowed Uncle Claude and Bertrand to come and live in the dower house. Bertrand has been the estate manager for the past eight or nine years, I think." She added somewhat defiantly, "Bertrand is a good man, regardless of what ye might be thinking of Penderleigh. 'Tis no easy task to keep us all fed and pander to Grandmama's whims with so little to work with!"

"I see," he said, wondering an instant at her sudden fierce defense of Bertrand. What does she expect me to do, he thought, toss Bertrand off the estate? He wondered if Lady Adella had plans to reinherit Claude and Bertrand, just as she was legitimizing Percy. He realized that it would not do at all for him to underestimate this possibly wily old woman. He said aloud, "And just what, Brandy, would you have to say about Lady Adella?"

Brandy wondered what he had been thinking, but she replied only, "Oh, Grandmama is rather odd at times. I think she prides herself on being eccentric."

"And you, Brandy, what do you pride yourself on being?"

"I, yer grace? I suppose that from yer point of view I am naught but a provincial female with no dowry to speak of, a poor relation."

Her matter-of-factness took him off his guard this time, and he found himself suddenly angry at such cynicism from one so young. He realized that he was now her guardian and had it in his power to alter her future, a future that indeed seemed rather bleak from his perspective. He mentally dressed her in a fashionable gown. She would be eighteen within the year and of marriageable age. It occurred to him that Felicity could take the girl under her wing and bring her out in society. He said, "I am now your guardian, Brandy, and you are in no way a provincial female to me. I am to be married in August, to a charming lady who, I am certain, would be delighted to teach you how to get on in society. Would you like to visit London?"

"No, I should not like it at all!" At the stunned look on his face, Brandy leaped to her feet and shook out her skirt. Bright yellow flowers landed in a heap. She ground some of them under her heel as she turned quickly. How dare he treat her so condescendingly!

She drew her pride about her and said coldly, "Excuse me, yer grace, but I must see to Fiona."

"Brandy!" he shouted angrily after her. Damn, but Felicity and Giles were right. The Scots were an unaccountable lot!

She turned and stared down her nose at him.

"You want manners, my girl," he said with icy hauteur. To his surprise, she raised her chin stubbornly, reached in the pocket of her skirt, and flung something at him.

He stared down to see the two guineas sparkling in the sunlight at his feet. The guineas he had given to Fiona.

"There, yer grace, I am already learning manners! Ye have been paid back in kind!" She turned and raced away from him, toward the path that led down the cliff.

"Dammit!" he yelled after her, "you know that was a

misunderstanding!" She did not respond to him and but an instant later, disappeared from his view.

He kicked the guineas with the toe of his boot, furious with her that she had hurled his very understandable mistake in his face. He found that he could not long maintain his anger, though, for she had indeed paid him back in kind. He wiped the grass stains from his breeches and strode to the edge of the cliff. He saw that Brandy had joined Fiona on the beach, next to a pile of mud that was, he supposed, Penderleigh Castle. He frowned, wondering why the devil she had so angrily refused the trip to London. He thought through the words he had spoken, but could find no clue. He turned away from the cliff, still perturbed, and made his way back toward the castle.

"Yer grace!"

The duke drew to a halt and sought out the source of the voice. He saw Bertrand, his red thatch of hair as bright as a cock's comb, striding toward him.

"Good morning, Bertrand," he called, planting a smile of welcome on his lips. He dismissed the gaggle of females, one in particular, from his mind.

"Ye've been enjoying our bright spring morning, I see," Bertrand said with his gentle smile.

The two men shook hands and the duke gazed ruefully down at his breeches. "I must hope that my baggage arrives soon, else I shall be dunning you for a pair of corduroys."

"Or perhaps one of my father's kilts."

The duke tried and failed to picture himself in the Scotman's traditional short skirts.

"Ye've the legs for the kilt," Bertrand said with a twinkle in his blue eyes, having seen the duke's unsuccessful attempt to hide how appalling he found the idea.

"I'll stick to my breeches, grass stains and all, for the moment. As for my legs, they thank you for the compliment."

Bertrand smiled at the duke's reply, and was silent for a moment. "I daresay ye would wish to see the Penderleigh ledgers, and perhaps visit some of our crofters to get the feel of life here."

"I should like that very much," Ian replied, wondering why Bertrand was so very diffident. "Brandy has told me that 'tis you who have run the estate for many years now."

"Aye. I do all my work at the dower house. If ye would like to come with me, we shall not be disturbed, for my father is at the castle with Lady Adella."

In all likelihood, they're discussing my earldom, the duke thought. "Let us get on with it, Bertrand, and please, call me Ian."

"Very well, Ian," Bertrand said, the scattered freckles on his tanned face flushing darker.

The Penderleigh dower house proved to be very little more than a two-story weathered stone cottage, with heavy green vines looping in and out of the crevices. A neat, well-tended garden surrounded the cottage, in startling contrast to the wild, unkept castle grounds. "You look as if you get along quite well here."

"Fraser takes good care of us," Bertrand said. "We are very nearly self-sufficient, what with all the vegetables he coaxes out of this arid ground. We are fortunate to be protected from the sea by all the beech hedges."

Bertrand unlatched the narrow front door and motioned to the duke to duck his head. "Incidently," he said under his breath, "do not mention Morag in Fraser's presence. They are married, ye see, but hold each other in truly remarkable dislike."

"Morag is the woman who scratches."

"Aye, a characteristic that, I believe, helped to sour their happy union."

The duke looked up to see a slightly built, balding man coming toward him, a gardening tool in his hand. "Och, Master Bertrand, yer father's up at the castle."

"Aye, Fraser, I know. This is his grace, the Duke of Portmaine and now also the Earl of Penderleigh."

"Yer grace." Fraser acknowledged the duke's presence with a slight bow and frank, assessing eyes.

"Fraser, be so kind as to fetch us tea. His grace and I will be in the study."

"Aye, Master Bertrand." He gave the duke a rather odd salute with the trowel he was carrying and, with a sprightly step, retreated in the direction he had come.

"Good man," Bertrand said as he led the duke into a small sunlit room, whose furnishings, although old and time-faded,

54

were distinctly respectable. Piles of papers and large velum ledgers were stacked neatly atop a large oak desk.

Bertrand tugged uncomfortably at the shock of red hair that lay over his left temple. " 'Tis not Holyrood House ye've inherited, I fear." He reluctantly picked up the top ledger.

"It matters not," the duke said calmly.

Bertrand seated himself beside the duke and opened the ledger to the most recent page. He began to painstakingly read aloud the entries.

Ian, after some minutes of this incomprehensible recital, grinned and shook his head.

"Words I understand better than numbers. Tell me this, Bertrand, can Penderleigh maintain itself?"

Bertrand said readily, closing the book, "Aye, it could if our crofters could be brought into this new century. Ye see, we have rich farmland in the lowlands to our east and south that is admirably suited for growing corn. But our crofters have not the tools nor the experience to sow the land. What happens most of the time is that they join with the fishermen from the small villages to our north whilst their bairns shepherd a few black-faced sheep."

There came a knock on the door and Fraser entered, balancing a sparkling silver tray on his arm. "Yer tea, master," he said, and with a nod, pulled the trowel from his pocket, and left the room, whistling.

"Cream, Ian?"

"Yes, please," the duke replied, his forehead furrowed in thought. "Could the land support more sheep?" he asked after taking a long drink of the strong tea.

"Aye, it could, but stocking with more sheep is shockingly costly. Ye see, the black-faced sheep are noted for their coarse wool, good really only for making sturdy carpets and the like. It is the Cheviot sheep whose wool makes fine clothing."

"Sheep require yearly shearing. Have we enough crofters?"

"Nay, but we could hire some of the roving tinkers at sheering time."

"And the wool would go to Glasgow? To the mills?"

Bertrand nodded and sat forward, dangling his hands between his legs. He eyed the duke uncertainly, wondering miserably if he thought him a sorry steward.

The duke set down his tea cup and sat forward in his chair. "I think, Bertrand, that you and I should pay a visit to some manufacturers in Stirlingshire. Sheep or corn—we must assess which is the more profitable for Penderleigh's future."

Bertrand blinked. "Ye know of Stirlingshire?"

"Yes, and Clackmannanshire as well." The duke added with a grin, "I didn't come up here totally ignorant, you know, though unfortunately what I did discover about Scottish industry gives me about as much knowledge as you have on the tip of your thumb! You must instruct me, Bertrand. I would not have you believe me a frivolous ne'er-do-well."

Bertrand flushed. "Nay, never that, yer grace! It is just that I . . . we. . . ."

"You did not believe that an English duke would concern himself with a Scottish estate?"

"Aye," Bertrand admitted, dropping his gaze.

"Come, Bertrand," the duke said briskly, "I have no intention of becoming like many English absentee landlords in Ireland. With a little capital and your management, Penderleigh will come to maintain itself with none of the fruits of your labor flowing out of Scotland. Now, if you think it worthwhile, I should like to spend the afternoon visiting the crofters and making out a list of repairs for the castle."

"I thank ye, Ian," Bertrand said, his eyes lighting up. "Penderleigh was once a great estate, but of course time and politics brought disastrous results."

"There is naught we can do to change the past. The future, though, is quite another matter. Brandy has told me what an able master you are. You need never fear the future. I hope that you will trust me in this."

Ian did not really expect Bertrand to reply to his somewhat vague assurances and, indeed, he was grateful that he did not, for the duke was not yet certain exactly what he had intended with his words. His thoughts went to Brandy and her sisters. Their futures were far more uncertain than Bertrand's. He spoke aloud his thoughts. "I was speaking with Brandy this morning about a number of things, including her future." He thought a moment about her inexplicable refusal to visit London, but said only, "Both Brandy and Constance are nearing marriageable age. Penderleigh is rather isolated and I gather there is little social intercourse. As the girls' guardian,

I will, of course, provide dowries, which should help in some measure."

"That is a fine idea," Bertrand said without enthusiasm.

Ian questioned him with his dark eyes.

Bertrand's indifferent shrug was belied by a rather interesting huskiness in his voice. "Constance is quite young yet, not in need of society or a dowry. As concerns Brandy, ye must do what ye feel best, of course."

Ah, the duke thought, the woman-child with the long black tresses and the provocative pouting lips, the sister who should have been the eldest. He was hard pressed to keep an amused smile from his lips. "Undoubtedly you are quite right about Constance," he said calmly. "As to Brandy, yes, I shall do what is best for her." Despite her protestations, he thought to himself.

"Fraser is an excellent cook," Bertrand said, rising. "If ye would have luncheon with me, we could continue our discussion."

"An excellent idea. You will be dining at the castle this evening, will you not?"

"I should be delighted," Bertrand said.

The duke made his way back to the castle late in the afternoon. The visit to the crofters had had to be postponed, for the duke discovered very quickly that there was much for him to learn about the relative merits of sheep and crops. Bertrand's enthusiasm had been catching, and Ian found himself quite pleased with the progress they had made. Brandy was right. Bertrand was a fine man who cared mightily for Penderleigh. But more than that, the duke ruminated, he was knowledgeable and possessed of an excellent mind.

The duke strode into the front entrance hall, dim in the late afternoon light, and wondered how a great hanging chandelier would fit with the ancient medieval tapestries and rusty suits of armor. There was no one about, and he made his way to his bedchamber, his thoughts turning to a hot bath. He was beginning to believe himself alone in the castle when he opened the bedchamber door to see an elderly woman laying out his evening clothes. Her gray hair was tucked neatly under a large mobcap and her voluminous black wool dress encased a rather scrawny figure. She turned and straightened at the sound of his footsteps.

"Yer grace?" she asked in a deep voice, and curtsied before he replied.

"Yes. And you are?"

"Marta, yer grace, her ladyship's maid. Said she did that ye didna fancy that scratchy trollop, Morag, aboot yer clothes an' such. Be there anythin' else ye be needin', yer grace?"

"Yes, a bath. Are there boys to fetch up the water?"

"Aye, I'll fetch Wee Albie out of the kitchen. 'Tis strong he be, but fuzzy in the head, if ye ken my meanin'."

"I ken," the duke said.

Marta swished from the room and the duke stripped off his clothes. He found a towel and wrapped it about his waist.

Wee Albie, the duke soon discovered, was a huge raw-boned lad who had the muscled appearance of a prizefighter. He had large vacant blue eyes and wore a wide grin, showing a gap between his front teeth.

"Yer water, sir," he said, all that business about graces and bows having long since fled from his mind.

"Thank you, Albie," the duke said.

Albie unearthed a well-used bar of soap and clumsily dumped the buckets of hot water into a large wooden tub. Small rivulets of the water began to seep from the bottom of the tub and stream across the floor. The duke gazed at the water with a fascinated eye. Albie, however, appeared to take no notice of such a trifling matter. He straightened and beamed at the duke. "Ye'll call if ye need aught else, sir?"

"You may rest assured that I shall call immediately," the duke replied, striving to maintain his gravity. He was still smiling as he shut the bedchamber door on Albie's retreating hulk.

He lowered himself into the wooden tub, wondering if he was likely to impale himself with splinters. He began to lather himself when to his dismay, he realized that the soap was scented. He grinned ruefully to himself. Damned but he'd smell like a Soho trollop. He wondered if Marta had filched the soap from Lady Adella.

He was leisurely in his scrubbing and stepped out of the tub only after the water had turned uncomfortably cool. He stood in front of the fireplace, naked and dripping, savoring for a moment his natural state.

At the sound of the door opening, he turned about to see Brandy standing in the entrance, panting as if she had been running.

He stared at her, wondering just where the devil he had put the damned towel.

She stared back at him, pointedly.

She gasped, "Why ye're not at all like me . . . ye're beautiful!"

He expected a delayed display of maidenly embarrassment, accompanied possibly by an outraged shriek. Instead, she said calmly, "Please forgive me for disturbing ye, yer grace. I did not think ye had yet returned. I'm trying to find Fiona, ye see."

"She is not here," he said, absurdly.

Brandy inclined her head in a most dignified acknowledgment and walked from the bedchamber, closing the door quietly behind her.

The duke suddenly regained command over his body. He grabbed the towel and wrapped it about his loins, only to realize the next moment how foolish his action was, since Brandy was not likely to return.

Brandy ran a few steps down the corridor, Fiona forgotten, and leaned against the wall, closing her eyes tightly. The duke's naked body was vivid in her mind. She ran her tongue over suddenly dry lips. She had never before seen a naked man and realized that she was trembling, not from embarrassed shock, but from waves of delicious sensation that brought color to her cheeks and a strange, insistent warm feeling to her belly.

"Brandy, here I am!" Fiona suddenly emerged a few paces down the hall. As her sister made no response, Fiona playfully danced toward her. "I was hiding all the time in the old blue room. Brandy?" She edged closer. "Are ye all right? Did I give ye a fright?"

"Nay, poppet, ye didn't give me a fright," Brandy managed to say, her voice breathless. "Come," she said, trying to get a hold on herself, "it is time for yer bath and bed."

Ian dressed quickly and mangled his cravat into a dismal,

lopsided knot, his powers of concentration apparently having deserted him. He tried first to shrug off the entire matter, thinking with a certain condescension that in England, such a thing as a young lady dashing into a gentleman's bedchamber would not be likely to happen. Well, he was in Scotland, he scowled, as he ripped off the mangled cravat and fetched another, and evidently that meant dripping wooden tubs, undisciplined servants, and a young girl with huge amber eyes gazing at him with awed curiosity.

Ye're not at all like me . . . ye're beautiful! What a curious, strange girl she was. He thought of Marianne, his ever modest, shy wife, and wondered if she had believed him beautiful. Absurd thought, for during their one year together, she had always blown out the bedside candle whenever he had entered her room. He had always been tender and gentle with her, but yet there was many a time when she would whimper and cry into his shoulder.

He looked with disgust at his cravat. It would simply have to do, since he had no others left. He very much hoped that Mabley, with his skilled hands and his trunks, would arrive on the morrow.

He carried the branch of candles with him when he left the bedchamber. Their glowing orange light made wispy images along the dimly lit corridor. So I am beautiful, am I, Brandy, he thought, and a small smile played about his lips.

As he neared the drawing room, he heard Lady Adella's powerful, dominating voice, and then Claude's familiar cackle. Brandy would be there, of course, and he determined that he must speak to her, if for naught else to assure himself that she was not mortified by her behavior.

He turned the door handles, large curved brass affairs whose knobs were griffins' heads, and entered the drawing room. Lady Adella held court from her high-backed chair, and, as usual, all eyes were turned to her. She was a proud old relic, he thought, and her behavior piqued his interest. As he gazed at her thick snow-white hair arranged in a knot high on her head, with small sausage ringlets dangling about her narrow face, he grimaced, for such a style was suitable for a woman at least forty years younger.

Claude sat opposite her, for all the world like a crumpled old roué, appearing many years older than his age. Bertrand

and Constance shared a long settee, and Percy, a glass of sherry in his outstretched hand, leaned negligently against the mantelpiece. He searched for Brandy and saw that she was seated on a small stool just behind Lady Adella's chair. She was wearing the same gown that she had worn the evening before, and the same tartan shawl was knotted tightly about her shoulders. She looked up and he smiled gently at her.

Lady Adella called to him. "Well, Ian, my lad, Bertie here has been telling us of your intoxicating pleasures today." Her jovial voice blended strangely with the snide words. He saw Bertrand lower his gaze to his large hands and wished he could tell him not to pay the old meddlesome woman any heed.

Ignoring her words, he strode toward her chair and said calmly, "A good evening to you, lady." He lightly kissed her age-spotted hand.

Percy took a long drink from his sherry and set his glass upon the mantelpiece. "Tell me, yer grace, is it true that ye intend to turn us all into farmers and shepherds?"

Damn, but Percy should learn to be more subtle in his insults, Ian thought. He said, "Bertrand and I have not as yet decided, Percy. You must be patient. It requires time to grow a profitable corn crop, thought I must admit that Penderleigh appears to have a surfeit of sheep dung in its confines right now."

Bertrand grinned openly and Claude cackled, slapping his hand to his knee.

"Ye'll mind yer tongue now, Percy, eh?" Lady Adella chortled and thumped her cane on the floor.

"I'll mind my tongue whenever it pleases me to do so, my lady!" Percy snapped, his eyes narrowing on the duke's impassive face.

"Good evening, yer grace," Constance said softly. She dimpled pertly and held out her hand to him.

"Good evening, cousin," the duke said, and obligingly dropped a light kiss upon her wrist. "You're looking quite lovely tonight."

Constance preened like a sleek, cream-fed cat. She slewed her green eyes pointedly in Percy's direction.

Damnation, the duke thought, the chit wants the wrong man.

He nodded to Brandy before turning toward Claude. "I trust you all approve Bertrand's and my plans?"

"Ye make me fair loathe to answer ye, me lad," Claude wheezed, displaying a row of blackened teeth. He turned to Percy and guffawed. "Yer talk of sheep dung makes me think of some men's morals."

"Ach, uncle," Percy cut in, "ye tumbled many a wench afore yer manhood shriveled up like yer brain! Yer moralizing rings as hollow as yer head!"

Lady Adella threw back her head and roared with laughter and Constance giggled. Ian found himself angry at such crudeness and a stinging retort rose to his lips. Brandy's angry voice cut him off.

"How dare ye say such things, Percy," she cried. "Such talk belongs in the stables! Hold yer vile tongue, do ye hear?"

Ian was mentally congratulating Brandy when Percy taunted her, his voice affecting a husky depth. "Ah, my little cousin, ye are troubled by thoughts o' tumbling with a man?"

The duke saw her slender hands curl into fists, and said coldly, "If Brandy is troubled, Percy, it is undoubtedly because you have turned the drawing room into a stable yard, fit only for the ears of pigs."

A deep growl tore from Percy's throat, but he was called to attention by Lady Adella. "I tell ye, Percy, to leave the girl alone! She's my wee innocent, and I'll not have ye turning her ears red!"

"Nay, lady," Percy said softly, ignoring the duke, "our Constance must be the wee innocent. Is not our Brandy seventeen and a woman grown?"

" 'Tis nay true, Percy," Constance cried breathlessly, drawing Percy's eyes to her. "I am a woman grown, not a braided, dowdy child! Years be not the yardstick."

"As ye will, lassie," Percy said, proffering her a mocking bow.

At that moment, Crabbe entered. "Dinner be served, yer grace!"

Lady Adella said sourly, "I'll wager yer miserable flat ears were plastered against the door!"

While Lady Adella fussed with her many shawls, Ian saw Percy straighten and make his way purposefully toward

Brandy. He moved quickly, neatly cutting him off, and offered her his arm.

"Will you accompany me to dinner, Brandy?"

She threw him a grateful look, rose quickly, and slipped her hand into the crook of his arm.

As they crossed the flagstones to the dining room, he said quietly, "I would speak to you, later perhaps."

She nodded. As if aware of Percy behind them, she lengthened her stride, pulling him with her.

As he readied to seat her beside Constance, Lady Adella said loudly, "Ye'll sit over here, child." She imperiously waved Brandy to the chair held solicitously by Percy. "Ye must get to know yer cousin, girl. He'll broaden yer view of the world."

What the devil is the old hag up to now, Ian wondered, frowning at her. Her eyes were mocking and her lips drawn into a thin line. He could think of no civil way to gainsay her. It came as something of a shock to him that she was using her granddaughter as a cat's paw, to stir up enmity between him and Percy. She is not only an eccentric, he thought, but also damned perverse.

Brandy sent a startled, confused look toward Lady Adella, but her eyes were now resting on Percy, glistening with mischief.

Percy laughed softly as Brandy hesitantly slipped herself into the chair. "Come, little cousin, as Lady Adella says, we must get to know each other better."

"I have no desire to even see ye, Percy, much less be forced to eat my dinner in yer company."

Unperturbed, Percy continued in a low, caressing voice, meant only for her hearing, "Don't ye want to become a woman, fair cousin? I can see ye now, yer thick, long hair freed and flowing, passion lighting yer virgin's eyes——"

"Stop it, ye pig!" Brandy hissed, and jabbed him in the leg with her fork.

Lady Adella chuckled maliciously. "It appears ye've suffered a setback, my lad. Speak to her of Edinburgh and yer travels, not o' yer randy disposition."

"Yes, Percy," the duke said, "I am certain that all of us would be much amused to hear of your travels. Perhaps, too, you would be so kind as to give us your opinion of the merits of Cheviot sheep?"

"One bleater speaking of other bleaters," Claude said, and laughed aloud at his own wit. "I vow there would be no benefit in that, yer grace!"

"Father, please," Bertrand said, wishing only that the wretched meal would be over without everyone flying into a passion. He gazed uncomfortably toward Ian, wondering what he must be thinking of all of them. As much as he had wanted to dislike the new Earl of Penderleigh, he had found after their afternoon together that the duke was not at all what he had expected. For one violent instant, he wished he could draw Percy's cork.

"Ah, our Bertrand, the peacemaker," Percy mocked, and forked down a bite of fish.

In the minute of silence, Ian turned to Bertrand and questioned him about the fishing along the coast. Brandy wished she could add something to this benign conversation, but could only think of her own small boat, nestled in a calm protective cove. She started to open her mouth when Percy leaned toward her. Repulsed, she drew away, all thoughts of boats and fishing fled from her mind. She chanced to gaze over at Constance, and saw her green eyes resting upon her, hard and glittering.

Brandy looked down at her plate, feeling awash with misery. Nay, Connie, she thought to herself, Percy is a wretch and a philanderer, not worthy of yer affection. If ye were indifferent to him, 'twould be the same as with me.

When the interminable meal had drawn to a relatively calm close, Lady Adella made to rise. Brandy was out of her chair and standing beside her grandmother before the old lady had even planted her cane upon the floor.

"We will leave ye to yer port, gentlemen," she said grandly, and sailed majestically from the room. Brandy close on her heels. Constance lagged behind as long as she dared, her eyes upon Percy.

Ian wondered if Lady Adella had decided to leave the gentlemen this evening with the hope of stirring up more mischief. He resolved to keep a firm hold on his temper, if for naught else, to spike her guns.

As Brandy helped to settle her grandmother close to the

roaring fire, Lady Adella said softly, "Ye're a coward, child, and have no notion of how to handle a gentleman."

"I would hardly call Percy a gentleman," Brandy whispered, aware of Constance coming into the drawing room.

"He'll be one soon enough, child. That shifty old eagle, MacPherson, prepared the papers today. Perhaps ye'll think better of yer cousin when he's not a bastard."

"Never!"

"Mayhap," Lady Adella continued, her eyes boring into Brandy's, "when he becomes a true Robertson of Penderleigh, I will see to it that the duke settles an income on him. Would ye want him then, child? Robertsons make weak husbands, lassie, and Percy would be no different . . . if ye knew how to hold his reins."

Brandy shuddered, despite the sweltering heat from the fireplace. She realized that her grandmother's turnabout as regarded Percy was intended not only to discomfit her but also to raise the duke's hackles. "Nay, Grandmama," she managed, " 'tis Constance who wishes Percy, not I."

"The eldest weds first," Lady Adella said with finality, thrusting out her pointed chin. "Our Constance will suit Bertrand."

Brandy was too startled by this abrupt disclosure to speak. She looked over at Constance, who was obviously bored, and watched her stroll to the windows to gaze at her reflection in the panes. Did not Lady Adella realize that Constance regarded Bertrand as a brother and nothing more? She decided to hold her peace, as she was certain Lady Adella would only become more outrageous if she dared to gainsay her.

Lady Adella looked up and snorted as the gentlemen filed in, a gleeful expression lighting her eyes.

"I see ye didn't take long over yer port! Ye didn't enjoy each other's company?"

"Our conversation was most stimulating, Lady Adella," Ian said calmly. "Percy has been telling us about Edinburgh."

Lady Adella tried to hide her disappointment by turning to Constance and ordering her to the pianoforte.

Brandy saw Percy making toward her and whispered urgently to Lady Adella, "Let me go, Grandmama, I wish to see to Fiona."

Lady Adella eyed her speculatively, but said only, "Ye're a coward, girl. Very well, off with ye."

Brandy breathed a sigh of relief and swept a slight curtsy toward the gentlemen. "I bid ye all good night."

Ian forestalled her departure. "A moment, please, Brandy, I would have a word with you, if you do not mind."

Percy laughed softly. "Perhaps, little cousin, after his grace is done, I may also speak with ye."

"Since ye ask, Percy, I will roundly tell ye no!"

Percy shrugged and turned to Constance, who was tugging at his sleeve. "Do come, Percy, I want ye to turn my pages."

"I will walk you to the stairs," Ian said to Brandy. "I'll be back presently, Lady Adella," he added smoothly. He turned and followed Brandy from the drawing room.

Brandy halted and looked up at him questioningly, her thoughts still muddled by her grandmother's startling pronouncements.

The duke drew up to his full height and gazed down at her kindly. "I am sorry about Percy, my dear. His wayward tongue needs to be tamed. I shall contrive to see that he doesn't bother you." He wasn't quite certain exactly how he would accomplish this, particularly in the face of Lady Adella's perverse encouragement of Percy.

"'Tis strange, a mystery," she said, still pondering her grandmother's inexplicable behavior.

"What is a mystery?"

Brandy smiled rather wanly. "Grandmama tells me that she intends Constance to wed Bertrand. Constance cannot approve that notion, I assure ye."

There is no end to the old harridan's plotting, Ian thought wryly. In this instance, though, her intention was not far removed from his own. "I see," he said evenly. He called himself back to his purpose and said gently, "I wished to speak to you, Brandy, because I wanted to . . . apologize to you for causing you upset."

She frowned at him, then suddenly remembered her outburst of the morning. He had meant only to be kind, offering her a trip to London, and she had behaved churlishly.

"Nay, yer grace—"

"Ian."

"Nay, Ian, the apology comes from the wrong mouth. It

was I who behaved in an unseemly manner." She had believed herself angry at his offer because he seemed to view her as a gauche provincial, a Scottish girl whose manners needed mending. But after she had fled from him, she was forced to admit to herself that her sudden fury had more to do with the thought of living with him and his future duchess. It had galled her, and she wasn't certain precisely why.

He thought that she had indeed behaved outrageously, but he said firmly, "No, your behavior, although unexpected, was not at all unseemly. After all, how could you have known?" Although he still saw no shyness or embarrassment in her amber eyes, he could not bring himself to add that what she could not have known was that he would be standing naked and wet in his bedchamber.

"Aye, but I should have guessed. I should have known that ye'd already have a lady."

The duke blinked. "What does my being betrothed have to say to anything? That Miss Trammerley would have been mortified and berated me for my carelessness?"

"Mayhap she would, Ian. 'Tis not likely that she would approve of me."

"I assure you, Brandy, that my future wife has nothing at all to say in this matter. Indeed, I cannot imagine a good reason for telling her."

Her eyes filled with hurt. "I've offended ye. Ye don't want me now."

He blinked at her. Damn, but this was ridiculous! She was an innocent young girl who simply did not understand what she was saying. " 'Twould be most improper of me to . . . want you, Brandy. I only spoke to you because I did not want you to feel awkward or embarrassed in my presence."

She drew herself up proudly. "If ye didn't want me, then whyever did ye—" She broke off and turned away. "I'll not hold it against ye, Ian, indeed, I'll never bring it up again."

He felt himself mired in confusion. "Good God, child, I only wanted you to understand that I harbored no base intentions! Rest assured that I shall keep the door locked after this!"

Brandy had the inescapable feeling that Scottish was a far

different language from the King's English. "Whatever does locking yer door have to say to anything?'

"Dammit, if I lock my door, you'll not burst in upon me again! Really, Brandy, I am not in the habit of allowing young girls to see me naked!"

"Naked! Oh!"

He watched a dull red flush spread from her neck to her hairline. She said in a small, choked voice, "I thought ye were apologizing for this morning, when I was angry at ye for inviting me to London . . . with yer wife."

He threw back his head and gave way to a booming laugh. So they had been speaking at cross-purposes! "No, cousin, 'twas not this morning I was talking of. What a blow you've dished up to my masculine ego! You didn't give the . . . incident a second thought."

She felt a strange tightness in her chest. She forced her eyes to his face and said, "Nay, Ian, ye're wrong."

Before he could speak, she grasped her skirts and fled up the stairs, leaving him to stare after her.

5

Ian awoke with a start the next morning. He turned a bleary eye toward the weathered window panes to see gray drizzle streaking down the glass, then glanced at the clock at his elbow. It was barely after five o'clock in the morning. Although he laid his cheek against the pillow and firmly closed his eyes again, he found that he was unable to fall asleep again and with a grunt of disgust, threw back the warm covers.

Mindful of splinters from the bare wooden floor, he walked gingerly to the fireplace, and after some well-enunciated curses managed to coax a decent flame from the wood and peat. He shrugged into his dressing gown and decided, without much enthusiasm, that he might as well pass the time until breakfast penning a letter to Felicity.

He dug out paper, quill, and ink pot and settled himself in a large winged chair close to the fire. He chewed absently on the end of his quill for some moments, forming phrases in his mind as was his habit. He smoothed out a sheet of his ducal stationery and set his quill to its task. "My dearest Felicity," he wrote, frowned a moment at nothing in particular, and wadded up the sheet of paper.

He began once again, "Dear Felicity. . . ." The blank page stretched before him endlessly. He stroked his chin a moment, then attacked with his quill, mindful that he did, after all, owe his betrothed some account of his journey and Penderleigh. "I arrived safely at Penderleigh three days ago. Unfortunately, my poor valet, Mabley, who was riding in the luggage coach, endured a mishap near Galashiels (a town to the southwest of here) and I pray to the stars that he will ar-

69

rive today. I swear I shall embrace the fellow! If he doesn't arrive, I suppose I shall be obliged to borrow a change of clothing from Bertrand Robertson, a cousin of mine. He and his father, Claude (an old curmudgeon of the first order), reside in the dower house, quite happily from what I can gather, and Bertrand has and will continue to run the estate. For some reason I have not yet been made privy to, Claude's father, Douglass, elder brother to the last earl, was disinherited many years ago, thus altering the inheritance line. 'Tis a pity really, for Bertrand cares much for Penderleigh and would make it a fine master. Lady Adella, the late earl's widow and an unaccountable old woman to boot, may wreak some magic and reverse the disinheritance. I might add that she has already begun to legitimize Percival Robertson, a cocky young buck who hates Englishmen in general and me in particular. If you find all of these family entanglements confusing, you can well imagine how I felt until I sorted everyone out! The 'gaggle' of females, as Giles calls the three girls, also cousins, are delightful, each in her own way. The youngest, Fiona, is a scarlet-haired little vixen who leads her eldest sister, Brandy (an odd name to be sure and shortened from Brandella), a merry chase. The middle girl, Constance, all of fifteen years of age, fancies herself much the grown-up lady and flirts outrageously with Percy. Brandy, the eldest, though, is the different one."

He paused in his writing and sat back in his chair, rubbing his fingers along the line of his jaw. He found that thinking of Brandy brought words quickly to his mind. "Strangely enough, her eyes are a deep amber and match her to her nickname quite aptly. She is an unusual girl and rather vulnerable at present, for Percy, in this odd ménage, is enamored of her and makes no bones about it. She, however, holds him in the strongest dislike."

Actually, he thought, she is the beauty of the family. He smiled, somewhat bemused at this admission.

"Everyone speaks with the soft, blurred Scottish brogue that, contrary to our snobs in England, is most pleasant to the ear. I, myself, find that I've slipped easily into some of their forms of speech." He paused yet again, realizing that he had completed a full page, which, normally, was not at all his way. Felicity would wonder at his sudden verbosity. He cramped together the last few lines.

"Bertrand and I plan to leave for the Cheviot today, if this accursed rain stops, to purchase, or at least inspect, what he informs me are the most profitable of Scottish sheep. After that, we are off to Glasgow to speak to local manufacturers at the mills. I am sorry, my dear, but I must revise the length of time I must remain from London. There is much to be done here at Penderleigh. I trust that Giles is escorting you to all the soirees and assemblies. Yours, Ian."

After affixing Felicity's direction to an envelope, he rose and stretched lazily, casting a dubious eye toward the sleeting rain. He refused to let the weather dampen his spirits and as he dressed quickly in riding breeches, a frilled white shirt, and hessians, he whistled the Robert Burns ballad that Brandy had sung.

Everyone appeared to be still abed. Only Crabbe was downstairs to bow and greet him good morning. He opened the door to the breakfast room and without precisely intending it, smiled broadly at the sight of Brandy, hunched over the table, dawdling listlessly over her porridge.

"Good morning, Brandy," he said, and found that his smile lingered.

"Yer grace . . . Ian! 'Tis so early!"

As he walked toward her, he saw a dull flush spread over her cheeks. Why the devil was she blushing, she wondered. "You believe me a sluggard, Brandy? Surely, I have done nothing to merit such a lowering thought."

She gazed at the snowy white lace at his throat and wrists. His riding breeches were molded to his muscular thighs and she thought yet again that she was a sorry specimen compared to his elegant appearance.

He regarded her with some amusement. "Do I meet with your approval?"

Her eyes flew to his face and she thought he was laughing at her. She said stiffly, "Aye. I was just thinking that ye do quite well without yer valet."

"I thank you, Brandy. Ah, porridge, I see." What he would give for just one slice of rare sirloin and a plate of eggs and kidneys!

"It's rather lumpy this morning. I think Cook must be in a miff about something."

She spooned a liberal amount into a bowl and placed it at the head of the table.

Ian seated himself and added some clotted cream and sugar to the brownish porridge. "Where is your wee bairn, Fiona, this morning?"

"She has the sniffles so I ordered her to stay in bed. Poor child, she detests not to be dashing about."

"If Mabley arrives this morning, I shall have him take a look at her. My valet," he added, as she cocked her head to one side questioningly. "He always carries with him a formidable array of potions, salves, and the like. Indeed, if he arrives after I leave, Brandy, do make use of his services."

"Ye're leaving?" she asked, hating the quiver in her voice.

"Aye, with Bertrand. I do not leave for England yet. We reached the decision last evening after you had gone to bed. We go to the Cheviot to look over sheep, then on to Glasgow. I fancy we shouldn't be gone too very long."

"I see," she said, feeling absurdly relieved.

He studied her a moment, wondering what she was thinking. He thought again of their cross-purposed conversation of the evening before and her bald statement before she had fled from him, and repressed the desire to ask her to more fully explain her parting words. Better to forget the entire ridiculous incident. He turned his thoughts to another topic. "I trust that you have reconsidered and will now come to London in the fall. You will have ample time to learn your way about before you are presented in the spring."

She regarded him steadily, and managed to cloak the hurt his words made her feel. "Scotland is my home, yer grace. I cannot imagine why ye are so insistent at having a graceless Scot about to embarrass ye in front of all yer fine friends and yer . . . wife. I would, yer grace, that ye would leave well enough alone."

"It seems to me, Brandy, that whenever you are displeased with me, I suddenly become 'yer grace.'" He saw the mulish set of her chin and said only, "We will discuss the matter when I return." Before she could disagree with him further, he said, "You are, of course, aware that Lady Adella is behaving outrageously, particularly where you and Percy are concerned. I would that you take care whilst I am gone, for he shows no signs of wishing to leave Penderleigh."

"I assure ye, yer grace—Ian, that I am well able to take care of myself! Percy is naught but a blustering, ridiculous bag of wind."

"I would not be too certain of that," he replied. It suddenly came to him that he could protect her without her knowing of it. He silently examined his idea for a few moments, and nodded to his porridge bowl, satisfied with his plan. Stubborn chit! He would see to her safety and avoid raising her hackles in the bargain.

She caught him off his guard when she said abruptly, "Yer future . . . wife, what is she like? A very fine lady, I suppose."

Ian had no particular wish to speak of Felicity, indeed, he had not much desire to even think about her at the moment. His black brows drew together and he said only, his voice repressive, "Yes, I suppose she is a fine lady."

"What does she look like?"

"Her hair is dark, her eyes green, and her size rather small. Does that satisfy you, Madame Curiosity?"

"Aye," she said, not at all satisfied. She stirred the remains of the porridge with her spoon for some moments. "What do ye think of Scotland, Ian? And the Scots?"

"I suspect that people are much the same wherever they live," he said calmly. "As to Scotland itself, I shall be in a much better position to answer you when I return."

"Ye . . . ye do not despise us?"

"Good God, Brandy, what a ridiculous question! Pray tell me why you think I should ever draw such a conclusion?"

"Ye are very polite," she said somewhat obliquely, and slipped out of her chair. "Bertrand thinks highly of ye. I suppose that like the rest of us, he expected another arrogant Englishman who would rob our lands and grind us under like so much dirt."

He said steadily, "And what do you think of me, Brandy?"

"As well as being polite, ye are also very . . . kind," she said, and turned away. She paused at the door and added over her shoulder, "I wish ye good fortune on yer trip, Ian."

"Thank you, Brandy." An invisible imp made him add, "I

think that I prefer being beautiful in your eyes rather than
. . . kind."

If he expected her to flush in embarrassment, he was disappointed. She said softly, her amber eyes widening with mischief, "Since to me, ye are both kind and beautiful, I can see no reason for ye to quibble!"

He was obliged to laugh, but before he could say anything further, she had gone.

To Ian's incalculable relief, Mabley arrived not an hour later, delighted to be again with his master, but determined not to show it. "A fine sight you are, your grace!" he said sourly, following Ian up to his bechamber.

"Ring a peal over me, Mabley, but do pack a portmanteau, for I am off for several days. No need to polish my hessians," he added hastily, as his valet looked near to apoplexy at the sight of his less than immaculate boots. He rather hoped that Mabley would not make the acquaintance of Morag too quickly, for he could well imagine how the poor old man's veiny nose would twitch in disgust at her exceptionable person. He left him grumbling and puttering about the room and went in search of Lady Adella, determined to see her before the weather cleared and he and Bertrand left Penderleigh. Now I will spike your guns, Brandy, he said to himself, as he made his way to the seaward side of the castle to Lady Adella's suite of rooms.

The door was open, and as he drew near, he heard two women's raised, angry voices. One was Lady Adella's and the other, he realized after a moment, was the old servant Marta's.

"Ye're a cold and heartless old bitch!"

"An old bitch I may well be," answered Lady Adella's drumming voice, "but at least I was never a plucked bag o' bones! Little ye did to warm the master's bed!"

"It's not true, damn ye. The master came to my bed when ye berated him and made him feel less the man."

"Ye're a fool, Marta, make no mistake. 'Twas always I who was the master and mistress of Penderleigh. When he took to tossing up yer skirts, 'twas but another hold he gave me."

"I loved him, do ye hear," Marta's voice trembled.

Lady Adella laughed rudely. "Love! You're a stupid slut!

Ye got naught from the earl save his ruddy cock! And that, Marta, I never minded in the least."

"But ye're nay master and mistress of Penderleigh anymore, lady! The duke be not a weak Robertson male. It's strong he is, lady, and much used to having everything as he wishes it. He'll not let ye play off yer tricks wi' him."

The duke stood rooted to the spot, his ethical considerations having lost soundly to his curiosity. He was rather pleased that he compared favorably to the "weak Robertson males."

"What tricks, ye old trollop?" Her voice grew cunning. "I do naught but make right all the wrongs of that rutting old goat. As for yer precious duke, he'll be gone from Penderleigh afore ye know it, back to where he belongs in London. And I'll thank ye to hold yer infernal tongue, ye gape-toothed hag, else I'll—"

"Else ye'll what? Set me to scouring the kitchen floors?"

Lady Adella's voice grew silkily quiet and the duke had to strain to hear her next words. "Ye know, I have been thinking that an heiress is naught what our Percy needs. Indeed, when old MacPherson brings him to the right side o' the blanket, methinks he'll be quite suitable for our Brandy."

"Och, ye're a witch! The girl hates him, the rutting bounder! If ye've eyes in yer shrunken head, ye know that Percy doesna want to stay at Penderleigh. As for Brandy, he loves her not, 'tis her virginity that intrigues him, and aye, her aversion to him."

"Ye're a romantic fool," Lady Adella said, her voice deep with scorn. "Mayhap I'll encourage Percy, mayhap let him force Brandy and plant a bairn in her belly. 'Tis I who would see that he weds her. Aye, he'll dance to my tune, ye'll see, believing all the while that he is the player!"

"But 'tis nay right, lady. Brandy hates him. Do ye want to see the child miserable just as ye were?"

"Shut yer mouth, damn ye! The child is too young to know her own mind and she'll do what I tell her. And don't ye dare rant to me about love. Ye old slut, yer notion of love is a grunting, sweating male between yer legs!"

"Ye're wicked, lady, wicked!"

The duke heard the clip-clop of heavy wooden shoes and strode quickly back down the corridor. Damn, but the old woman was daft. If he had to drag Brandy, kicking and yelling, he would not let her remain under Lady Adella's perverse thumb.

He waited a few minutes, then retraced his steps to Lady Adella's sitting room. It was time that he let her know quite clearly exactly who was the master of Penderleigh.

He found her seated, her back ramrod straight, in a high-backed chair close to the fireplace. He gazed about her sitting room, hard put to imagine a more chill and forbidding place.

He seated himself opposite her and began smoothly, "I find myself faced with somewhat of a problem, Aunt, and I seek your good advices."

Her faded blue eyes sharpened with curiosity. "Aye, lad?"

"It concerns the girls, Brandy in particular, since she is the eldest. As I am now their legal guardian, I would like to provide them with proper dowries and, indeed, a season in London."

She gazed at him shrewdly under her thin lashes. "Why?" she demanded baldly.

Ian had no ready answer, their interview not as yet following the lines he had expected. "I would think," he said coolly, "that you would be delighted to have the girls so well provided for."

"I cannot gainsay that the dowries will help the Penderleigh coffers, but as for sending the girls to London for a season . . . ridiculous! Besides, it's not what I have planned for them."

"I beg your pardon, Aunt, but I have no intention of any dowry money making its way into the Penderleigh coffers. Indeed, the money will only be released when I have formally approved the future bridegrooms."

"The girls' futures are my concern, yer grace, and I'll thank ye not to meddle in what doesn't concern ye! Ye may with my blessing dower the girls, but it is I who will choose their husbands!"

" 'Tis not likely, lady, that I would allow you such control, particularly since I have remarked how you abuse it. Contrive to remember, Lady Adella, that it is I who am master of Penderleigh, and you can hold claim no longer to being its mistress!"

She sucked in her breath, realizing that she had pushed him too far. "And what do ye mean by that, my lad?"

"I mean that Percy, no matter what side of the blanket he finds himself at the end of your machinations, will not take Brandy to wed. Indeed, as her guardian, I will no longer allow him to make a nuisance of himself where she is concerned."

"What, do ye fear that he'll overturn yer claims to Penderleigh . . . or to Brandy?" She saw him stiffen and hastened to add in a wheedling tone, "Ye've not given the lad a chance to prove himself. 'Tis not a bad 'un Percy is. Think ye, yer grace, if ye dower Brandy and she weds with Percy, then the money rests at Penderleigh. The girl doesn't know her own mind and 'tis coy she's being. I'll see that Percy does right by her, when she's his wife."

"Heed me well, lady. Percy will never touch Brandy, or Constance, for that matter. If you continue to encourage him and badger Brandy to receive his attentions, here is what I shall do. I shall have you removed from Penderleigh land, provide you with a small widow's jointure, and never again let you meddle with the lives of your family. Do I make myself quite clear, lady?"

"Ye wouldn't dare!"

"You know that I would," he said, and stared steadily into her angry eyes. He added softly, "No matter your crooked intentions toward Percy and Claude, just remember that it is I who hold the power. If I allow you to carry out your legitimization plans for Percy, indeed, if you choose to reinherit Claude and thus Bertrand, it is because I permit it."

Lady Adella sank back against the chair cushions, sucked in her breath, and glared at him. "Ye dare to threaten me, duke. I much dislike threats, particularly from Englishmen!"

"They are not threats, lady, but assurances. Believe me that if you go against my wishes with Brandy, I will do exactly what I have said."

Although she quickly lowered her gaze to her clutching fingers, he saw a look of uncertainty in her eyes.

"As you know, Bertrand and I leave this afternoon and plan to be away from Penderleigh for some days. I expect you to take immediate steps to ensure that Percy does not go near to Brandy. After you have seen to that, Lady Adella, I would that you use your almost boundless influence with her and convince her that she must come to London once I am married."

Lady Adella couldn't help herself and asked in an incredulous voice, "Ye mean to tell me that Brandy already knows of yer plans and has refused ye!"

"Yes, but I expect upon my return that you will have changed her mind. Now, lady," he said, rising, "do I have your agreement to do as I ask?"

She shot him a look of loathing from beneath half-closed eyes and waved her veiny hand at him. "Aye, for the moment."

"You have set my mind at ease, lady," he said, and proffering her a slight bow, turned and left her sitting room.

Shortly after luncheon, the weather cleared and Ian and Bertrand decided to take their leave. Mabley, looking somewhat bewildered, packed his master's portmanteau, his eyes baleful and accusing.

"I'll not be gone long, Mabley. My only advice to you is that you avoid a woman called Morag." He grinned at his valet's look of confusion, and took his leave.

~ 6 ~

"Don't get wet, poppet," Brandy admonished, and watched Fiona until the child had gained the beach.

She sighed and turned away, very much aware of the cause of her sudden sadness. Ian had left with Bertrand only an hour ago and she had gazed after him until she could no longer hear the clop-clop of his horse's hooves.

The sun grew hot and she pulled off her shawl and rolled up her muslin sleeves to her elbows. For want of anything better to do, she sank down in the field of anemones and began absently to pull up the yellow flowers and weave them into a garland.

She felt someone's presence and turned to see Percy standing but a few feet away from her, legs spread, hands on his hips. He reached down and picked up her shawl, wadded it into a plaid ball, and threw it some distance from her.

She stared at him coldly. "How dare ye, Percy! Ye be not funny, ye know. Hand me my shawl and leave me be."

"And why do ye want yer shawl?" he drawled. "The sun is really quite warm." He let his hooded green eyes stray from her flushed face to her breasts, to her small waist. "Ye really shouldn't hide yer woman's charms, Brandy."

She realized that showing her discomfort would only encourage him to be more outrageous. "Really, Percy, both ye and yer observations bore me. I have always disliked being in the company of pigs and . . . bastards."

She saw a dangerous glint in his eyes and instinctively drew back.

"Ye are becoming hoity toity, lassie, what with the illustrious duke insisting that ye travel to London! Aye, don't look

79

so surprised, Lady Adella just told me of what she called 'yer good fortune.' " He didn't tell her that Lady Adella had also been explicit in her orders to him, the old bitch! "Tell me, little cousin," he continued, "just what did ye have to do for the duke to earn yerself a trip and a dowry?"

The color drained from her face and she rose jerkily to her feet. "Why must ye always think others as despicable as yerself!" Her anger fanned also toward Ian, for she realized that he must have gone behind her back to Lady Adella. Was he so blind not to guess how it would make her feel, being together with him and that *other* lady, who was to be his wife?

She drew a deep breath and forced herself to say calmly, "Ye're wrong, Percy. I have no intention of going to London. Ye must know that Grandmama is always meddling and plotting. As for the duke's providing all of us with dowries. . . ." She shrugged her shoulders.

"Ye're a strange lass, Brandy," Percy said finally, puzzled. "Just what do ye want?"

"What do I want?" she repeated slowly, her brow furrowed in an effort to dismiss what she knew to be an outlandish, altogether absurd desire. She looked out to sea and saw some crofters in a barely seaworthy little boat, heaving their tattered nets over the side into the water.

"I want naught but what I can have, Percy, and that is what I have now—Grandmama, Fiona, and Penderleigh." She faced him again. "Do ye intend to remain here or return to Edinburgh?"

He recalled Lady Adella's cold, mocking voice. "Ye'll leave yer hands off the girl, my randy lad. Mayhap it will be better to remove yerself from temptation. Yer heiress awaits ye, does she not?"

"Edinburgh," he answered Brandy. "I believe that I will leave on the morrow. 'Tis off to woo my heiress. Without her father knowing just yet . . . leastwise until the courts have tied me up with a new ribbon."

"Is that what *ye* want, Percy?" Brandy asked, feeling somehow that he was mocking himself. There was a bitterness in his voice that made her, for the moment, sorry for him.

He gazed down at her, taking in the soft tendrils of hair that curled about her face and the full curve of her breasts. "Nay, lass, 'tis not what I want," he said in a husky voice.

Before she knew what he was about, Percy grabbed her shoulders and pulled her roughly against him. She cried out in surprise and fear, only to feel his mouth grinding against hers and his tongue probing wildly against her teeth. A wave of revulsion swept through her and she struggled frantically against his hold.

"Don't fight me, Brandy," he moaned into her mouth, stifling her cries. "Ye know how long I've desired ye." Swiftly, he grasped her hips, lifted her from the ground and toppled her onto her back amid the bright yellow flowers.

She screamed once before he covered her mouth with his hand. She felt him moving on top of her, felt his weight crushing her down, and for a moment could not get enough air into her lungs.

He tore at the buttons on her gown, his fingers wildly groping for her breast. My God, she thought, he is going to rape me! She writhed beneath him, pounding at his shoulders with her fists, tearing at his hair. His breath was hot against her mouth and she felt a curious hardness pressing against her belly. She had seen animals mating, and knew that he would thrust himself into her. She felt terrified at her own helplessness.

"Brandy! Cousin Percy! Ye're playing and ye didn't invite me! Can I play the game with ye?"

Percy froze over her, his face ludicrous with dismay.

"Fiona!" Brandy pulled her bodice together, shoved Percy off of her, and scrambled to her feet. Percy pulled himself to a sitting position. His face was crimson with anger, and Brandy heard him cursing under his breath.

"Well, can't I play?" Fiona demanded, eyeing first her sister, then Percy.

"Nay, poppet," Brandy gasped, "the game is over!" Seeing the child's confusion, she stumbled on. " 'Tis a new kind of wrestling Cousin Percy was teaching me! As ye can see, I beat him handily!"

Brandy dared to look down at Percy as she spoke, and drew back at the fury in his eyes. Were it not for Fiona, she knew that he would have had his way with her. She noticed that she was trembling from fear.

"There'll be another time, little cousin," he muttered in a

low voice. "Ye need to be tamed, and, aye, I'm the man who will do it."

She took another step back, her distance from him giving her courage. "I'll see ye in hell first! There'll ne'er be another time!" Without another look at Percy, Brandy picked up her skirts and broke into a run. She cried over her shoulder, "Come, poppet, I'll race ye!"

Brandy left Fiona in Marta's care, assiduously avoiding the old woman's curious eyes, and made her way to Lady Adella's sitting room.

Clutching together the torn buttons on her gown, she drew a deep breath and walked into Lady Adella's line of vision.

"Ye look the perfect dowd!" Lady Adella exclaimed irritably, looking Brandy up and down. "I swear, why can't ye take more pains with yerself, like yer sister!"

Lady Adella's insult fanned Brandy's anger. "Mayhap I would be more presentable, Grandmama, if Percy had not just tried to rape me!"

Lady Adella's thin eyebrows snapped together. "He what?"

"He tried to rape me," Brandy repeated, the thought of his body pressing her down sending a shudder the length of her body.

"Och! Ye fought him off, then, did ye, my girl?"

At Brandy's silent nod, Lady Adella drew a sigh of relief. A smile deepened the lines about her thin mouth. Damn Percy anyway! She might have known that he wouldn't keep his hands off the girl, despite her threats.

"What are ye going to do about him, Grandmama?"

"Do? With Percy? Really, ye silly chit, there's aught for me to do since he didn't succeed in cooling his passion for ye! Such a prissy prude ye are, child! Surely ye know what men want of women, 'tis only natural . . . particularly for Percy!"

Brandy stared at her, appalled. "Ye wouldn't have cared had he succeeded?"

"Of course I would have minded! 'Twould have changed everything. But no harm done. Stop yer trembling, child, I'll see that our randy Percy takes his leave on the morrow. He'll not bother ye again, child."

"Before Percy attacked me, Grandmama, he said that ye had told him that I was going to London. Did Ian talk to ye?"

Lady Adella saw the angry gleam in the girl's amber eyes and carefully chose her words. "Certainly the duke spoke with me, stupid girl! If ye care not about yer future, he, as yer guardian, has every right to concern himself with yer affairs."

"I'll not go, Grandmama, and I told him so! How dare he come to ye!"

Lady Adella saw the ready sparkle of defiance and quickly retrenched. She splayed her gnarled hands in a display of defeat. "Very well, child, I'll not try to force ye to go to London, though I'll never ken yer mule's stubbornness. 'Tis like Old Angus ye've become."

Brandy breathed a wary sigh of relief. "Thank ye, Grandmama, for not forcing me to leave ye, for no matter what ye would say, nor what the duke said, I'll nay go."

"As ye will, child. I had thought ye'd prefer having a choice of husbands, for Ian assured me that he'd put many a proper gentleman in yer path. Since it isn't to yer liking, well, I'll ensure that ye'll have yer wish and stay at Penderleigh—"

"Oh, thank ye, Grandmama!"

"After what Percy tried to do to ye, I would not think that ye'd want him, but—"

Brandy drew back as though she'd been struck. "Percy! Nay, Grandmama, ye must know that I loathe him! Ne'er would I marry with him!"

"So ye want yer cream and the bowl too, lass! Well, it's no worthless spinster I'll have at Penderleigh. Ye'll marry Percy or ye'll go to London. The choice is yers."

Brandy tried to swallow down the lump of fear and revulsion that stuck in her throat. She bounded to her feet and cried in a wrenching voice, "Grandmama, do ye want to make me unhappy? Why do ye hate me? What have I done to make ye treat me thus?"

"I don't hate ye, ye silly chit! Damnation, child, I want to see ye well placed afore I join yer grandfather in Hades. 'Tis a fondness he had for ye, the old rutting goat, and I'll not spend eternity with him badgering me about failing in my duty toward ye!"

Brandy forced calm into her voice. "If that is so, Grandmama, I can't believe that Grandfather would have wanted me to be so very unhappy. He disliked Percy, ye know."

Lady Adella realized that she had buried herself in a losing argument and she knew that her threat was a hollow one. Never would the duke let Percy have the girl. She hastened to change her direction, gnashing her teeth impotently at the duke's implacable orders. She resorted to a fine display of rage. She slammed her cane hard into the side of a small table and sent it crashing to the floor.

"I'll run away! Do ye hear, Grandmama, I swear that I'll run away!"

Lady Adella drew up short and sucked in her breath. A cunning grin pulled up at the corners of her mouth. "Ye run away, Brandy, and I'll take Fiona away from ye—forever." She had no idea how she could accomplish such a feat were it required of her, but she saw that she had finally won the battle. The rebellious light faded from Brandy's eyes and her shoulders slumped forward.

"Aye, that's more the thing, lass. Fiona is like yer wee bairn, isn't she? Once ye're married—after yer season in London with the duke and duchess—she'll be all yers, I promise ye."

"Ye're wicked, Grandmama!"

"I may be, ye silly child, it matters naught! Now off with ye, for I wish to speak to yer Uncle Claude. It's waiting for me, he is, at the dower house."

Brandy whirled about and ran from the sitting room. She rushed from the castle, heedless of the fact that Percy could still be about, and made for a lonely stretch of beach, far away from prying eyes. She rushed to the edge of the water and gulped in the salty air. She stood staring blindly toward the empty horizon, wondering if anyone beyond that stretch of water could be as miserable as was she. Water lapped about her sandals and she retreated beyond the reach of the rising tide to a large outjutting rock.

She wrapped her skirts about her legs and sank her chin to her knees. She felt tears sting at her eyes and resolutely gulped them away. She would never give up Fiona. She would do anything, even wed with Percy, not to lose her little sister. Her mind brought her back to her other choice. London with Ian . . . and his bride. The thought brought with it such a sense of despair that she pressed her knuckles against her eyes to keep away the hated tears. To be in his company every day whilst that hated, faceless wife held his attention and his love. Unbidden, the words she had spoken to Percy rose in her mind. "I want naught but what I can have."

Ye're a witless fool, she told herself. Ye can't have the duke, so there's an end to it. She swallowed this bitter pill and forced her thoughts to London. She had no workable notion of exactly what a "season" entailed. Obviously, from the way Grandmama spoke, it must involve scores of single ladies and gentlemen coming together for the purpose of deciding who would marry whom. She tried to picture these gentlemen, but only Ian's face appeared before her. She rose abruptly and kicked a stone with the toe of her sandal. I might well be a witless fool, she repeated to herself again, but I do want him, and I'll have none other. She drew herself up and stared defiantly out to sea.

Lady Adella leaned heavily on her cane as she followed Fraser into the small sitting room in the dower house. "Don't ye get up, Claude," she said sourly, "there's no reason for the both of us to suffer."

Fraser assisted her to sit down, then offered her one of his freshly baked scones.

"Strawberry jam, my lady?" he inquired.

"Nay, Fraser, I like 'em just as they are, with the butter oozing over the sides." She gazed at him, a gleam in her faded eyes. "Morag would be a fat slut were ye still living with her! Claude, ye got the best of the bargain—would ye like to trade Fraser for Morag?"

As if I'm a miserable deaf stick of wood, Fraser thought to himself, all the while imposing a stern mask of impassivity to his round face.

Claude cackled, displaying bits of buttery scone against his black front teeth. "Fraser stays right where he is, lady. Besides, ye try to force him to be near that scratchy Morag, and 'tis likely he'd take himself off to Edinburgh. Have I yer measure, Fraser?"

Fraser pursed his lips into enforced silence and nodded pleasantly.

Lady Adella poked his leg with the tip of her cane. "Don't ye miss having a wench in yer bed, Fraser? I vow Morag gets scratchier by the day, seeing as how she has nay a man to tumble her!"

Fraser's nostrils twitched, as he remembered the noxious body odors of his wife. He said solemnly, "If ye'll allow me to say, my lady, 'tis nay a man Morag needs, 'tis a thorough scrubbing twice a day with a bar of lye soap."

Lady Adella choked on her scone, and Fraser delicately thumped her back. "I like a man who speaks his mind, Fraser! Indeed I do! Och, now off with ye, I must needs bore myself with yer master."

After Fraser had calmly bowed himself from the room, Lady Adella turned to Claude, smacking her lips free of crumbs.

"Well, my boy, now we can speak freely. Attend me well, for the subject will be closed after today."

Claude sat forward in his chair, his eyes aglitter. He said warily, "Aye, lady?"

"Ye know that the time has come to make . . . retribution, my boy. I suspect that old MacPherson is grinding his teeth at the tasks I've set him. But 'twill be done. Ye'll have yer claim to Penderleigh as will Bertrand after ye. As to what it'll bring ye . . ." She shrugged eloquently.

Claude said harshly, "Ye set me more trouble, what with yer legitimizing that scoundrel Percy afore ye reinherit me! And the English duke—what do ye plan to do with him, may I be so bold as to ask?"

Lady Adella raised a penciled eyebrow. "What would ye that I do . . . poison him like the Borgias? Come, my boy, know there was naught I could do whilst Angus cursed this world with his presence! After he died, I could do naught immediately, for the duke's claim carried the day. Look ye, Claude, the duke pours money into the estate. I have no intention of allowing the faucet to be turned off till the well is dry. Then we'll see. Ye, Bertrand, Percy. 'Tis a fine battle we'll have if ye've any blood in yer veins!"

Claude growled deep in his throat. "Ye've tied my hands, lady! And I can see that ye haven't even looked beyond the end of yer nose. If the duke's claim holds, then nay a one of us will ever benefit! Penderleigh will fall into the English line and be forever lost to us! Have ye any idea how I feel to see Bertie sing the praises of that damned English duke? Why I don't think the boy feels even now that 'tis I and then he who are Penderleigh's true heirs! And ye, lady, ye are under the duke's thumb, just as am I, and ye keep yer claws sheathed!"

Lady Adella leaned forward and said softly, "Aye, ye're right, Claude. But remember ye, the duke has no direct heirs as yet. Right now, there's naught but a cousin—an *English* cousin—to succeed him. Surely, ye can't believe that a Scottish court would rule in favor of the English cousin who has no blood ties with the Robertsons!" She raised her hand as Claude looked ready to protest. "Enough, my boy! I've done all I can for ye and Bertrand, and, aye, for Percy too. 'Tis up to ye now. I'll be saying no more on the matter!"

"I want only what is my due," Claude said, his anger rising. "Ye give me the horse's saddle, but nay the horse!" A crafty look settled into his small eyes. "What if, lady, the world were to discover the cause of my father's disinheritance? What if, lady, ye were—"

Lady Adella threw back her head and roared with laughter. "Douglass was ne'er as doltish as ye, Claude! I'd call ye a miserable liar and hound ye as far as the Highlands! Yer father held his tongue until he reached his deathbed. 'Twas his only mistake in telling ye, my lad! If ye've a brain in yer head, ye'll not tell Bertrand, though," she added with thoughtful maliciousness. "Methinks he's a spineless creature, lapping about the duke's heels!"

"I'll not let ye speak thus of Bertie. I think, lady, that ye've far more the taste for bounders like Percy than for gentlemen like my Bertie!"

Lady Adella held up a conciliating hand. "Hold ye, Claude, afore ye burst yer heart." She took a noisy sip of her tea and changed the topic. "I haven't told ye, but I intend our Constance for Bertrand. I'd thought we would have several years yet, but the girl has blossomed more quickly than I expected. If I don't miss my guess, yer son's hot for her."

Claude reared back his head in patent disbelief. "Wee Connie? Why Bertie's ne'er spared a thought for a wench in all his life, more's the pity, save that trollop in the village!"

"I am surrounded by witless fools! Open yer eyes, my boy. Connie's not like Brandy—she thinks herself a woman grown. If Bertrand plays his gentleman's game with her, he'll soon find himself left in a ditch, with naught but himself to blame."

Claude thoughtfully stroked the stubble on his chin. "Bertie tells me that the duke plans to dower all the girls."

"Aye, but ye needn't worry about Constance trekking off to London, as the duke intends for Brandy. Lord, we'd have to wait another two years, and I tell ye, she'd have lost her maidenhead long afore that!"

Claude shifted painfully in his chair. Bedamned but that gouty foot was paining him today! "Very well, lady," he said finally, wearied of the topic, "I'll speak to Bertie. But don't expect him to ravish the chit!"

Lady Adella endeavored to picture such an event, but failed. "I can't even imagine Bertie without his breeches. More likely, I think, if we are to get anywhere at all, 'twill have to be Connie who seduces Bertie."

7

Brandy discovered during the next two weeks that the idyllic existence she had sought to cling to held less and less pleasure for her. Her thoughts centered more and more upon the duke, on what he was doing and whether his thinking ever included her. She even allowed herself the fancy of picturing herself as an elegant young lady whose Scottish accent had miraculously disappeared, surrounded by London gentlemen, with a jealous Ian standing close by.

She was in the midst of seeing herself languidly waving a fan to and fro when she heard the rumble of carriage wheels and drew her thoughts back to the present.

She walked slowly back to the castle, wondering who had come to call. MacPherson, most likely. Grandmama had mentioned that he was to visit. As she rounded the last outcropping of rhododendron bushes along the drive to the castle, she drew up dead in her tracks. There in front of the castle steps stood the duke's carriage.

She suddenly became aware of her fly-away appearance. Salty, damp tendrils of hair clung to her forehead, and her old gown hung about her with all the style of a crofter's wife's. She thought to skirt the front entrance and creep through the servants' door and up the back stairs, when she heard her name ring out.

"Brandy!"

The duke and Bertrand stood in the doorway, looking toward her. She gnashed her teeth at the picture she presented, and forced herself to wave toward them.

"She always has the look of a little mermaid," she heard Bertrand say to the duke.

A porpoise, more like, she told herself witheringly and forced her feet to move forward.

"Yes," the duke said with a smile. He drew in a deep breath of the fresh sea air, aware that he was glad to be back at Penderleigh. The huge gray rambling ediface no longer appeared to him as a crumbling old castle and a ready drain on his purse. It was more like a proud symbol, he thought, of Scotland's rich tradition.

"Come, Brandy, don't dawdle," Bertrand said good-naturedly. "We've much to tell, and the spice goes out of the telling if it must be repeated."

"Good afternoon, Bertrand . . . Ian," Brandy said with forced formality. "I trust yer trip was successful."

"Aye, that it was," Bertrand said. "Lord, my girl, ye smell salty as the sea itself."

In that instant, Brandy hated the sea. She looked up to the duke's face to see his eyes alight with jocular good humor. Her pounding heart plummeted to her toes. She said stiffly, "I . . . I will go change, if ye will excuse me."

"Don't be a silly goose," Bertrand said, clapping her on the shoulder. "It matters naught if we have a mermaid in the castle."

Ian added kindly, "Come, Brandy, I have brought you a present and I don't want to wait in the giving of it."

"As ye will," she mumbled, the image of the elegant young lady fast disappearing from her mind.

As she passed beside him, Ian had the fleeting desire to wind his fingers around the salty tendrils of heavy blond hair that curled absurdly over her brow. He sternly repressed this momentary weakness.

As the three of them entered the drawing room, Ian found himself wondering just how Lady Adella would treat him. He had not, he grinned to himself, left her on exactly the best of terms.

Lady Adella, Claude, and Constance were in the drawing room having afternoon tea. It was, Ian thought, Lady Adella's only concession to her English heritage.

"Well, ye're back from mucking about in yer sheep dung," Lady Adella said, and snapped her tea cup back on its saucer.

"That we are, lady," Ian said, eyeing her closely. He could

see naught in her face or her words save her usual sour humor and added, "I see you are in good health."

"Aye, no thanks to ye! Well, Bertie, yer presence relieves me, 'tis a maudlin bore Claude's become in yer absence."

She saw that Bertrand was in conversation with Constance and said in a loud voice, "I can see that ye've missed yer cousin more than yer father!"

"Indeed I have not," Bertrand said calmly, and made his bow to Claude. "I was just telling Connie that Ian and I spent several days in Edinburgh, seeing the sights."

"I had not thought ye interested in brothels, Bertie," Lady Adella said slyly, hoping to make him flush.

Ian laughed. "Nothing so decadent, I assure you, Lady Adella. 'Tis a beautiful city, in fact, London's undisputed northern rival. I might add that it boasts excellent shops."

"Aye, and ye might guess that Ian insisted upon visiting them," Bertrand added, his eyes caressing Constance's face. He straightened and pointed to Crabbe, who stood in the doorway, several wrapped boxes in his arms.

"Ye brought me a present!" Constance exclaimed, hopping to her feet.

"We brought all the ladies presents," Ian said, gazing at Lady Adella to see her reaction.

She snorted, but readily accepted the prettily wrapped box from Ian's outstretched hand.

"What is it, a shroud to cover my old bones?" she said with a fine show of indifference.

"Nay, lady, nothing so final," Ian retorted with a grin.

"Impudent," she snorted, but was unable to contain her excitement as her fingers pulled away the layers of silver paper. "Och!" She withdrew an exquisite shawl of Norwich silk, the varying shades of blue shimmering like spun sky in her hands. " 'Tis not fit for an old woman," she grumbled, her eyes all the while glittering with delight.

"That is just what I told the shopkeeper," Ian said, "but I see that he went against my wishes."

Lady Adella appeared not at all put out by his teasing remark, and the duke betook himself to hand Brandy her present whilst Bertrand placed a wrapped box into Constance's hands. He wondered how Brandy would react to a gift that was more for a woman than a young girl.

Brandy's hands trembled as she brought forth what seemed to be yard upon yard of dark blue velvet. She stood slowly and shook out the gown in front of her. She saw no sash or belt and wondered where the waist was. She looked doubtfully up at the duke.

"It is the empire style, made fashionable by Napoleon's Josephine," Ian said, smiling at her ignorance. He wanted to add that such a gown hugged a woman's breasts most flatteringly, but of course did not.

"It is beautiful," Brandy breathed, stroking the soft material. "I don't understand, Ian. It has no waist. I fear I would look quite odd in it."

"Not at all," he replied, forcing all amusement from his voice. "It is designed to fall in straight lines from . . . above your waist. The style is all the crack in London."

His mention of London reminded her of his perfidy in going behind her back to Lady Adella. She would certainly take him to task for his underhandedness, she had decided, when they were alone. She looked closely at the small gathers in the bodice of the gown and realized that the small expanse of blue velvet above was meant to cover her bosom. She paled at the thought.

Ian watched the myriad of emotions playing over her face. Despite her assurances that she was a woman grown, he wondered if the modish gown made her feel uncomfortable, perhaps embarrassed.

"Brandy, if the style does not please you. . . ." he temporized, his voice gentle.

"Nay," she cried, clasping the soft material against her protectively. "It is the most lovely gown I've ever seen. I thank ye, Ian, for yer kindness."

"It is nothing," he said stiffly, wondering at his own sudden formality. He turned away abruptly at Constance's crow of delight. He grinned to himself, for he had insisted that Bertrand choose Constance's gown. It was a deep green muslin, with row upon row of delicate lace covering what would otherwise be a most inappropriate expanse of bosom for a fifteen-year-old girl.

Brandy lovingly wrapped the gown and placed it back in the box. She looked up at Ian. "Fiona, yer grace?" she asked meaningfully.

"I would never forget your wee child," he said with a smile, and pointed to a large wooden crate near the door.

She raised eyes brimming with love to his face and he was startled into looking away. She intends it for the child, he told himself stoutly.

"Let me fetch her!" Brandy dipped a slight curtsy and scurried from the room.

Bertrand said to Constance, "The green matches yer eyes, Connie, though the material could never be as bright."

Lady Adella shot Claude a look fraught with meaning. "I see ye have become a poet, Bertie," he said gazing at his son with new eyes. "So ye got naught for yer old father, eh?"

"Nay, father, only the ladies," Bertrand said, looking quickly away from Constance. She looked rather puzzled at this exchange.

A bright mop of red hair appeared in the open doorway, announced by a child's high squeal of delight. Fiona stood speechless in front of the large wooden crate, so overcome that her mouth was agape.

"Come, poppet, I'll help ye open it," Brandy said, giving the child a quick hug.

"Allow me to assist you, Brandy," Ian said, and joined her before she could answer.

Together they tugged at the boards until the contents were laid bare. Brandy rocked back on her heels.

"It's a horse!" Fiona cried, and began to tug frantically at the lifelike mane.

"Hold a moment, Fiona," Ian interrupted, and leaning over, gently lifted the large wooden rocking horse out of the crate.

"It even has a saddle and bridle," Brandy said. From her kneeling position, she gazed up at the duke and said softly, " 'Tis a grand present, Ian. Ye shouldn't have spoiled the child, but I thank ye."

He looked again into her amber eyes and felt a small shaft of guilt turn like a knife within him. He found that he could only nod and damned himself roundly for being a churl.

"I say, Ian," Bertrand said, "don't ye think it's time we informed everybody of our other purchases?"

Ian gave himself a mental shake and planted a smile on his lips. "Aye, 'tis a large and woolly purchase. Seriously, we purchased sheep from a rather dour old man in the Cheviot, near to Fort David."

"A man by the name of Hesketh," Bertrand continued. "Have ye heard of him, Lady Adella? He owns a large old stone manor house which looks as time-honored as Penderleigh."

"Hesketh," she repeated slowly, and shook her head. She looked sourly over at Fiona, whose crows of pleasure were becoming more enthusiastic. "Brandy, remove the child and her horse, afore my head splits with her noise."

"Aye, Grandmama," Brandy said, and quietly removed her little sister and the wooden horse from the drawing room. "Come, poppet, we can pretend he's the great wooden horse that sat before the gates of Troy."

She settled Fiona and her horse near the small fireplace in her bedchamber, then pulled the exquisite velvet gown from its silver paper. She quickly stripped off her clothes, not even bothering to keep on her shift. She wanted to feel the sensuous material against her skin.

She slowly slipped the gown over her head and let it float over her body. With some difficulty, she managed to fasten most of the small hooks up the back. She felt the small gathers, sewn into a stiff band of material, pushing her breasts upward and forward. Hesitantly, she walked to the long narrow mirror in the corner of her room and gazed speechlessly at her image.

She felt her face flush with embarrassment. Her full breasts rose from the bodice of the gown in rounded white splendor, forming a deep cleavage that seemed to start nearly at the base of her throat.

"Brandy! Ye don't look like yerself!"

Brandy tried to cover her breasts with her hands.

"Ye look like a . . . queen!"

Brandy gave an embarrassed laugh. "Nay, poppet, 'tis still me. Ian bought ye the horse, and for me he bought this gown. Is it not lovely?"

Fiona stepped gingerly forward and softly fingered the material. " 'Tis furry, like a rabbit," she allowed finally, "but I prefer my horse."

Absurdly, Brandy asked, "Do ye think it's a proper dress to wear downstairs to dinner?"

"If Cousin Percy were here, he would be sure to like it," Fiona said with appalling innocence.

Brandy remembered how Fiona had come upon Percy struggling atop of her, and tried to say in a light voice, " 'Tis a silly thing to say, poppet! To begin with, Percy isn't even here."

Fiona, who was fast losing interest, shrugged her small shoulders and said, "Well, I think it's stupid the way he's always looking at ye. And Connie, always batting *her* eyes at *him!*"

"Aye," she said only, and walked across the room toward the windows, savoring the delicious feel of the gown against her body. Her eyes were drawn to a light carriage that was pulling to a halt amid clouds of dust before the castle. She sucked in her breath as she watched Percy alight. She quickly backed away from the windows. What in God's name was he doing here?

She walked back to the mirror and gazed long at her image. With a sigh that sounded suspiciously like a sob, she drew off the velvet gown and lovingly laid it back into its box. Although she felt herself to be far too bosomy, even misshapen, she realized that her breasts were a sign of her womanhood and that Percy, damn him, would not let her forget it.

She thought of Ian and how she simply must do something about her appearance, else he would always think of her as a dowdy child. She quickly dressed in her waisted muslin gown, tightened the laces of her chemise over her breasts, and came to a decision. Ruthlessly, she unbraided the long tresses and pulled a brush through the deep rippling waves. She fashioned a braided coronet high atop her head and drew the long masses of hair through the circle, curling the ends about her fingers. She looked in the mirror and was satisfied with the appearance she presented, at least from the neck upward.

Brandy entered the drawing room rather later than usual that evening, for Fiona, still excited over her wooden horse, had been loathe to go to sleep. She prayed to be unobtrusive, but realized the moment she stepped into the room that this was not to be. Her eyes first fell upon Constance, lovely and terribly grown up in her new gown, and she choked back a stab of jealousy.

Lady Adella roared at her, "Stupid girl! I thought we'd banished the ugly duckling! Ye look like a scraggly weed next to yer sister." She paused a moment, taking in Brandy's new hair arrangement, and snorted, "At least ye've gotten rid of yer child's braids. 'Tis some improvement, I suppose."

Percy said languidly to Lady Adella, "As ye say, lady, our ugly duckling has changed some of her plumage."

Ian thought her hair looked stunning, but could not prevent a frown of disappointment.

Brandy hastened to say with as much calm as she could muster, "The gown is quite lovely, Ian, truly it is. It is just that it did not fit quite right and I must make alterations before I can wear it."

She turned quickly to her sister. " 'Tis lovely ye are, Connie. The green matches yer eyes, just as Bertrand said."

Constance nodded her head gracefully, but her green eyes gleamed triumphantly. Aye, she thought, Brandy does look like a scraggly weed, just as Grandmama said.

She was gratified to the tips of her toes and bestowed a pouting smile upon Bertrand, for he seemed to be gazing at her with undeniable admiration. Perhaps, she thought, trying to untangle her budding woman's wiles, if she paid more attention to Bertrand, Percy would take more interest in her. She turned to Bertrand and moistened her lips with the tip of her tongue. "Do ye really like the gown, Bertie?"

Bertrand, fascinated by the pointed pink tongue, allowed himself most willingly to be drawn in. "Aye, Connie, ye're the fairest lass in all of Scotland."

Constance shot a look at Percy and was chagrined to see his attention elsewhere.

Percy said in a low voice to Brandy, "Ye don't appear much discomfitted to see me, little cousin."

"Nay, the devil roves all about the land, the Bible says."

Percy threw back his head and roared with laughter.

"Dinner be ready, yer grace!" Crabbe announced from the doorway.

"Ye needn't sneak in like a limpet, Crabbe!" Lady Adella shouted at his wooden face. She gave a loud creak of laughter at her own joke. "Come here, Brandy, and make yerself useful! If ye can't look like a lady, ye might as well forget yer hoity toity manners and help me on with my shawl."

"Aye, Grandmama."

Percy whispered, "So ye've a new gown from the master, lass. I ask myself why ye must make . . . alterations on it." He looked meaningfully at her flattened breasts. He remembered her writhing beneath him, struggling to be free of him. She would not have fought me long, he assured himself silently.

Brandy arranged Lady Adella's new Norwich shawl about her shoulders before saying coldly, "Why did ye return to Penderleigh? Did yer heiress discover yer true nature and tell ye to take yerself to perdition?"

"What a sharp tongue sets on yer woman's shoulders, little cousin! Nay, my heiress pleaded with me to remain with her, if ye must know."

" 'Tis a pity ye did not see fit to comply with her wishes."

"I will agree with the child, Percy," Lady Adella interrupted, "if ye don't behave yerself." She gazed at him sharply from beneath furrowed brows and he realized with a start that she knew of his amorous bout with Brandy.

He felt a sudden stab of fear, for the old woman could still, he supposed, prevent him from becoming legitimate. Damn the girl, anyway, he thought angrily. "I shall be as meek as the Cheviot sheep the good duke has just purchased, lady," he said.

"Percy thinks himself much in demand," Bertrand said with barely veiled dislike.

"Eh? Percy in demand?" Lady Adella said. "The only ones to demand ye, my boy, are the constables from debtors' prison!"

"Not for very much longer, as ye know, lady," Percy replied in a silken voice.

～ 8 ～

Brandy walked quickly toward the stables, some ten minutes late, having waged an exhausting battle with an old and very snug riding habit that had belonged to her mother. She could take only short breaths because of the painfully tight lacing of her chemise.

Her step lagged as she drew near to the rickety stables. What an idiot she had been to so gaily assure Ian that she much loved riding, and all for the purpose of having him to herself for an entire morning. After all that, how could she then gainsay his conclusion that she must be a bruising rider?

At least, she thought, brightening somewhat, the old hack who had for several years moldered lazily in the stables would hardly send her flying ignominiously onto her bottom. After all, her infrequent rides in the past had been conducted at the speed the old mare chose herself. She glanced up at the stables, seeing them for the first time through Ian's eyes. They had not been mucked out for weeks, as Wee Albie assiduously avoided this task, and the loose, unpainted boards creaked ominously with the slightest wind from the sea.

"So there you are, Brandy. I had begun to give up hope." Ian smiled at her flushed face, wondering if she had run all the way from the castle. "You're looking lovely, my dear," he added unthinkingly. Actually, he thought, any change from her old gowns and the tartan shawl could not help but be an improvement. She had braided her hair high atop her head and set a plumed riding hat squarely over her forehead.

Brandy took several small gulping breaths, afraid that at any minute the buttons on the fragile blouse would pop open.

"Thank ye, Ian," she said, her eyes shifting nervously toward one of Ian's huge gray stallions.

Ian followed her eyes. "I trust you will like him. His name is Cantor, one of my favorite mounts."

As she was gazing at him blankly, he explained, "That poor old, slope-shouldered mare in the stall seemed hardly enthusiastic about an outing. Since you are an accomplished horsewoman, I thought you would prefer Cantor. He is a bit frisky, but nothing, I am certain, that you cannot handle."

Cantor had wicked, shifty eyes, Brandy saw at once. Though he stood quietly enough, tethered to the duke's hand, she thought he was but biding his time until he felt her own hand upon his bridle. She gulped. "He does look rather spirited, Ian."

"He's itching for a gallop, as is my own stallion, Hercules. I unearthed a side saddle for you." As she hesitated, he teased, "You mustn't think that I cannot properly girth a saddle, for I have gotten much practice in Scotland. Here, let me assist you to mount."

Brandy gulped yet again and nodded. Well, my girl, she told herself, ye must turn yer bragging into fact. She placed her booted foot on his laced fingers. Her resolution very nearly failed her when Canton sidled to one side as Ian tossed her into the saddle.

"Be polite, Cantor," the duke scolded lightly, patting the horse's silken nose. He placed the reins into Brandy's trembling hands and turned to his own horse.

Brandy sent a silent plea heavenward whilst Ian's back was turned to her. "Please Cantor," she whispered toward the twitching ears, "I promise ye carrots by the dozen if ye'll not shame me."

Ian brought Hercules prancing neatly to her side and she marveled enviously at his easy confidence.

"Where would you like to ride, Brandy?"

With sudden inspiration, she said, "Ye lead the way, Ian, and I'll follow behind. I've covered all the land ye see, and wish to follow someone else's lead."

"As you will. We'll go slowly for a bit, but then I promise you a treat. Whilst Bertrand and I were visiting some of the crofters, I spotted a wide flat meadow that will be perfect for a gallop," He smiled at her broadly, displaying strong white teeth.

He gave Hercules a gentle dig and the horse moved forward. Brandy had no time for a simple click click, for no sooner did Hercules break into a slow measured trot than Cantor, oblivious to the ineffective tug on his reins, snorted and pranced forward.

Brandy gripped the pommel and concentrated upon keeping her seat. She thanked God that Ian could not see her ineptitude.

She forced an easy smile to her lips when Ian pulled up Hercules and waited until she came alongside of him. "The wooded area around Penderleigh reminds me somewhat of the home wood at Carmichael Hall, though, of course, I do not have the sea at my back door."

"I think I should very much miss the sea if I ever had to leave Penderleigh."

"I have nothing so awesome, but there is a long winding lake that sits like a beautiful blue gem in the middle of the forest."

"I should much like to see it," she said, half her attention focused on Cantor's flattened ears.

"Do you like to swim, Brandy?"

"Aye, indeed I do. I wager, Ian, that ye would have a difficult time beating me. The sea currents make one a strong swimmer, ye know."

He raised a disbelieving black brow, trying to picture the slender girl beside him stroking through the choppy waves.

She took affront at his amusement. "Ye'll sing a different tune, yer grace, once I have ye in the water! I am very strong, ye'll see."

The black brow remained cocked upward and he grinned. "Bertrand called you a mermaid, but I doubt he was referring to your prowess as a swimmer."

"Nay," she admitted, "it is because I am often damp and smell salty. He much likes to tease me. But ye know," she added with a pert smile, "I must doubt that he would ever wish Connie to be like me."

"Ah, so you've seen that the breeze blows in that direction! Bertrand is much smitten. Actually, it took hardly any encouragement from me during our trip for him to laud your sister in the most glowing terms. Unfortunately, Constance does not as yet return his regard."

"Aye, Percy again! If only she would realize that there is naught that is worthy of affection in him. He is all vain strutting! I pity his poor heiress."

"Perhaps once he has the Robertson name and his heiress, he will forget about all that he cannot possess."

She looked at him sharply, but he merely smiled. "I had thought that I . . . we would be rid of him. Odd that he arrived on yer heels yesterday. Do ye know why he returned?"

He shook his head. "Percy adores making mischief. In that regard he much resembles Lady Adella. I suppose that he heard of Bertrand and me being in Edinburgh and thought it safe to return."

Brandy had no chance to reply, for Ian drew up suddenly and said, "The meadow, Brandy. I can see that you're itching for a race. Our first race will be by land and, if you're willing, our second will be by sea."

"Conceited man! I'll beat ye to flinders at both! What a blow to yer consequence to be trounced by a mere female!"

"Ho, the lady becomes cocky! As for this race, Brandy, Cantor has all the speed of Hercules, so you get no beginning start. The last one to the trees yon must pay a forfeit!"

Brandy gazed across the broad stretch of meadow and felt her courage begin to fail her. But she saw the smiling, challenging light in his eyes and forced herself to nod brightly. "I have all the advantage I require, Ian," she cried, and with sublime disregard for her person, dug in her heels and slapped the loosened reins against Cantor's neck.

For a brief moment, she forgot her fear, so smoothly and speedily did Cantor race across the meadow. She felt her riding hat loosen in the wind, and slapped her hand down on it, pressing her body close to Cantor's neck. She saw Ian close rapidly beside her, and in a moment of foolhardiness, fiercely dug in her heels.

The once faraway trees loomed closer and closer, and Brandy, with the sudden insight of one who has awakened from a fool's dream, wondered just how the devil she was going to halt the steaming piece of horseflesh beneath her. She heard Ian's deep laughter as he pulled ahead of her. She watched him draw up the mighty stallion at the edge of the trees and whirl him about to face her.

She told her riding hat to fend for itself, and with both gloved hands pulled back on Cantor's reins with all her might. Although he slackened his speed, he otherwise ignored the weakling on his back.

She tugged frantically and closed her eyes as Cantor headed full tilt toward Ian.

She heard a shout of laughter, felt Cantor rear back on his hind legs, and dropped the reins, grasping the pommel with all her strength. It was over in a flash. Cantor had pulled to a panting stop, Brandy still miraculously in the saddle, and Ian held her horse's reins, his eyes alight with amusement.

She could hardly believe her ears when he said, "What ploy is this, Brandy? Did you think to run me out of the way and thus claim victory? Are you equally intrepid when you are swimming?"

She heard her own voice ring out with appalling audacity, "Hercules is the faster, Ian! I demand another race . . . sometime," she quickly added.

"Hercules faster indeed! Better horsemanship, Brandy, come, admit it!"

"Aye—this time!"

"What forfeit can I claim?"

Forfeit . . . she had forgotten all about a forfeit. Just so long as he did not wish another race, she would grant him anything. She slipped quickly out of the saddle, relieved to have the ground beneath her feet. She said breathlessly, "Whatever ye wish, Ian."

He dismounted and tethered the horses to a yew bush. "Whatever I wish, eh?" He grinned and walked over to her.

She gazed up at him and found that her eyes strayed to his firm mouth.

"Brandy," he said uncertainly.

She took a half step toward him, her lips slightly parted.

He stood rigid before her, forcing his arms to stay at his sides. Before he had time to applaud his strength of character, she stood on her tiptoes and locked her hands around his neck, drawing him down to her. Shyly, and not without trepidation, she kissed him, with all the tenderness in her heart. She felt the strength of him, the curious gentleness of his mouth, and sighed softly as the awareness of desire grew within her.

Ian felt his control near to breaking, but forced his lips not to part, and pulled her hands away. He said in a raspy voice, "No, Brandy, you—we must not."

She backed away from him, her body alive with tingling feeling. "Yer forfeit, Ian," she whispered, her voice husky and deep.

He felt her vulnerability, the innocent tentativeness of her longing. "That is not exactly the forfeit I had intended," he began.

"But it was the forfeit I wanted to give to ye. And after all, I did lose the race."

He groaned and ran his hand through his hair. "Brandy, you must listen to me. Dammit, I am your guardian and more than that, I am engaged to another lady. You're an innocent child, and I would be the most despicable of men to take advantage—"

"Damn ye, Ian, I am not a child! Ye call me a child so ye won't have to think of me as aught else!"

He drew up and stared at her.

Furious that he did not answer, she rushed on, "I knew exactly what I was doing, and I'll not allow ye denying it with yer nonsensical words of taking advantage!" Visions of his faceless wife-to-be rose in her mind's eye, and she cried with perverse logic, "Ye can't force me to go with ye to London! I'll not live in the same house with that—hateful woman! I'll have Percy first, do ye ken!"

She whirled about on a sob and rushed to Cantor. She jerked his reins free of the bush, and without a thought to her fear of him, gracelessly climbed up into the saddle.

"Brandy, wait! I must talk to you, explain to you—"

"Nay! I hate ye . . . yer grace!" Foolishly, she dug in her heels. Cantor sensed that the insignificant burden on his back had absolutely no control over herself, much less over him. With a happy snort, he dove forward, back across the meadow.

Ian stared after her a moment, his own anger rising. Damn her for not allowing him to explain. God, how very simple everything had been before he came to this outlandish place!

He jumped on Hercules's back, loosed his full strength,

and galloped after her. He drew alongside just as Cantor broke through the trees back to the main road. He leaned over to grab the reins from her hands when she jerked back on the bridle and tried to wheel Cantor away. Cantor, recognizing the hand of his master, reared back on his hind legs, tore the reins from the ineffectual bundle on his back, and planted himself in a stubborn halt.

"Ye wretched beast!" Brandy cried, panting. She lunged forward to grab the reins from Ian's hands, but he pulled them from her reach.

They stared at each other a moment, silently. Brandy, her anger having melted, wished for something akin to oblivion. Ian found for the next few moments that his mind was occupied picturing her with her hair flowing free down her back, with not one accursed braid.

He said finally with painstaking correctness, "Now, if you would not mind, Brandy, I would that we continue our ride. I have no intention of giving rise to uncomfortable speculation amongst your family."

She gazed at him, baffled at this calm, possessed speech.

She merely nodded, not trusting herself to speak. He placed Cantor's reins back into her hands and they proceeded back along the path, away from the castle.

Ian was cursing himself silently for sounding the pompous ass—like a pompous *English* ass, he amended to himself, straightlaced and stiff in the collar.

He chose a much traveled path that forked off the road, past crofters' huts, away from the sea. He became aware that the sky was darkening dangerously, but kept riding, telling himself that he would not mind in the least if Brandy was in for a good soaking.

After some time, he thought he had discovered a quite correct and proper string of phrases to present to her, and drew to a halt in a quiet wooded area, a few feet from the path.

"Would you like to dismount here, Brandy?"

As he spoke, he began to dismount. No sooner were the words unloosed than the darkened sky was split by a dazzling bolt of lightning. A crashing boom of thunder followed quickly in its wake.

Brandy's voice caught itself in a scream as Cantor, frightened and blinded by the jagged flash of lightning, reared up with a wild snort, tore the reins from Brandy's hands, and plunged forward. She made a mad grab for the reins but they were beyond her reach. For an instant, she was frozen with terror.

"Ian, help! I can't stop him! The reins, I can't reach them!" She felt hollow with fear. Her riding hat was torn from her head by a low hanging branch and she believed that at any instant she would follow her hat and be ground under Cantor's hooves.

There was another loud clap of thunder, and Cantor lengthened his stride and crashed all the faster through the dense undergrowth.

A sliver of hope flashed through her mind as she heard Ian closing fast behind her. She jerked around in the saddle to measure his distance from her, when the reins, hanging loose, tangled themselves under one of Cantor's hooves, and inevitably, he stumbled.

Ian had nearly reached her when he saw Cantor fall to one knee and Brandy fly over his head. Her name died in his throat as he watched her fall to the ground amid masses of tangled ivy.

He drew up Hercules and leaped from his back. His first instinct was to gather her up into his arms, but reason asserted itself and he knelt down beside her and placed two fingers against the pulse in the hollow of her throat. The beat was steady, if somewhat rapid. Gently, he felt each of her arms for broken bones, then her legs. He was only partially reassured, since she could have quite easily injured herself internally.

"Brandy," he said, leaning close to her still face. He gently slapped her cheeks, but she did not respond. He rocked back on his heels, wondering what to do. As if the heavens had already not done enough with the accursed lightning and thunder, several large rain drops suddenly splashed on Brandy's face.

"Damnation," he muttered under his breath, and looked about for some sort of shelter. He slipped out of his riding jacket and covered her. He gazed a moment grimly down at her still face, then rose and strode into the woods. He had not gone too far when he espied a crofter's hut. He would take Brandy there and send one of the children back to Penderleigh for help.

The rain was coming down in earnest by the time he reached her side again. He saw that his coat had done little to keep her dry. As gently as he could, Ian lifted her into his arms and carried her to Hercules.

Holding her in the crook of one arm, he grasped Cantor's reins in the other hand, and slowly moved the small cavalcade toward the hut.

As he drew nearer, he saw that the hut had long been abandoned, its thatched roof sagging precariously over the stone walls. The thatch was supported in the front of the hut by two skinny poles and would afford, at least, some shelter for the horses.

He dismounted slowly, shifted Brandy's weight to his right arm, and tied the horses. With the toe of his boot, he kicked open the narrow front door. It creaked ominously on rusted hinges, and he prayed that it would not collapse on him.

It took him some moments to adjust his eyes to the dim interior of the hut. There was only one small room, its floor still covered mostly with rotting boards. He stepped gingerly toward a crudely wrought fireplace and gently laid Brandy beside it, smoothing his coat under her.

Another booming crash of thunder brought him to his feet. Cantor whinnied, but he did not tear away. Ian spotted a pile of peat clumps in one corner and thanked the lord for at least something of use.

The beauty of peat was that it needed very little coaxing to burn itself. Though a goodly amount of smoke gushed into the room, Ian contented himself that his efforts did provide some warmth.

He pulled out his handkerchief and gently wiped the rain from Brandy's face. He stared at her firm chin, her very straight nose, and her thick brows that flared ever so slightly toward her temples.

He felt damnably helpless. A memory he had thought long buried rose suddenly to taunt him. Vividly he remembered the wrenching helplessness he had felt when, at last, he had realized that there was naught he could do to save Marianne. Even when he had managed to reach Paris, stealing into that revolution-racked city under the cover of night, he had known that he was too late.

"Dammit, Brandy, wake up!" he shouted at her.

"Ye don't have to yell at me, Ian," Brandy whispered, forcing her eyes to open. His sigh of relief was audible, and her mouth moved to a painful smile.

As much as he wanted to hear her voice, he said quickly, "Don't talk if it pains you."

Brandy gulped down a bout of dizzying nausea and tried to raise her hand to her head.

"For God's sake, Brandy, hold still!" He forced her hand back to her side.

"I hit my head," she said inconsequentially.

"Yes," he acknowledged, and gently probed the lump under the damp braid.

She whimpered softly and turned her face away, for she did not wish him to see the tears that were woefully near to the surface.

"I don't know why the devil you must needs braid your hair so tightly," he muttered to himself.

"Aye, it hurts." she admitted.

"Then we simply must do something about it. I'll try not to hurt you more." He picked up the end of the long thick plait and gently began to pull it free. Damp, springy waves fell over his hands and he smoothed down the deep ripples. Finally, he finished his task, and Brandy breathed a small sigh as pressure from the heavy braid was eased away.

"Is that better?" he asked, gazing at the small face, surrounded by a rippling halo of thick blond tresses. "You must stop braiding your hair," he said. He turned quickly away and tossed several more clumps of peat into the smoking fire.

The duke's words had floated gently over Brandy's head, for she felt so near to retching that it required all her will not to succumb. Another wave of nausea passed and she was brought quickly to her own perfidy and her ignominious fall.

"I lied to ye, Ian," she rasped out, immediately feeling better for her confession. She fastened a wary eye on him, waiting for retribution to fall.

He gazed at her uncomprehending, wondering if she was delirious. "You what?" he ventured gently.

"Ye needn't be a gentleman about it! It's my wretched pride, ye see, and now I have paid the full price."

He frowned and unconsciously gathered a mass of blond hair in his hand and smoothed it next to her face, off of the filthy floor. "I would most gladly roar at you in a most ungentlemanlike fashion, if you would only tell me what you're talking about."

Huge amber eyes widened on his face. "Ye—ye don't know?"

He nodded slowly, understanding dawning. He felt again her soft lips against his mouth, and heard her fiery, angry words. She regretted it now. He should have been inordinately relieved, but instead, he felt sorry at what could not be.

She gave a miniature sigh, thinking that with Ian, confession was quite an easy matter. And she had been such a braggart! "Ye don't think . . . less of me?"

Dammit, why did she persist in pushing the matter! He said shortly, not looking at her, "No, of course not." His conscience forced him to add, "You see, Brandy, it was as much my fault as yours."

"Nay, Ian, ye mustn't shoulder any of the blame. 'Twas all my fault, for I didn't wish ye to know of my cowardice. I have paid full measure, but I might have hurt ye, too. 'Twas unforgivable." If only he would rant, if just a little. Could he not shout at her just once, like Grandmama?

It dawned on him suddenly that their conversation was suspiciously like another held that long-ago evening. At least this time, it wasn't a matter of his being naked! He laughed and lightly touched his hand to her cheek. "I fear, little one, that we are again at cross-purposes. We shall begin at the beginning. Now, what exactly do you mean with all this cowardice talk?"

"Oh," she whispered, "ye mean when ye were naked and I thought ye were talking about the London trip." She gazed up at him with such intensity that he felt himself quite naked once again.

"Stop thinking what you are thinking, Brandy," he ordered.

"Very well," she sighed.

"Cowardice?" he prodded.

A slight flush stained her cheeks and she blurted out, "I've always been frightfully afraid of them. I think perhaps that one of the nasty beasts bit me when I was an infant! Cantor is a lovely horse, truly, it is just that horses make me so very skittish!"

He could not help himself, and burst out laughing. "And here I thought you a bruising rider! All that bravado! That trick of nearly running me down—in truth, you couldn't stop Cantor?"

"Aye," she whispered miserably. "I didn't want ye to think me not up to snuff! You're so *perfect* at everything, whilst I am—"

"Hush, Brandy! I am not perfect. Indeed, I have more than my share of foibles. As to your so-called cowardice, I think rather you were quite brave, mayhap foolishly so. You needn't have to prove your worth to anyone, do you understand?"

"Ye don't mind that I am afraid of horses?"

"Not at all," he said, laughter still lurking in his voice. "Are you going to tell me now that you can't swim a stroke either?"

"Nay!" she said with some spirit. "I am certain to beat ye at that."

She shivered suddenly and closed her eyes tightly. He saw that she was quite white about the mouth, and instantly forgot both horses and swimming. He eyed suspiciously the drops of rain that were seeping through the thatched roof not three feet away from them.

"I am sorry, my dear, but I cannot remove you back to the castle. Do you feel quite wretched?"

"Not terribly so," she assayed gamely, shivering as the words left her mouth.

"Well, the least I can do is remove your wet jacket. Hopefully, your blouse will dry out closer to the fire."

He gently drew her up into his arms to slip off her riding jacket, and she stiffened perceptibly. "Hold still," he said with a hint of impatience, "I have no intention of offending your modesty!"

She painfully sucked in her breath, hoping that he would not notice that she was not willowy slender. She thought of the gaping buttons across her bosom and felt near to tears with mortification.

He pulled off her jacket and frowned at the frayed white blouse. It was so very tight on her—she must have worn the riding habit since she was ten years old.

"There, is that better, Brandy?" he asked, still holding her against his chest, hopeful that his body's warmth would protect her from taking a chill.

"Aye," she whispered, savoring his strength and nearness. She shivered again, not with cold, and was rewarded when he drew her more tightly against him.

Quite unintentionally, he dropped a light kiss on her hair.

Brandy raised her hand and wonderingly touched his cheek. Once again quite unintentionally, he leaned down and kissed her soft mouth. She forgot her aching head and her uncomfortably damp body and unhesitatingly parted her lips.

The rational, prudent man made an ineffectual protest, only to lose soundly to masses of silky hair tangled in his hand and a trembling mouth that brought forth a moan of passion at the pressure of his lips. He kissed her forehead, her straight nose, her chin, and savored the softness of her skin. He felt her fingers run through his damp hair, and heard her softly murmur his name.

He yielded to the growing ache in his loins and let his hand caress her shoulder and throat before moving gently to her breast. He was thwarted by the layers of clothing and began to pull open the buttons on her blouse.

She tensed for an instant, knowing that he wanted to touch her, to see her breasts.

Damn, he had frightened her! He dropped his hand and drew a shaking breath. He had come very close to dishonoring her. He turned away from her wide, questioning eyes, angry with himself at his weakness. He was a rutting bounder, just like Percy.

She felt him withdraw from her. He did not want her, but rather that faceless lady who was to be his duchess. She smoothed down her riotously curling hair and rose shakily to her feet. He made no move to hold her back.

Ian rose and grasped her slender shoulders. Even to his own ears, his voice sounded aloof, formal. "You must forgive me for being . . . overly affectionate. It is not at all what I intended." She looked away from him and nodded, unable to speak.

He said more gently, "Are you feeling just the thing?"

She replied in a tight voice, "Aye, I've naught but an aching head. If ye please, Ian, I should like to return to Penderleigh. The rain has slackened."

"Very well, but I shall lead Cantor."

She flushed angrily, thinking he mocked her.

"Nay, Brandy," he said, guessing her thoughts. "I want you to expend all your energies on your aching head." He stooped and retrieved both of their damp jackets. He was somewhat surprised when she pointedly turned her back to him as she shrugged hers on.

Later, when she was gently tucked into her bed by a clucking Marta, Brandy thought she had borne up rather well under the shrieks of concern and demands to know what had happened. That Ian had taken firm control of the situation, calmly telling everyone that she had met with an unavoidable accident, bothered her not at all. She considered it quite a feat that she had not fallen into a faint in the process. She fell asleep from the laudanum the duke had ordered Marta to give to her, her last cogent thought, her relief at being lifted off Cantor's back.

❧ 9 ❧

Brandy awoke early the next morning with a slight head-ache, ravenous hunger, and an urgent desire to speak to the duke. Crabbe raised a surprised face as she crossed the front hall toward the breakfast room.

"Surely, ye shouldn't be out of yer bed, miss!"

" 'Tis fit as a new penny, I am, Crabbe. Is the duke about yet?"

"Nay, miss. 'Tis even earlier he was this morning. Off with Master Bertrand, to Clackmannanshire, I believe. The Cheviot sheep, ye know."

She tried to hide her disappointment and walked ahead of Crabbe into the breakfast room. She served herself a large bowl of porridge, as Crabbe hovered like a clucking mother hen next to her.

"Master Percy also took his leave early this morning," he offered, still eyeing her closely.

"Good heavens," she exclaimed, relief lacing her voice. "Ye'll be telling me that we're alone at Penderleigh, Crabbe!"

"Nay, miss. Lady Adella ordered him to be gone, last evening. Told him that she didn't want to see him again until he was no longer a bastard!" Crabbe added with a rare smile, "Leastways as regards his name, she said."

"I fear that that is all that Percy will achieve," she said with an answering grin.

After Crabbe left the breakfast room, satisfied, she supposed, that she would not expire from her riding accident, Brandy finished her porridge at a leisurely pace, her thoughts turning to Ian. With the sheep purchased and on their way to Penderleigh, it could not be long now until he took his leave back to England. After what had happened yesterday, she had to admit the likelihood that the dreadful *other* lady would have him. There was simply no help for it. She was silent for some minutes. Finally, she forced a smile to her lips and went to the nursery to fetch Fiona. She wanted to get away from the castle, with all of its prying eyes, and thus bundled up Fiona and took her to the small cove where her boat was moored.

It was late in the afternoon when she bore Fiona back to the castle, the both of them saltily damp and windblown. There was a strange equipage standing at the front of the castle. "Perhaps it is one of Grandmama's friends," she muttered to Fiona, and drew the child with her into the front entrance hall. Her feet came to a paralyzed halt at the sight of the most beautiful lady she had ever beheld. She was small, with a gloriously willow-slender figure encased in a golden traveling gown that fit snugly under her bosom and fell in straight lines to her delicately shod toes. Her black curls elegantly framed her face under a bonnet of matching gold straw with bunches of darker gold ribbons, glossy as a raven's wing. Her eyes were slightly slanted and a deep leaf green, fringed by thick black lashes.

The lady was speaking to Ian, and Brandy saw that he was clasping one of her slender gloved hands. She knew without being told that she was the duke's betrothed.

The lady turned, as if sensing her presence, and gave a light trill of laughter. "Why, your grace," her voice sang out, "Scotland is indeed a strange country! But look, you allow your servants to enter through the front door!"

Brandy's eyes flew to Ian's face and she saw that he had stiffened.

"Careful, my dear, you are treading in uncharted water," a gentleman said in a silky smooth, almost mocking voice. At any other time, Brandy would have been sorely tempted to laugh at his outlandish attire, so many gold buttons and fobs were there on his coat and waistcoat. But instead, she stood in wretched silence, her hand tightening painfully about Fiona's fingers.

"Brandy, ye're hurting me!" Fiona cried, and tugged at Brandy's arm. She released Fiona's hand as Ian stepped resolutely forward.

"Brandy, I am glad you are returned. I would like you to meet Miss Felicity Trammerley. Felicity, this is Brandy, the eldest of my female cousins." Seeing Fiona's bright eyes staring in unabashed curiosity, he added, "And this is my helter-skelter Fiona, the youngest."

"Indeed! How very delighted I am, to be sure," Miss Trammerley murmured, only slightly inclining her graceful neck. So Brandy is the *different one*, she thought, those were the duke's glowing words. Different indeed! To think that she, an earl's daughter and an acclaimed beauty, could ever have imagined that the Duke of Portmaine could possibly be interested in such a disheveled, froozy brat!

Brandy blurted out, "Fiona and I have been fishing!"

The faint light of contempt burned brighter in Miss Trammerley's slanted eyes, and she turned back to the duke. "How very . . . odd," she tossed over her shoulder.

Brandy was trembling with humiliation and outrage. How dare this uppity lady treat her like she was some sort of crofter's brat!

The gentleman with all the fobs stepped forward. He said with faint amusement, "Brandy, is it? A quaint name, my dear. I am Giles Braidston, you know. Ian's *English* cousin."

Brandy choked out a strangled "How do ye do," and managed to dip a curtsy.

"Are those buttons *real* gold?" Fiona demanded, in awe over the strange gentleman's remarkable plumage.

"Yes, Fiona, most assuredly they are! You have my leave to touch them. But, my child, I think it only fair, since you have been fishing, that you wash your hands first!"

Such a promised treat was too much for Fiona's unformed sense of propriety, and she dashed away from Brandy toward the stairs. "I'll be back in but a moment, sir! Ye'll not forget yer promise!"

Giles merely laughed and waved Fiona away.

"Have you taken leave of your senses, Giles?" Brandy heard Miss Trammerley utter. "Given half a chance, she will probably tear them off your coat!"

Ian frowned, peeved at Felicity for her want of manners. He was at the point of calling her to order when he was forcibly struck by his own first impressions of Penderleigh and Scotland. It was certainly not what Felicity was used to, and he admitted that it must all be quite a shock to her. She gazed up at him at that moment with melting eyes, and he forced a smile to his lips.

Brandy saw that look and felt weak with misery. "Excuse me," she said to no one in particular, and walked quickly toward the stairs, trying as best she could to keep her back straight and her chin proudly in the air.

"So this is Penderleigh Castle, eh, Ian?" Giles said, breaking the brief tension. "At least you're not wearing kilts yet, old boy!" He glanced smugly at his cousin's severe riding attire.

"Nay, not as yet, Giles. But Bertrand, another cousin, informs me that I have the legs for the kilt!"

"*Nay* and *kilts*, dear sir?" Miss Trammerley inquired sweetly. "I fear that if you do not speak English, I shall be sadly at a loss to understand you."

The duke was quickly brought around to remembering his duties as a host. "Do forgive me, my dear. I have told Crabbe—that leathery old butler you saw—to inform Lady Adella of your coming. Will you not come into the drawing room?"

Felicity allowed herself to be seated in a faded old chair, that was, she thought, a relic worthy of a servant's lodgings.

Ian turned to Giles. "Now tell me, whatever do you do here in Scotland?" he asked in a low voice. "Surely such a journey has been very uncomfortable for Felicity."

"Your betrothed missed you sadly, cousin," Giles said by way of explanation, his tone sardonic.

"I suppose I have been gone from London much longer than I had originally anticipated," the duke said, knowing all the while that his defense was quite unsatisfactory. "There has been much to occupy my attention. Bertrand and I have been to the Cheviot to purchase sheep, and, of course, there have been several trips to Glasgow, to the mills, you know." He ground to a halt, seeing that Felicity was eyeing him with incredulity.

"Cheviot sheep! Good God, Ian, what a bore! Poor fellow. You see, dear Felicity, I was right in assuring you that Ian had not forgotten his . . . obligations!"

Miss Trammerley was quite rigid with anger. "You mean

to tell me, Ian, that you, a duke and peer of the realm, have been playing at being a shepherd!"

"Nothing quite so mundane as that," Ian said coolly. "You see, I wish to make Penderleigh self-sufficient. All the raw materials are here in abundance. All that was needed was capital."

"Indeed, I have to agree that there are certainly *raw* materials in abundance here!" Felicity said sharply. She saw the duke's eyes narrow briefly in what she recognized as his autocratic stubborn look, and quickly retrenched. "What I mean to say, my dear, is that I have missed you sorely and begrudge all the time you have spent away from me."

She was rewarded for her pretty speech by a quick smile. "It has been difficult for me also, Felicity," Ian said, realizing that his meaning did not precisely match up to his words.

Giles cleared his throat, and Ian turned to see Lady Adella walk in a most stately manner into the drawing room.

He rose quickly to his feet. "Lady Adella, I would like you to meet my cousin, Mr. Giles Braidston, and my betrothed, Miss Felicity Trammerley. They have come to pay us a visit."

Lady Adella gazed upon the dashing Giles and instantly liked what she saw. Now, there was a true gentleman! No grubbing about an estate for that one! She took in every elegant line of Miss Trammerley's apparel and her well-bred countenance, and decided that Brandy could well learn style from living in the same house as this girl.

She nodded welcome down her long nose and allowed Giles to kiss her veined hand. "Most charmed, my lady," he said at his smoothest.

As she sailed past Miss Trammerley, the girl gave her a tight-lipped smile. What a ridiculous old relic, Felicity thought, lowering her eyes. That black gown was at least thirty years out of style, and the way she was wearing her hair! The abundant sausage curls made her shudder with distaste.

"So when do ye wed with Ian?" Lady Adella asked Felicity without preamble.

"In August."

"Ah! I'll allow ye some time for yer wedding trip afore I send Brandy to ye."

Miss Trammerley's mouth fell unbecomingly open and she

turned a frigid eye upon her betrothed, who, at the moment, appeared to find his cravat too snug about his neck.

Ian said, "Actually, Lady Adella, since Felicity has just arrived, I have not as yet had time to discuss the matter with her."

Giles said softly, "I can't imagine why not, Ian. Felicity has been here for the better part of fifteen minutes, and has, old boy, made Brandy's acquaintance."

Ian sent a quelling glance toward Giles, and rose. "Lady Adella, which bedchamber may Miss Trammerley use? She is fatigued from the journey and is needful of rest before dinner."

Lady Adella nodded and bellowed, "Crabbe! Get yer stiff bones in here, ye old sot! We've guests and there's work for ye to see to!"

Felicity flinched, and looked contemptuously down her nose.

"Aye, my lady?" Crabbe looked inquiringly at his mistress.

"Have Marta prepare two bedchambers—mind ye, not Morag. We don't want our guests to wake up itching from that licy old trollop!"

Ian swallowed a smile at this baldly phrased command and offered Felicity his arm. "Crabbe will see to you, Giles," he said over his shoulder as he escorted his betrothed from the drawing room.

"The Green Room for the lady, yer grace," Crabbe said.

Ian escorted a silent Felicity to a guest chamber of an indeterminate shade of green, down the corridor from his own bedchamber. Upon his initial inspection of all the rooms some time ago, he had thought the room rather plain in its furnishings but not of an inferior nature. He quickly disabused himself of his original opinion, seeing it now through Felicity's eyes. He chose to ignore her sharp intake of breath and inquired, "Would you like a bath, my dear?" It immediately occurred to him that he must ensure that she was not beset by either Wee Albie or the leaking wooden tub.

She nodded, tight-lipped. "That would be fine, Ian. It has indeed been a long trip and quite fatiguing." She added smoothly, "You mustn't worry about the proprieties, my dear, for my abigail was with me."

"I would that you had written me of your intent to come

here," was all that he said. He thought to ask. "How many servants did you bring, Felicity?"

"Only Maria and Pelham, Giles's valet. Surely there is room in this beastly castle for them!"

"Certainly," he snapped. He pulled out his watch and consulted it. "Dinner is served at six o'clock, my dear. The family meets in the drawing room shortly before that time."

Felicity failed to suppress a shudder at such an unstylishly early dinner.

"I will see to your bath," Ian said, and turned to leave.

"Ian," she blurted out, "whatever did that wretched old woman mean about Brandy coming to London? Surely you do not intend for me to take that dowdy child about . . . in *English* society?"

"Brandy is not a child," he said, at once amused at himself for this admission. "She will be eighteen in the fall. As to her appearance, I fear you did not see her at the most sterling of moments."

"You expect me to turn that one into a lady?"

"She is already a lady, Felicity. Contrive to remember that she is an earl's granddaughter. As to her appearance, I daresay that a proper wardrobe would solve that problem."

"I suppose," Felicity said in a scathing voice, "that I shall have to watch her boating about in the Thames!"

Ian drew his lips into a thin line. "I think you have sufficiently abused the topic. Now, if you will excuse me, Felicity, I will see to your bath."

Miss Trammerley raged silently, upon his firmly closing the door. How dare he dismiss her in such a highhanded manner! She tore off the stylish confection that sat atop her black curls and hurled it into a faded brocade chair. She paced the length of the dismal little room until her anger calmed. There was not, after all, any reason for her to be so upset. What did it matter that the duke was being particularly autocratic and disagreeable? She did not doubt that once married to him, she would be quite able to sway his opinions, particularly about that disgusting girl!

The duke made his way back downstairs to the drawing room. He drew up at the open doorway to see Giles sitting close to Lady Adella. That lady, it appeared to him, was enthralled by his cousin. He heard Lady Adella give a creak of delighted laughter. "Aye, indeed, my boy, old Charles had quite a reputation in those days!"

Ian walked forward. "You must excuse me, Lady Adella, but I must take Giles upstairs, else he will never achieve his exquisite appearance by dinner time."

She gave a grunt of disappointment. "Very well, lad, if ye must! We've plenty of time, I suppose." She waved a bony hand toward Giles. "Sharpen yer wits, my boy, 'tis fifty years worth of gossip I'll want from ye."

"I shall do my pitiful best, my lady," Giles said smoothly, and followed Ian from the room.

"Fancy that," Giles said as they climbed the stairs. "She knew old Lord Covenporth. Killed himself with womanizing and drink, you know. His grandson, Aldous, is treading much the same path, I fear. He'll run out of his pleasures soon enough, for Coven Manor is heavily mortgaged and the better part of it is entailed."

The duke grunted, wondering to himself why Giles seemed to prefer such a set of rakehell men.

Giles drew to a halt at the top of the landing to gaze back down at the old hall. "Dear me, Ian, what an outlandish place to be sure! There isn't much here to remind one of Carmichael Hall, is there?"

Ian thought of the huge, sprawling estate in Suffolk, with its forty bedrooms aind indecently large ballroom, and shook his head. "I should have to say, perhaps, that Penderleigh is more . . . quaint. It's alive with history and tradition, Giles, and I think even you will admit that the view toward the sea is breathtaking. Certainly there is none of the filth of London here."

Giles cocked an incredulous brow, but said only, "I am certain you are right in your opinion, old boy."

As Ian shepherded Giles to his bedchamber, in the opposite direction from his own, he asked, "Now, Giles, just what the devil do you mean by escorting Felicity here?"

"Don't rip up at me, Ian, I beg of you! It was your damned letter that quite set her mind to it. Actually, I had little choice in the matter!"

"My what?"

Giles shook his head, a ghost of a smile playing about his lips. "Your letter, Ian. Lord, never have I seen you set so many glowing words on paper! That chit, Brandy, found herself the subject of much too many sentences. Jealousy fairly dripped from dear Felicity's lovely eyes. Indeed," he paused casting a sardonic look at his cousin, "were I you, Ian, I would think twice about leg shackling myself to such a termagant."

"I trust, Giles, that you did not encourage Felicity in such an improper opinion. You, of all people, should know that I would not turn my back on my . . . obligations. As for Brandy, I am the girl's guardian, and as such, I intend to do what is best for her."

"Rest assured, old boy, that I in no way encouraged Felicity's thinking. Indeed, I found myself forced to be an unwilling recipient of her venom all the way to Scotland." He drew to a halt as Ian opened the door to his bedchamber. "Good God, I do hope that you will tell me that this is where you expect my valet to sleep!"

"Dammit, Giles, I simply haven't had the time to see to the refurbishment of the castle. This room is perfectly adequate, and I've already suffered similar observations from Felicity. You are snobs, the both of you. Since you're here, though, I would be quite happy to allow your artist's talents full rein!"

"I would be hard pressed to know just where to begin," Giles murmured, dusting off a chair top with the tail of his coat.

"It matters not to me. Order that valet of yours—old stiff-necked Pelham—to turn your room into proper form. If you must know, my Mabley is quite enjoying himself now, after his initial shock."

Giles sighed in gentle suffering and walked to the window. "No wonder it's so devilish damp, the place is very nearly hanging into the sea. To think that I let that ice maiden talk me into coming here."

"Ice maiden? I thought she was a termagant."

"Unfortunately, I believe that dear Felicity is both. If I do not miss my guess, she will be all ice and coldness at night and a termagant during the day." He brushed a speck of dust from his coat sleeve and added softly, "Poor Ian, she is not at all like Marianne, you know." He ignored the tightening of his cousin's lips and the rush of color to his cheeks. "Much the same looks and appearance, I grant you. Of course, if you wish to make a marriage of convenience——"

"You go too far, Giles," the duke said at his most frigid. "Marianne has been dead these eight years and has naught to do with anything. As to Felicity's character, either during the night or the day, I think you must grant that I am in a much better position to judge than are you."

"Don't fly into your high ropes, duke! Undoubtedly you are quite right, but then, you have never spent the better part of a week with her!"

"Giles, do not presume further on our kinship! She needs a firm hand, and, as I have told you before, she will do my bidding."

"You make her sound like some sort of filly to break to bridle." He looked as if he would have said more, but only shrugged. "Have you been much in the company of Felicity's brother, Lord Sayer?"

"He's an out and outer, I suppose, but I do not dislike him," the duke said, relieved to be on unexceptionable ground. "He strips well in the ring and shows a good account of himself."

Giles shivered delicately and regarded his beautifully manicured nails. "I find him rather indelicate, rather outspoken, mayhap vulgar."

"Why? Because he doesn't wear gold buttons the size of saucers?"

"I pray you, Ian, do not draw attention to your own lack of style," Giles chided with ready laughter in his eyes.

The duke threw up his hands. "Damn you, Giles, stop pinpricking me! Lord, but you and Percy will have a fine time of it!"

"Percy? Another Scottish relative?"

"He's a bastard," Ian said, smiling to himself as he remembered Brandy's bald delivery of this fact. At Giles's arched brow, he added, "His father, now dead, was one of Lady Adella's two sons. Percy was born on the wrong side of the blanket but is in the midst of becoming legitimate at this very moment."

"Good lord," Giles exclaimed, "and I thought to be bored here!"

"Ah, here is Pelham. I'll see that Wee Albie sends up your

bath." The duke laughed, most incomprehensibly, Giles thought, as he stared after his retreating figure.

When the duke finally gained his own bedchamber, he gazed about the large, somewhat gloomy room. Of a certainty it was quite different from his magnificent suite of rooms at Carmichael Hall, but, in his opinion, not at all to be despised. He caught himself wondering idly what Brandy would think about his ducal residence, and in the next minute walked over to a wooden chair and kicked it violently toward the fireplace.

Mabley came bustling into the room. "We mustn't dawdle, your grace! Lady Adella is very particular about gathering in the drawing room before dinner."

Ian eyed the bald head and the cherubic face, and found himself smiling in spite of himself. "Do with me what you will, Mabley."

"My, my, whatever happened to this chair, I wonder?" Mabley muttered to himself.

Brandy could not seem to stop herself from furiously pacing back and forth across the threadbare carpet in her room. How dare that bitch call her a servant! She chanced to see her own flushed countenance in the mirror and was forced, albeit reluctantly, to admit that she might have had some justification. She was windblown, her face and hands sticky with salty seawater. Her nose twitched as she got a whiff of her own fishy scent.

Constance chose that moment to fling into her room, in a state of trembling excitement.

"Och, Brandy, I got a glimpse of her! Did ye see her gown and that gorgeous bonnet? And so small she is! I vow I felt the perfect clodpole just being near to her. Why she can't possibly even reach Ian's shoulder!"

"I didn't see anything so very special about her," Brandy said between gritted teeth.

Constance took no notice and let her tongue continue on its runaway wheels. "That gentleman—Giles Braidston! He is most elegant, far more so than the duke. Grandmama told me that he is Ian's cousin, and even though she called him a rattle pate in that sour way of hers, I could tell she was much impressed. Ugh—fish! Brandy, do ye wish to give them a disgust for ye? Ye look and smell like a fishmonger's wife! Do take a bath. I do wonder if my new gown is stylish enough for Miss Trammerley's taste."

She dashed to Brandy's mirror and peered closely at her black curls. She saw an angry gleam in her sister's eyes, and turned about to face her, her brows drawing shrewdly together. "Her coming distresses ye, does it not, Brandy?"

"She is a rude bitch!"

"Mayhap, but she is also betrothed to the duke. Even if she dripped charm, I can't imagine ye liking her."

"Yer tongue talks without yer brain thinking, Connie! I'll thank ye to keep your nonsensical thoughts to yerself!"

Constance shrugged. "As ye will. Ye might try wearing the new gown Ian bought for ye." As Brandy did not reply, Constance shot her a saucy smile and turned to go. "I think I shall have Marta do something special with my hair," she said over her shoulder.

After Constance left her, Brandy thought a moment about the beautiful velvet gown and dismissed it with a sigh. Ian would be sure to think her a perfect cow, with her bosom so exposed. She was so unlike the petite, exquisitely slender Felicity. She gazed toward the closed door. Had she been so obvious in her feelings that Connie had guessed them?

After biding her time for a good hour until a tub was free for her use, she managed to convince herself that the famed Robertson pride (at least it was famed according to Lady Adella) must see her through this hateful time. She arranged her long hair into the Grecian style, pointedly ignored the lovely velvet gown, and yanked down a waisted green muslin. She added the crowning touch of her mother's faded shawl, and trudged doggedly downstairs.

Felicity, after driving her maid to distraction with conflicting orders and demands, finally achieved a result that pleased her, and walked down the wretchedly dim corridor downstairs to the drawing room. She knew that she was some minutes late, but did not care, for she was determined not to let Ian dictate orders to her.

Ian proffered her a stiff bow, and made brief introductions to Claude, Bertrand, and Constance. Felicity looked closely at Constance, for this girl, unlike her sister, gave the impression of budding beauty, with her carefully coiffed black hair and her green dress.

"Ye're late," Lady Adella said, not mincing matters, even with a guest. "And I, for one, don't like my haggis cold. Give me yer arm, my boy," she commanded Giles.

Felicity gazed beneath her lashes at Ian, as he drew her arm through his. How stern he appeared, she thought, particularly after the week she had spent with the laughing, stylish Giles. She shuddered delicately, her eyes drawn to his large hands, to the long fingers, blunted at the tips, touching her.

As Ian seated her at the long dining table, he said in a conciliating tone, "You must see that it is important to Lady Adella that everyone is punctual for dinner. I trust you will pay more attention to the clock in the future, if for no other reason than to avoid her sharp tongue."

She pointedly ignored him and turned her attention to Lady Adella, who was saying to Giles, "Tell me more about Dudley, my lad. Ye know I fancied myself in love with his grandfather once, the old scoundrel! I heard that he ran aground against Fox and was forced to rusticate."

Giles willingly cudgeled his memory, but as the event described happened before his entrance into the world, he was forced to dwell upon the grandson. "A dull sort of chap, my lady, turned squire in a corner of Somerset, and has quite half a dozen brats hanging onto his coattails." He sent a wicked look toward Ian, and added, "Much like our Ian here, I fear, perfectly content to ignore his ducal advantages and consequence, and trudge over his acres. Admit it, Ian, you scorn town life and if you have your way," this said with a pointed look toward Felicity, "you'll want closer to a dozen brats! From the size of him, Lady Adella, I venture he'll breed giants, more's the pity for his wife!"

"Hush your stream of nonsense, Giles," the duke ordered. He added seriously, his eyes upon his betrothed, "Though I must admit that I do prefer country life. And if I could be assured of half a dozen little Fionas, I would most willingly populate Suffolk with my offspring."

Felicity dropped her fork into what she considered to be an inedible plate of food, and turned on Ian with ill-concealed shock. "Ian, surely you jest! I cannot imagine anything more vulgar and common than redheaded children!"

Brandy clutched her wine glass and said in the coldest voice Ian had ever heard from her, "My little sister is not vulgar, Miss Trammerley. Vulgarity, I think, is that quality in people that makes them quick to hurt others' feelings."

Felicity forced a laugh that held no mirth. "La, Miss Robertson, I meant no insult! After all, your dear sister is your fishing companion, is she not?"

Ian said sharply, "Little Fiona is many things, Felicity. I think, though, that Brandy regards her more as her own child, rather than her sister—her wee bairn, as we would say in Scotland."

"Wee bairn, your grace? All these strange words, *ye* for *you* and *wee* for *small*, I vow I am in a foreign country! Do contrive to speak English, I beg of you."

Claude, who had not bothered to attune himself to any unpleasant undercurrents, said with his grating cackle, "I daresay ye're quite right, Miss Trammerley! For a lady such as yerself, we must all mind our speaking and treat ye in the manner in which ye're accustomed."

Felicity searched for sarcasm in this speech, found none, and decided that perhaps this one Robertson had a modicum of wit. She nodded graciously to Claude.

Lady Adella, however, kept the pot boiling. "So ye don't like the distraction of town life, eh, Ian? I hope I can count on ye for one season to launch my Brandy into the *ton*."

Miss Trammerley said coldly, "I fear, Lady Adella, that his grace and I intend a rather extended wedding trip. Have you no suitable relatives in, say, Edinburgh? Surely, such society as Edinburgh offers would be more to her liking and more suited to her abilities."

Giles looked sharply at Felicity, saw the mulish set of her mouth, and shrugged. He gazed beneath his lids at Brandy. Surely Felicity could not have noticed those huge amber eyes.

"Nay, 'tis not Edinburgh I wish for the chit," Lady Adella continued serenely, seemingly oblivious to Felicity's insult. "What with Ian providing the girl with a proper dowry, and she being, after all, part English, I wish her to find a suitable husband in London."

"What about me, Grandmama?" Constance cried.

Claude grinned widely and poked Bertrand in the ribs.

" 'Tis other plans we have for ye, girl! Ye need have no worry about yer future. Be that not right, Bertie?"

"There is a proper time and place for most things, Father," Bertrand said stiffly. "I find that ye have missed on both counts. I'll thank both ye and Lady Adella to let me mind my own affairs."

He avoided Constance's wide-eyed gaze and turned back to his dinner.

"Just see that the hair on yer head isn't gray by the time ye make up yer mind, lad!" Lady Adella admonished, waving her fork at him.

"I find that Bertrand always shows remarkable good sense," Ian said, then quickly added, seeing Cook's attempt at trifle nearing the table, "It has been a most filling dinner. It is my wish that we save dessert for later and adjourn to the drawing room."

Brandy could not contain a small wicked smile and said, "But, Ian, trifle is such an *English* dish. Are ye certain ye have no wish to try it?"

"Nay, Brandy!" He shot her a quelling look, but her impish grin remained.

He received unexpected assistance from Giles, who rose and began solicitous removal of Lady Adella. "The sooner we retire to the drawing room the better, old boy! Your cane, my lady. Now, where were we? Ah, yes . . . Dwyer. Do you remember that old curmudgeon, Viscount Dwyer, my lady?"

"Dwyer, Dwyer," Lady Adella muttered. "Can't say that I do, my boy," she finally admitted, the furrows in her brow deepening in disappointment.

"It doesn't matter, my lady," Giles said smoothly, "he really isn't worth the bother." Actually, to the best of Giles's knowledge, there was no Viscount Dwyer. Ian caught his eyes, but Giles greeted his sardonic grin with sublime disregard.

"I say, my boy," Lady Adella said, once she was settled in her chair in the drawing room, "why don't ye tell me about yer own family, and the duke's? I know my sister's daughter married a regular sawed-off little creeper, and I'd like to know how Ian gained his giant's body!"

"Mayhap your sister's daughter played the little creeper false, my lady."

Lady Adella chortled loudly, in Claude's best tradition, and gave Giles a light buffet on his immaculate shoulder.

Brandy, who could not bear to see Ian solicitously assist Felicity into a chair—as though she were some sort of helpless baby, she thought with a silent snort—inched closer to Giles and her grandmother and felt emboldened to inquire, "Seriously, Giles, we know so little of yer family. Ian never speaks of them——"

"What!" Giles interrupted, his eyes mocking, "our illustrious head of the family has not even bothered to tout his proud lineage! I say, Ian," he called to his cousin, "you leave it to me to puff up your consequence."

"Puff away, rattle pate," the duke returned with a wry smile. "Mind you, though, don't put the ladies quite to sleep with boredom."

Felicity found this dampening of ducal antecedents not at all to her liking. "Really, your grace, how can you make light of your noble ancestors!"

Brandy added soulfully, "Aye, Ian, to be such a vaunted peer of the realm is no mean thing! I, for one, am quite ready to be suitably impressed, that is, as soon as Giles has seen to Grandmama's creature comforts!"

Felicity snapped, "I would have you know, Miss Robertson, that the Carmichael family has a noble and proud lineage. Pure *English*, mind you, not tainted with any foreign blood."

"How quickly you forget the Comte and Comtesse de Vaux, my dear," Giles interjected in a silky voice.

"Giles!"

Brandy heard the threatening tenor in the duke's voice, but could not help herself. "Who were the de Vaux, Giles?"

"That is for our dear duke to answer, Brandy."

Felicity said with finality, "I, for one, Giles, do not see what difference the de Vaux made. After all, they added no French blood to the Portmaine line."

"Quite so, my dear," Giles agreed, and withdrew his snuff box from his floral waist coat pocket.

"Brandy," the duke ordered sternly, "go and play for us."

Her eyes flew to his face only to see that he was glaring at Giles. She was too startled at his command to refuse.

She sang a sad Rabbie Burns ballad, but earned at the end

127

of her endeavors only Miss Trammerley's sniffing comment, "How difficult it is to enjoy a song when one cannot understand the words."

Brandy was thwarted in discovering more of Ian's family and the mysterious de Vaux, for Felicity rose with a delicate yawn and prettily begged the duke to escort her to her room. "The corridor is so very glum, your grace, I fear I will lose my way."

"I wish she would break her ankle," Constance whispered with undisguised malice.

" 'Twould only make her stay here longer," Brandy said, pleased that Constance had changed her opinion of Miss Trammerley.

Claude rose painfully on his gouty foot and gallantly kissed Miss Trammerley's hand.

"Don't be an old fool, Claude," Lady Adella snorted. "Miss Trammerley certainly has no wish for yer arthritic attentions!"

Miss Trammerley appeared to think otherwise, for she smiled graciously at Claude, before saying vague good nights to the company in general.

The duke was feeling much the butt of everyone's ill humor, and thus took no pains to soften the autocratic set of his jaw.

"As much as it must please me to see you," he began as he escorted his betrothed up the stairs, "your manners have been sorely wanting this evening!"

Miss Trammerley, feeling every bit as misused as the duke, sucked in her breath and gritted her teeth against unladylike vindictives.

The duke continued, "I know it must all be very strange to you, but you must make a push to be pleasant . . . in the short time you will be here."

"Pleasant!" She turned on the huge, altogether too dark man who was to be her husband, and said with dripping sarcasm, "How very *easy* it is to be pleasant in this moth-eaten household! And how very *pleasant* you make it, your grace, with your talk of populating Suffolk with half a dozen brats like that wretched Fiona! Indeed, what a *pleasant* thought it is picturing myself as some sort of breeding mare locked away in that huge mausoleum, Carmichael Hall! If you ever believe I would give up London life, you sorely mistake the matter, your grace!"

"Are you saying, Felicity, that you do not wish to bear my children?" Her eyes unconsciously flitted over him and he sensed her distaste of him.

She splayed her hands in front of her, and drew a measured breath. "What a ridiculous question, to be sure! I am overtired, yes, that is it, and am in need of a good night's sleep."

"Yes, certainly," he said, and opened the door to her bedchamber, calling on the same tolerance he had always given to Marianne. "I will see you in the morning."

～ 10 ～

The nursery overlooked the front drive at Penderleigh and it was from this vantage point that Brandy observed the duke toss Felicity, dressed in an exquisite blue velvet riding habit, onto Cantor's back. She felt close to choking with jealousy, for Felicity sat tall and straight in the saddle, quite at her ease. How very elegant and self-assured she appears, Brandy thought and with a growl, turned away to resume Fiona's lessons.

This morning, Brandy laid aside the ponderous tome of Brandenstone's history of Scotland and instead unearthed a crinkled map of England and set Fiona to the task of locating Suffolk.

"Suffolk," Fiona said, rendering the word Scottish. "Where is Suffolk, Brandy?"

" 'Tis in England, poppet, where Ian lives when he is not in London."

"His *ducal* residence," Fiona said matter of factly as she ran a stubby finger down the eastern side of England.

"Good heavens, poppet, wherever did ye hear that?"

"Grandmama," Fiona replied, her concentration still on the task. "Brandy," she asked, looking up from the map, "what's a *ducal*?"

Brandy looked startled a moment, then threw back her head and laughed aloud. "Oh, poppet," she said merrily, "ye make it sound something like a porpoise! A *ducal*, my love describes what Ian is, since he's a duke." Brandy realized that her definition could have been a bit more accurate and polished, but Fiona appeared satisfied.

Fiona finally laid her forefinger upon Suffolk, then raised

130

her eyes to gaze pensively at her sister. "When is that nasty lady going to leave?"

Brandy, whose thoughts were on a ducal residence named Carmichael Hall, jerked her attention back to Fiona and gave a tight little laugh. "I don't know," she said, not bothering to improve upon Fiona's description. She murmured more to herself than to Fiona, "I do wonder, though, why she came here. 'Tis obvious she dislikes all of us and Penderleigh."

"Well, I hope she doesn't drag Ian away with her. Maybe if I put a toad in her bed——"

Brandy caught Fiona up in a tight hug. "Nay, poppet, ye mustn't. Though it would be fun!"

Ian rode beside Felicity at a decorous pace along the road that lay parallel to the cliff. It occurred to him to wonder just why he persisted in remaining at Penderleigh. Getting the Cheviot sheep settled and all the accounts straight leaped to the fore as plausible reasons, but he realized that the huge pair of amber eyes that gazed up at him as though he were the only person on the face of the earth ranked above the sheep. He thought again of the hour he had spent with Brandy at the hut. Her beautiful soft lips and the innocent, ever so natural moans of pleasure that she had breathed into his mouth as he had kissed her.

"Ian! Slow down, if you please! I have no inclination for a gallop, particularly on this rutted path. There appear to be no decent roads in this accursed country."

Ian drew in his horse as he did his breath and turned to Felicity. "Sorry my dear," he said shortly.

"Ian, whatever is the matter with you? You are not behaving at all like yourself, you know."

"Felicity," he said, reining in Hercules beside Cantor, "why did you come to Penderleigh? I did write you explaining my delay here."

Miss Trammerley, who to this point had borne his inattention with what she considered more than a modicum of patience, said sharply, "I told you that I missed you, Ian. Surely that is enough reason to pay my betrothed a visit."

A black brow arched a good inch. "Come, Felicity, all the way to Scotland? Carmichael Hall, perhaps, I can credit."

Felicity smoothed the wrinkles from her gloves, an activity designed to control her anger. "It would appear," she said finally, her voice cool, "that I am to be cross-examined. I—I find you somewhat changed, your grace."

"Changed, my dear? I think it is just that you have never before seen me away from our London acquaintances. Further, I admit to being somewhat surprised that you would forego your pleasures in the midst of the season to come to a place that you obviously despise."

"Is it so unbelievable that I wished to see you? Or, perhaps it is that you are discomfitted, your grace, that I have dared to interrupt *your* pleasures. Do not think, I pray you, that I don't realize that the wretched little slut is trying to make you forget what you owe to your rank, and to me! She doesn't fool me with her ridiculous dowdy clothes. Did you really believe that I would not notice how very fondly you wrote of her in your letter?"

For a moment, Ian considered telling her the truth of the matter, but her cold, insulting tone held him silent. He said finally, "What is it you mean to say, Felicity?"

Felicity turned her face away, forcing herself to remember that she was, after all, the petted daughter of the Earl of Braecourt, and not some flyaway little ragamuffin in the wilds of Scotland.

"I suppose it is quite natural for you to wish to take your . . . pleasure, even in this hateful, uncivilized place. I only ask that you do not bring your whore to London after we are married."

"Ah, so that is why you traveled all the way to Penderleigh—because I wrote of Brandy and you, Felicity, you assumed that she must be my mistress. I think that I begin to understand you."

"I trust that you do, Ian. You will not then bring her to London?"

"Brandy refuses to come to London, though, of course, it is my wish that she do so." He abruptly changed the topic before she could properly assimilate this distressing fact. "I asked you last night, Felicity, if you wished to bear my children. Now, I believe, I must require an answer from you."

She lowered her eyes in a maidenly pose, but her voice trembled. "I—I will, of course, do my duty."

"Your duty," he repeated in a level voice.

"You must have an heir, I suppose, though why it must

needs be so important, I cannot imagine. After all, there is Giles. But you need not doubt that I will do what is expected."

"Do you love me, Felicity?"

She was so taken aback by this calmly asked question that she blinked several times, then gave a brittle laugh. "How perfectly quaint! My dear duke, I begin to believe that your wits have become addled in this backward country! I certainly have a great *regard* for you and your family, as I trust you would expect in the future Duchess of Portmaine. Surely, you have not succumbed to notions suitable for the lower classes and silly females who read novels filled with romantic drivel!"

"A duke and duchess are so different from everyone else, then?"

She gazed at him with strained tolerance. "A duke and duchess should set the example for those of lesser birth. Maudlin sentiment, of a certainty, has no place in such elevated circles. I cannot imagine that you would want the Duchess of Portmaine to distress you with ill-bred clinging scenes, fit only for the stage!"

He gazed at her, saddened. Perhaps he had agreed with her at one time, but now he realized that she was right, he had somehow changed, had become a man he wasn't certain that he understood. He sighed inwardly. Even if he were not a duke, he was still a gentleman, and a gentleman did not break an engagement formally announced.

"I think it time we returned to Penderleigh," he said shortly, and wheeled Hercules about.

Felicity inclined her head graciously, a forced smile firmly pinned to her lips, and followed his lead.

Percy's arrival later in the day did little to elevate Ian's spirits. He was surprised, however, to see the armor of cynicism that Percy habitually displayed replaced by open joviality. He announced that he was now a true Robertson and no longer a bastard, the Scottish court, under obdurate pressure from MacPherson, having legitimized him the afternoon before in Edingburgh.

Ian saw Bertrand pale visibly at the news. As for Claude, he snorted angrily, fastening his rheumy eyes upon Lady Adella. She appeared vastly amused and clapped Percy smartly on the back before turning to Claude. "Yer turn will come, don't fret yerself," she said snidely. "What's another week or month, for that matter! One thing at a time, old MacPherson's not capable of more."

It was Felicity's reaction to meeting Percy that surprised Ian the most. He had fully expected that she would elevate her patrician nose, repulsed at being in the same house with a bastard, a *former* bastard, he mentally revised. He was wrong. Percy possessed himself of one of her small hands, murmured silken phrases, and planted a light kiss upon her wrist. He would have sworn that she actually preened at Percy's cavalier antics.

Giles, as was his way, accepted Percy's acquaintance with his usual urbanity, and remarked to Ian in pensive undertones that regardless of the fellow's antecedents, he was possessed of a rare way with the ladies. With the exception of one lady, Ian thought to himself.

At dinner that evening, Percy recounted with relish his brief visit after his legitimization with Joanna's father, Conan MacDonald. "Ye should have seen the look on the old man's face when I told him I'd kept to his wishes and not returned until my name was fixed up right and tight! He turned positively purple! He could no longer gainsay my hand for his fusby-faced daughter."

"Why, sir," Felicity inquired in her most charming manner, "do you court a lady who holds so little attraction?"

"Methinks," Giles interposed, a gleam in his eyes, "that mistress Joanna is an heiress!"

"Indeed," Percy agreed with a satisfied laugh. "And a plump little pigeon for the taking, ye may be certain. Of course, for all his wealth, Conan MacDonald still carries the smell of the shop, but I think I can easily bear the odor."

Ian noted with a silent grimace that Felicity appeared to have no difficulty whatsoever in understanding Percy's thick Scottish brogue.

"MacDonald will have ye then, my boy?" Lady Adella asked.

"Can ye doubt it, lady? Old Angus, may he rot in hell, still exercises a powerful influence amongst the Scottish gentry. Ye may well guess too that I was not backward in extolling the rank and virtue of our current Earl of Penderleigh. The old man's mean eyes bulged when I made it known that it is an English duke who now holds the title."

Lady Adella bent a penetrating look toward Percy. "Ye didn't tell him, did ye, ye rascal, that ye were the duke's heir?"

Ian set down his wine glass with a decided snap. "The duke's heir is yet to be born! I trust that he will make his appearance in the next year or so."

Giles murmured close to Felicity, "Ah, 'tis well occupied you'll be, my dear. The master has given his orders."

Brandy heard his soft words and pressed her napkin hard against her mouth.

"Hold your tongue, Giles," Ian commanded sharply.

Unabashed, Giles gave a crooked grin and said to his cousin, "A toast, Ian. May you have better luck this time!"

Brandy jerked up her head and watched Ian's face pale beneath his tan. Whatever did Giles mean, "this time"?

Constance, to this point seated very quietly beside her, suddenly tossed her napkin unceremoniously on the table and rushed from the dining room, flinging a disjointed excuse over her shoulder.

"Whatever ails the chit?" Lady Adella demanded of no one in particular.

"I shall take care of her," Bertrand said, rising quickly. "Pray continue, Ian," he added and left the room.

He was drawn by the sound of angry hiccuping sobs coming from a small parlor at the back of the castle. The door stood ajar and he drew up, seeing Constance flung face down upon a sofa, sobbing wildly.

She looked so heartbreakingly lovely with her black hair streaming over her bare shoulders that it required great effort for him not to gather her up into his arms. He sat down beside her and said softly, "Nay, lass, don't cry."

" 'Tis ye, Bertrand," she said without enthusiasm, and dashed her hand across her eyes.

"Aye, 'tis I," he replied, undaunted.

"Did Grandmama or Uncle Claude send ye after me?" she demanded between broken hiccups.

"Nay, I came because I'm . . . concerned about ye." He pulled a handkerchief from his waistcoat pocket. "Here, Connie, dry yer eyes and tell me what troubles ye."

She daubed her drenched lashes and looked away from him, twisting the handkerchief between her fingers.

"Come, lass, ye know ye can trust me. Haven't I always been yer . . . friend?"

Constance saw no condemnation in his eyes, only kindness. She blurted out, "Percy will wed that dreadful Joanna, he now makes no bones about it! Ye know he does not love her, 'tis only her money he wants! He's despicable!"

Bertrand forced steadiness into his voice. "Perhaps, Connie, but ye surely must understand Percy's position. He loves his gay life in Edinburgh. Without the capital to maintain his pleasures, he would assuredly be miserable. He has chosen what he wants, and if it must needs be a marriage to a lady he doesn't cherish, then, in a way, I can only pity him."

"But I thought him more *noble!*" she cried. "And ye, Bertrand, ye defend him!"

"Nay, lass, 'tis not that I approve of what he does, 'tis merely that I understand his motives. Ye must forget him, Connie, he has never been worthy of yer affection."

She was silent a moment and he hoped that she was pondering his words.

" 'Tis not fair," she said in a tight little voice.

"Life does not always bring us what we think to be just."

"But Brandy, why should she go to London, whilst I—I have never even been to Edinburgh!"

Bertrand felt a tug of amusement at this new grievance. At least, he thought, she is no longer thinking about Percy. "Brandy is the eldest, Connie, although," he added with brilliant insight, "some think her less the woman than ye are."

"Aye, 'tis true," she said with strong conviction.

"I do not think, though, that she will go to London. It is the duke who desires it, not Brandy. Can ye believe that Miss Trammerley would wish either of ye in her home?"

"She's a witch!"

"Mayhap she is like most of the English ladies in London. I cannot see ye having much enjoyment in her company. Edinburgh, though, is quite another matter. 'Tis a beautiful city, Connie, and before long, I am certain ye will pay a long visit there. Ian told me that London boasts no finer shops and attractions than our own Scottish capitol."

Although Constance did not appear entirely convinced, she

said nothing more. She rose and straightened her shoulders. "Ye're kind, Bertie." She lifted her face to his. "Can ye see that I've been crying?"

He gently took the handkerchief from her hand and rubbed away the tears from her soft cheeks. "Nay, ye're as lovely as ever. If anyone asks, we shall simply say that ye had the heachache."

"Thank ye, Bertie."

When they returned to the dining room, no one made comment about Constance's sudden flight, though Ian saw Lady Adella give a sly wink to Claude.

Brandy gazed at her sister, knowing that Percy was responsible for her upset. She was surprised to see her quite composed now, and she wondered what Bertrand could have said to her.

After dinner, Brandy managed to work up the courage to speak to Giles. Her opportunity came when Felicity, prettily entreated, sat herself at the pianoforte and executed a Mozart sonata. Her stumblingly phrased question brought a wry smile to Giles's well-formed lips.

"My poor Brandy, you didn't know about Marianne?"

"Nay."

"When I wished Ian better luck this time, I referred to his first wife. She died under the guillotine, you know."

"Marianne was French . . . a de Vaux?"

"You've an excellent memory, my dear. Yes, she was a lovely, fragile little creature."

"I see."

Giles gave a start at the misery he read in the girl's amber eyes. Poor child, he thought, Ian has obviously unleashed a woman's emotions in the girl's breast. He shrugged, rather philosophically. She was young, and young hearts didn't break, only bruised a bit.

∼ 11 ∼

After spending his morning with Bertrand and the crofters herding together the scores of Cheviot sheep into their enclosures, Ian felt he smelled rank enough to baa. Unwilling to present such an odiferous presence to the rest of the family, he strode toward the small, protected cove, trusting that the salty sea would cleanse away the worst of it.

He glanced only cursorily about once he reached the pebbly beach to ensure that he was alone, and quickly stripped off his clothes and dropped them unceremoniously upon a rock. His skin tingled as the cold seawater lapped about his legs. He ignored this minor unpleasantness, waded in waist deep, and struck out with long firm strokes into deeper water. When this pastime paled, he flipped upon his back and floated, gazing lazily up at the cloudless blue sky. What a glorious place, he thought. If he were never to return to London, he fancied that it would be no great loss to him. London, with all of its unremitting social demands, and Felicity. He sighed and closed his eyes against the sun's glare, willing himself not to think about anything at all.

Brandy walked along the promontory, too downcast to notice that her tartan shawl was making her gown stick to her back from the trapped heat. She thought of Fiona, and a slight smile tugged at the corners of her mouth. One afternoon each week, Lady Adella insisted that the child spend several hours with her in her sitting room, to learn the manners of a lady born, she said. Fiona was relegated to sitting on the cushion at Lady Adella's feet, setting crooked stitches into a swatch of embroidery and listening to fifty-year-old stories of Grandmama's long-ago conquests.

She made her way carefully down the steep path to the beach and did not at first notice the pile of men's clothing heaped on a rock. She shaded her eyes with her hand and gazed out over the water.

She knew it was Ian, even before he stood and walked toward shore. She stared at him as intensely as she had that other evening when she had inadvertently bounded into his bedchamber. Surely there could be no man to compare with him, she thought. His thick black hair was plastered about his head, making him look rather boyish. He stepped from the water and stood a moment on the rocky beach, stretching his arms above his head.

Brandy was beginning to believe that she was cursed with divine ill luck that fated her to see her love achingly naked, yet so far out of her reach.

The black hair on his massive chest dripped rivulets of water that ran down over his muscled, flat belly into the curling hair below. She knew that she should not be staring at him, but she could not help herself. She drank in all of him, acutely aware of the rampaging feelings that welled within her. With vivid memory, she thought of their short afternoon in the abandoned crofter's hut, his mouth hungrily upon hers, his strong arms holding her against his chest. The thought of being naked against him, molding her own body to the length of his, having him make her a woman, made her gasp with longing.

Ian finished buttoning his white shirt, that garment still, unfortunately, reeking of sheep odor. He threw his rumpled cravat over his arm and prepared to leave the beach. It was a bright patch of color that brought his eyes slewing in Brandy's direction. It took him but an instant to recognize the faded plaid of Brandy's tartan shawl.

"Brandy! You little witch, come out here at once!"

Brandy took a hesitant step toward him, her face so flushed that he could not help but notice.

"Just how long have you been standing there?"

Her voice sounded ridiculously breathless. "For a . . . long time."

He felt a powerful surge of desire that he managed to mask with a convincing show of anger. "Brandy, dammit, this is the second time you have placed me in an altogether ridiculous position! Don't you realize, you little fool, that you shouldn't stare at naked men?"

She drew a shaking breath, unable to bear his condemnation, and turned on her heel to make her escape.

"Wait, dammit!" he yelled, and broke into a run after her.

At that instant, Ian felt a tremendous force strike his back. It hurtled him forward, face down, onto the beach.

Brandy froze in her tracks, the sound of the shot stunning her. She stared stupidly at Ian, who lay motionless, his blood beginning to ooze through his white shirt, forming a spreading stain of deep red. She screamed his name and ran to his side. She looked wildly in the direction the shot had come from, the enormity of what had happened searing into her mind.

Another shot rang out, and she felt its hiss as it whizzed harmlessly past her head. She threw herself down over Ian, covering his body as best she could with her own. Dear God, someone was trying to kill him!

She opened her mouth and screamed as loud as she could, until her voice grew raspy and hoarse.

Time was her enemy, an eternity of minutes that held her motionless with Ian bleeding beneath her. She did not realize she was crying until she saw Bertrand and Fraser through a haze of tears, running down the snaking path toward her.

"Bertie, thank God ye've come! Hurry! Someone has shot him!" She quickly rolled off Ian and ripped open his shirt to bare the wound.

She pulled off her shawl, rolled it into a ball and pressed it with all her strength against the bloody wound in his back.

"Good God, Brandy! What the devil!"

Bertrand pulled her from Ian's side and shouted to Fraser, "Hurry, man, fetch the others! Send someone for Wee Robert!" He pressed his fingers over the wound to slow the bleeding. "We heard shots, then your screams. Who was it, Brandy? Did you see him?"

"Nay, I saw no one. Bertrand, will he be all right?"

"I—I don't know, Brandy, the wound is deep, but I do not think the ball has hit a vital organ."

Percy and Giles came running down the path. Giles said nothing until he had examined his cousin. "Surely you must have seen who it was," he said sharply, staring up at Brandy's white face.

She shook her head, mute.

Giles nodded her back. "Come, Bertrand, Percy, we must get him back to the castle." The three men lifted him carefully and with agonizing slowness gained the top of the cliff path.

"Damn, but he's pale as a sheet," Bertrand said shakily.

"It's just as well that he's unconscious," Giles said calmly, shifting Ian's weight.

They finally reached the castle. Brandy dogged their heels, past a shrieking Morag and a gaping Constance, staying as close to Ian as the men would allow, until they had reached the duke's bedchamber.

Bertrand turned to her and said gently, "Come, Brandy, ye must go now. We must undress him and put him to bed."

She did not move and he shook her shoulders. "He'll live, I promise ye. There's naught more ye can do. Go now, ye must speak with the others."

She pulled her eyes away from Ian's motionless figure to Percy's face. His eyes appeared to her more hooded than usual, his mouth drawn in a cold tight line. She turned frantic eyes to Bertrand.

"Ye'll not leave him alone," she cried urgently, plucking at his sleeve. "Promise me, Bertrand!"

"I promise, lass."

Brandy did not take the time to strip off her bloodied clothing, but instead made her way downstairs to the drawing room.

"Take this, child," Lady Adella ordered, handing her a glass of brandy.

She gulped down the fiery liquid, coughed violently as it burned down her throat, and set the empty glass on the sideboard with shaking fingers.

"What did you do to the duke?" Felicity demanded, instinctively drawing away from Brandy and her bloody gown.

"Someone tried to kill him, on the beach in the protected cove. The bullet went into his back."

Felicity screamed and collapsed to the floor.

"Useless frilled chit!" Lady Adella snorted at Felicity's prone figure.

Brandy and Constance each took an arm and dragged Felicity up onto a sofa.

"Brandy, the blood on yer gown—ye're covered with it," Constance cried.

"Hush, Constance. The girl doesn't need ye to state the obvious." Lady Adella turned to Brandy. "Ye must get a hold of yerself, child. Fraser's gone to fetch the magistrate, Trevor. Now, tell me before ye go and change yer gown, did ye see who did this terrible thing?"

"Nay, Grandmama, I saw no one. Whoever shot him must have been hiding in the rocks atop the cliff."

Lady Adella lowered her gaze from Brandy's distraught face and stared thoughtfully down at her gnarled fingers.

"A poacher! It must have been a poacher," Constance cried.

She repeated her belief to Mr. Trevor, the magistrate, some while later.

"There are no poachers within fifty miles of here," Brandy said harshly, her eyes fastened upon the drawing room door. She had heard Wee Robert's familiar voice some minutes before. Surely, he must come down soon!

Mr. Trevor stared meditatively at Brandy. "We can decide upon that matter after I've heard yer sister's story." He frowned, his bushy brows drawing almost together over his craggy forehead as Brandy related the few facts she knew. "It would appear to me that ye saved the duke's life, lass." He turned to Lady Adella. "I understand, my lady, that Mr. Percival Robertson no longer stands in, shall we say, an ambiguous position."

"Aye, that is true," she replied slowly. She then drew herself upright and added in her most imperious voice, "Ye'll stop yer nonsensical thinking, Trevor! I'll thank ye not to involve any of the family in this affair! I suppose ye'll be asking me next if Claude Robertson's gout is aught but a wily trick and he pulled the trigger! A lawless tinker must be the culprit, and it's time for ye to go find the wretch!"

The lines about Mr. Trevor's mouth deepened at this diatribe, but outwardly he remained calm. " 'Tis a serious matter, my lady, and I but do my duty. I ask ye to forget, at least for the moment, any tinker, for there aren't any about to the best of my knowledge, and tell me who in yer judgment would wish the English duke dead."

Percy's name stood stark on Brandy's lips. But she held herself silent, for could not every Robertson, each in his own way, have perceived some gain by Ian's death?

Lady Adella thwacked her cane hard against the floor and snorted with disgust. "Damn ye, Trevor, why does any villain show his true colors? I'll tell ye again, ye are sniffing in the wrong foxhole!"

Mr. Trevor held his peace. It seemed to him that Mr. Percival Robertson was the likeliest suspect, as his becoming legitimate had made him next in line to the title, though he had no intention of dismissing other members of the family. What an altogether wretched situation! And in his county, too.

He rose slowly to take his leave. "Let us trust, Lady Adella, that his grace will be able to provide me more information on the morrow."

Lady Adella snorted and waved him away. She turned a contemptuous eye toward Felicity, who was sitting dazed on the sofa. "Brandy, call for Miss Trammerley's maid. She'll do better in her own room."

Brandy did as she was bid, thankful for any activity that would keep her mind occupied.

As the morning lengthened into afternoon, Wee Robert still had not come downstairs.

"Tearing yer shawl to shreds won't make him come down any faster, child," Lady Adella said.

"Aye, Grandmama." But she continued fretting mercilessly at the fringe.

Crabbe entered the drawing room a step in front of the doctor. "Wee Robert, milady."

"I've eyes in my head, Crabbe! Well, Wee Robert, how fares the duke?"

Wee Robert, Elgin Robert by name, took no offense at this appellation, having grown quite used to it over the past fifteen years, and walked wearily into the room. He was a man whose body had betrayed him, rendering him a mere five feet tall in his stocking feet. He rubbed a chubby hand over his brow and advanced toward Lady Adella.

"His grace will, I think, recover, my lady," he said in a gentle, almost girlishly soft voice. "The ball entered his back just below his left shoulder. I might add that yer kinsman was a stoic to the point of causing me concern. Not one sound did he make when I drew out the bullet. White and blown he is now, to be sure, but resting more comfortably. There's only fever and infection to concern us now." Wee Robert gratefully accepted a cup of tea from Constance and took a long drink. "The duke is young and quite strong. Aye, he'll pull through quite nicely, quite nicely. Nasty business, though."

"Nasty, indeed!" Lady Adella said. "That fool, Trevor, left here as stupid as he was when he came! I vow that man is only good for catching urchins who steal apples!"

"Is his grace awake?" Brandy asked.

"Nay, lass, I gave him a hefty dose of laudanum. Sleep is the best healer, ye know."

Percy, Giles, and Bertrand entered the drawing room together, each man's face white and drawn.

Wee Robert turned to them. "I thank all of ye gentleman for yer help." He turned away abruptly, realizing that possibly one of them had brought the duke to his present condition.

Bertrand nodded, and asked, "Trevor came, Lady Adella?"

"Aye, I was just telling Wee Robert that the man brays like an ass! 'Tis his notion to lay the blame at a Robertson's door! Of course, it must be one of those demned tinkers responsible."

Giles raised a brow and gazed at Percy and Bertrand.

"Where is Uncle Claude?" Brandy blurted out.

"Good God, Brandy, surely ye don't think that my father could be capable of such an act!"

"For that matter," Percy interposed, "do any of us know where the other was when Ian was shot?"

"We might begin with where you were, Percy," Bertrand said coldly.

"Ah, dear cousin, do I detect a note of suspicion in yer voice? If ye must know, I was endeavoring to avoid the filthy stench of yer precious sheep!"

"I do not think that such haggling will get us to the truth," Giles said, "nor will it aid in cementing trust or friendship. Incidently, where is Miss Trammerley?"

"She went into hysterics, then fainted," Constance said, a note of satisfaction in her voice.

"A stupid question," Giles murmured. "I should have guessed as much."

Wee Robert, who had sat in pained, embarrassed silence to this point, rose and proffered a slight bow to Lady Adella. "I can see that my presence is no longer needed. I will pay the duke a visit tomorrow morning."

"But what if he worsens during the night?" Brandy asked in a panic.

"I'm but fifteen minutes away, lass."

After Crabbe, who unlike Wee Robert had no wish to leave the interesting contretemps in the drawing room, was prevailed upon to escort Wee Robert from the room, Bertrand turned to Brandy. "It was lucky for Ian that ye were on the beach, lass. But ye put yerself in grave danger, ye know."

Percy said, "Just why were ye there?"

"I was merely avoiding the . . . stench, like ye, Percy." She found herself gazing about from one face to another, searching for any sign that might betray the owner's guilt. But she saw nothing, and as she had no wish to hear any further pointless bickering, she slipped quietly from the room, her destination the duke's bedchamber. His valet, Mabley, had to be with him, and it was this gentleman that she wanted to see.

She walked quickly past Felicity's room, scowling as she did so at the closed door. How ridiculous that *she* should be having vapors!

She quietly opened the duke's door and slipped into the darkened room. She did not see Mabley and silently cursed him for leaving his master alone. She heard Ian's deep, even breathing and crept softly to his bedside. He appeared so natural in his sleep, the strain of his ordeal not evident on his face. A lock of black hair hung over his forehead, and tenderly, she smoothed it back.

"Miss Brandy!"

She spun about, automatically placing an admonishing finger to her lips.

"You shouldn't be here, miss," Mabley said. She turned beseeching eyes to him and he could not help but see the pain in their amber depths. Mabley felt old, much too old for this kind of excitement. His hands still shook from wiping the sweat from his master's brow whilst the doctor probed for the bullet.

She shushed him again with her finger on her lips.

"You needn't whisper, Miss Brandy, his grace is sleeping soundly."

She rose and beckoned him away from the bed. He followed her wearily, wishing only for a warm mug of ale to ease his tiredness.

She gazed up at him somberly and said without preamble, "His grace must not be left alone for even a moment, Mabley."

Affronted, Mabley said, "It weren't my intention to leave him take care of himself, miss!"

"Nay, ye don't understand. Ye know that someone has tried to kill him," she said, nearly choking over the word. "We cannot afford to trust anyone, do ye hear? He's helpless as a babe now, unable to defend himself." She adopted her grandmother's imperious tone. "If ye'll stay with him during the day, I'll not leave him at night."

" 'Tis most unseemly, miss! Surely, Mr. Giles or Mr. Bertrand——"

"Nay! I want none of them ever to be alone with him! Don't ye see, Mabley, we can't afford to take any risks."

Mabley rubbed his sagging jaw, trying to gather together his weary wits. "If it be dangerous, miss, like you say, then I'll not allow you, a small female, begging your pardon——"

Brandy interrupted him with a snap. "See here, Mabley, Grandfather Angus had a remarkable gun collection. I'll have one of his pistols with me. Does that make ye rest easy?"

Mabley was very much of the belief that guns and females were not fit company for each other, but the decisive glitter in the girl's eyes stilled his tongue.

"You'll wear yourself out, miss," he essayed feebly.

"Nonsense! Now, promise me ye'll not leave him. I'll bring ye yer dinner later and then ye may take yerself to bed." Brandy turned away before he could develop further arguments. She smiled as she heard his defeated sigh behind her.

The small clock on the mantel rang out a faint ten strokes, and Brandy rose from the hob, where a pot of broth lay hot and ready, and walked softly to the bed. She laid the palm of her hand on the duke's forehead. He was still cool to the touch, thank God. Still, Wee Robert had warned that a fever could strike at any time during the next few days.

"I'll let no one hurt ye, my love," she whispered, and lightly kissed his mouth. She straightened and walked back to the warmth of the fire. Quickly, she stripped off her clothing and pulled on her cotton nightgown over her head, tying the drawstring at her neck. It took her longer to unbraid her hair and brush out the masses of ripples. Finally, she fastened her shawl about her shoulders and walked back to the bedside.

Still he lay motionless. She settled into the large chair she had drawn up and tucked her feet under her. Before allowing her tired muscles to relax, Brandy gazed one last time at the locked door, then to the small pistol that lay on the night-stand beside her. Mabley was sound asleep in the adjoining room. That door was also locked, Brandy having insisted that he comply with her instructions. Her only concern was the corridor door to Mabley's room, for which there was no lock.

Only Lady Adella and Mabley knew of her vigil. To Brandy's surprise, Lady Adella had heard her out, regarding her in a rather peculiar manner, but did not gainsay her wishes. "It's just as well that we don't tell anyone else, child," she had said, looking away. "I have no desire for that milk-and-honey Felicity to be raising a ruckus!"

Brandy heard no ruckus from anyone that night, and was surprised when Mabley shook her shoulder the next morning to awaken her.

"Oh, Mabley! I had thought to be dressed and wake ye up!"

Mabley grunted and gazed down at his master. "Hie yourself off now, miss, I'll see to him."

Later that morning, Mr. Trevor arrived and asked to see the duke. Wee Robert gave his consent, and while both men shared a cup of coffee with Lady Adella downstairs, Mabley gently awakened his master.

Ian awoke, somewhat reluctantly, still dazed from the laudanum and with an irksome pain in his shoulder.

"Ah, your grace! 'Tis glad I am to see your eyes open again!"

Ian thought to change his position, but a searing pain made him quickly abandon the notion.

"You just lie still, your grace," Mabley said in his most soothing voice. "I'll fetch you some broth that Miss Brandy has kept warm for you."

In a slurred voice, Ian asked, "How long have I been asleep?"

"Since yesterday afternoon, your grace. Wee Robert gave you a powerful dose of laudanum, if your grace recalls."

"Wee Robert," the duke repeated, bemused.

"The doctor, your grace. A tiny little Scotsman, but fair good with his hands."

Ian winced at the vague memory of lying in exquisite agony as someone had dug the bullet out of his back. Other memories tugged at his mind, and he felt himself go pale. "Mabley, is Brandy all right? She was with me on the beach, just before I was shot!"

"Your grace mustn't upset yourself. Miss Brandy escaped injury. Indeed, the young lady, from what I can glean, your grace, saved your life." He did not think it wise to mention that the young lady was also the duke's self-appointed guardian during the night.

"Mr. Trevor, the Scottish magistrate, wishes to see you, your grace. Do you feel well enough to speak with him?"

Ian nodded and tried to clear his mind. A bushy-browed gentleman dressed in somber black came into his line of vision.

"It's just a few minutes I need to talk with ye, yer grace."

Ian nodded again, and tried to focus his wits away from the pain in his back.

"It appears to me that yer grace is a lucky man."

"Mabley told me that Brandy saved my life," the duke offered in way of response to Mr. Trevor's statement.

"Aye, that she did, yer grace," Mr. Trevor saw that his grace was not at all sharp in his mind, and allowed himself to become sidetracked. "Evidently, yer grace, when ye fell, she threw herself over ye, another shot barely missing her. Yelled like a banshee, she did, scaring off the killer. Her screaming and the gun shots brought the family arunning!"

"Little fool!" Ian muttered, "she could have been killed."

"Aye, but she wasn't. It's very worried all the family is, yer grace. Is there naught ye can tell me?"

"I don't think so," Ian managed in a shaky voice.

Mr. Trevor saw the duke's effort was making his brow furrow in pain. He rose. "I'll fetch Wee Robert, yer grace, 'tis him ye need now, not me. We'll talk more of this later."

Ian scarce heard him. He blinked several times in an effort to clear away the blurriness that was distorting the room around him. He saw Brandy, her face becomingly flushed, staring at him on a beach. Then someone was standing beside him and he felt the cool rim of a glass pressed against his mouth. He opened his mouth from habit, took several long drinks of a cool liquid, and closed his eyes and let the quiet darkness close over him.

"The wound is healing nicely, no infection there. But his grace has got the fever." Wee Robert sat on his black coat-tails in the drawing room, facing the assembled family. As he spoke, he eyed Miss Trammerley. A more weak-kneed, fainting lady he had yet to meet. She grew rather pale at his words, but retained her upright position.

Brandy asked quietly, "How long do ye expect the fever to last, sir?"

Wee Robert beamed at her with approval. "I won't mince matters with ye, lass. There be some who never recover from the fever. But like I told ye yesterday, his grace is young and a stronger man I've yet to meet. He'll pull through it, I'll wager."

"But he is a *duke*!" Felicity expostulated.

Wee Robert said with a touch of humor, "Aye, miss, that he is. Undoubtedly, the title will assist him greatly to get well!"

"I believe what Miss Trammerley is expressing," Giles said smoothly, with a quiet smile toward the flustered Felicity, "is that it is rather incredible that one of his grace's estate should find himself in such a situation."

Wee Robert rose. "That is a matter for Mr. Trevor, I think. There is naught more I can do for his grace, Lady Adella. I've given Mabley instructions for his care."

Bertrand walked with Wee Robert to the door.

"What a damned mess!" Claude said irritably. "I swear my gout has pained me more in this past day than in the last year!"

"I think I would prefer a little gout to a ball in the back," Percy said with barely veiled contempt.

Bertrand returned to the group. "Ye all know, I presume, that Ian could tell Trevor nothing."

"I agree with Lady Adella," Claude broke in. "It must have been one of those filthy tinkers. They're a damnable lot, ye know."

Brandy sighed and rose. "If ye'll excuse me, Grandmama, I must give Fiona her lessons. Then I wish to see how the duke fares."

"Don't cast such a long face, child, else ye'll give the girl nightmares." Lady Adella waved Brandy from the room, then eyed each of the assembled company in turn, her gaze speculative. "I dislike mysteries and I dislike scoundrels, having lived with one for over fifty years. That a man could be such a villain and on Penderleigh land, makes my stomach turn."

"I do not think, Lady Adella," Percy said softly, "that Trevor counts only men amongst his suspects."

"Come, Percy," Bertrand said angrily, "do ye believe that Lady Adella balanced a gun on her cane?"

"I merely speculate, dear cousin. If Trevor is going to continue poking about, asking us all sorts of ridiculous questions, I see no reason why the ladies should be excluded from such fine sport."

Felicity rose and said in a trembling voice to Giles, "I feel dreadful! Maria must bathe my temples with lavender water. Why did the duke ever insist upon coming to this wretched place? Look what it has brought him—to death's door by some scheming Scottish barbarian! Oh, how I wish none of us had come here!"

"Then why don't ye leave?" Constance asked sweetly. "Ye're doing naught for anyone, save causing a great pelter!"

Felicity turned on her, her eyes flashing daggers. "Scottish brat! You—you can't even speak English properly!" With this Parthian shot, she stalked from the drawing room.

"I have seen Ian, 'tis flushed with fever he is," Giles said, turning the company's attention from Felicity.

"Aye, Mabley says he's becoming delirious. Damn!" Bertrand suddenly smashed his fist against his thigh.

"Are ye damning the fact that the duke is ill or that the killer missed his mark?" Percy inquired in a mocking voice.

"What a despicable thing to say!" Constance cried.

Giles broke in, "Mabley tells me that his grace will not be

left alone for a single minute. I think that should cool our would-be killer's ardor. Now, I think, Lady Adella, that is if you do not mind, that we should have our afternoon tea."

"You'll not let anything else happen to Ian, will ye, Brandy?" Fiona asked with a worried litle pucker on her forehead. Brandy tucked in the bedcovers about her little sister's neck, shaking her head. "Nay, poppet, I'll let none hurt him again."

She left Fiona for the evening, and unwilling to endure more interminable hours of sly accusations and cutting remarks, took herself to her own room.

It was a pale, drawn figure that Mabley admitted to Ian's bedchamber as the evening advanced toward ten o'clock. Brandy's eyes flew toward the bed. "He's quiet, Mabley. Has the fever broken?"

Her voice was so hopeful that Mabley disliked having to dash her down. "No, miss. 'Tis only more delirious he's become, tossing about and muttering about this and that. Eight years it's been, yet it's her name that he cries out, over and over." Mabley shook his head wearily, unaware that he had turned a knife of misery in Brandy's breast.

"Ye mean Marianne?"

"Yes, miss. I think he's reliving that terrible time all over again." Mabley's old bones were so weary that he plumped himself down in a chair and closed his eyes. He could still picture the duke's white mask of a face the day he had returned alone from France. Aloud, he said, "His friends feared for his reason. Even the King sent his condolences, I remember. 'Twas a sad time, yes, a sad time indeed."

Brandy took a tight hold on herself. Marianne was long dead and she, Brandy, was very much alive. Ian needed her care. If she had to share him with a ghost, she would do so. Felicity, she refused to even admit into her thinking. "Go to bed, Mabley, ye're near to dropping."

Mabley readily obliged. He turned at the adjoining door. "You'll call me, miss, if his grace becomes overly restless?"

"Aye. Be certain to lock the door, Mabley. His grace is in enough danger with the wound. I don't want to have to worry about the man who was scoundrel enough to shoot him."

Mabley withdrew, locking the narrow door after him. He

stood for a moment in the middle of the small dressing room and eyed with disgust the lumpy truckle bed that had been his nightly companion for so many weeks now. Just knowing that Morag had changed the linen this very morning made him itch involuntarily. Like Miss Trammerley, he wished that they had never come to Scotland. He prayed that his grace would soon be on the mend, and once mended, would consent to leaving this land with all its strange foods, funny speech, and salty sea air.

As he slowly removed his black coat, he glanced toward the closed door and allowed his thin brows to draw together over narrowed eyes. It wasn't right that Miss Brandy should be protecting his grace, better one of the men, Mr. Giles, for example. A stubborn young lady she was, and more than just fond of his grace, he guessed. She was in for a bruised heart, he knew, for although he himself had no liking for the haughty Miss Trammerley, he knew the ways of the Quality. His grace was as good as leg-shackled, what with the formal announcement. If asked, he would have gladly enlightened his grace as to the differences between Miss Trammerley and the duke's poor first duchess. A pity, he thought, yes, it was a pity.

Brandy stood quietly beside the duke's bedside, gazing down at his flushed countenance. Tenderly, she smoothed a shock of black hair from his brow. He muttered something unintelligible and turned his face away on the pillow.

She dampened a cloth in his basin and gently daubed his forehead. He tried weakly to strike her hand away.

"Hush, my love," she whispered softly, and pulled the heavy goosedown cover up over his bare chest, mindful of his fever, even though the room was cozily warm. The white strips of linen bound about his chest and under his back stood out starkly against the curling black hair, and she had the desire to touch him.

His breathing became less ragged and he tossed about very little, but the flush of fever was still bright.

Brandy felt her eyelids begin to grow heavy and she tugged herself out of the large leather chair at his bedside. She stretched and went to build up the fire which had fallen into thick layers of orange embers. After she undressed and changed into her nightgown, she fastened her tartan shawl once more firmly about her shoulders and sank back into her chair, pulling a rough wool blanket up to her chin for warmth.

She was pulled from her sleep by the sound of garbled mutterings. In an instant she was beside him, gazing fearfully down into his face. She felt near to tears at his anguished voice.

"Marianne, Marianne. If only you had trusted me . . . told me, Marianne. I would have tried to save them. . . . Marianne, why did you doubt me? Too late . . . I was too late."

"Oh no, Ian, 'twas not yer fault! No, my love, do not blame yerself for her death. Hush, my love . . . hush." I love ye more than she could have, Ian, she cried to herself. I would not have left ye.

He began to twist about and Brandy, fearing the wound would open, resolutely blinked back tears and sat down beside him, holding down his shoulders as best she could. " 'Twill be all right, love," she crooned softly, "ye must lie still."

His voice rose, and she relived with him visions of the guillotine, the cruel blade that had severed Marianne's life.

" 'Twas not yer fault, Ian," she repeated again and again. She touched her fingertips to his lips and pressed her cheek against his, holding him fiercely to her.

Through her fingertips, he whispered yet again Marianne's name, and in her misery, Brandy closed her mouth over his, willing him to forget his ghost. He responded to her, and she was surprised at the desire she felt when his tongue explored her mouth. His arms went around her, his large hands sweeping down her back to her hips. She tried to pull away from him, but he held her so tightly that she could not move.

"Ian, no, ye mustn't!" she cried, her voice ragged with longing.

His lips were suddenly slack and she saw that he was staring at her, his eyes bright, penetrating.

"My love . . . my little love," he whispered, and pulled her face fiercely down to him. He found her mouth, and with an almost wild brutality, he forced·her lips to open.

He thinks I am Marianne, she thought dully, hopelessly,

and then she did not care at all. She willingly parted her lips and let the passion within her burst into life.

With sudden strength, Ian pulled her on top of him, and she felt his manhood hard against her belly through the down cover. She moaned softly as his hands caressed her hips, tugging at the offending nightgown. She helped him, eagerly, with no pretense, with no virginal terror. The thought of him naked against her made her groan with frustration as her fingers jerked away the cover from her body. She saw his swollen manhood springing from the mat of black curling hair, and trembled with excitement, knowing that he would enter her, engorge her with himself.

"Oh, Ian, I do love ye so," she whispered breathlessly into his mouth.

His hands were kneading her hips, more gently now, and she was eased once again atop him, her belly and legs naked and pressed hard against him.

With one surging movement, he clasped his arms tightly about her back and rolled over on top of her. His fingers stroked her and she gasped aloud with pleasure, her body not wanting to stop, her hips pressing upward against him.

She felt him parting her, probing into her gently, and felt a stab of pain. She wrapped her arms tightly about his neck and arched upward. She felt his huge manhood pressing against her, as his fingers kept her parted. She gasped aloud at the tremendous pressure as he pushed inside her, and though she was moist with desire, she thought that he would rip her apart.

But she was not prepared for the searing pain when he pressed deeper into her, hard against her taut maidenhead. She knew she mustn't cry out, that such a sound might bring Mabley dashing in from the adjoining room.

He pulled himself momentarily back, then fiercely, urgently, drove with all his might into her, ripping through the tiny passage, thrusting deeper until she engulfed all of him.

To hold the cries of pain deep in her throat, she dug her teeth into the hollow of his neck and let her tears streak along his cheek. She felt a tremendous tautness in him as he drove back and forth in her, his arms tight about her. Suddenly, he shuddered and tensed over her. A whimpering cry escaped her mouth as he thrust one final time deep within her, his seed erupting from him, filling her.

He collapsed on top of her, burying her beneath him. His breath came in deep, sighing gasps as his face fell beside hers on the pillow.

Brandy lay very still, though her body cried out in protest at his great weight. His breathing calmed, and she felt the warmth of his mouth against her cheek. He gave a deep moan and was quiet. She believed that he slept.

I am part of him now, she thought, and tightened her arms about his waist. She lay quiet until she could bear his weight no longer. As gently as she could, Brandy eased herself from under him and lay against his side. She gazed at his face in the dim candlelight, and let her fingers trace along the firm line of his jaw, featherlight, so as not to disturb him.

For tonight, at least, he was hers, and she would not allow Marianne's ghost or Felicity's presence to intrude upon her happiness. She pulled the covers over both of them and carefully rested her face against his shoulder, savoring the precious moments until she would have to leave his side.

Ian awoke with a start, feeling as though his mind had been gone from his body for longer than he could remember. For a moment, he was disoriented and gazed with some confusion at the bright shaft of sunlight that streamed through the windows. He planted his mind firmly back into his body and tentatively raised himself to his elbow.

"Your grace!"

"Mabley, good God, man, what is the day and the time?"

"Your grace is clear-headed?"

"I have my wits restored, I believe." He carefully flexed his back, and winced at the pain. "It's on the mend, Mabley."

" 'Tis Thursday, your grace, and near to ten o'clock in the morning."

"You mean that I've been unconscious since yesterday?"

The deep lines in Mabley's old face smoothed out as he smiled at his master. "Yes, your grace, that, and you were out of your head for some time with the fever. Your grace had all of us mightily worried."

"Out of my head? You mean I was delirious?" He frowned, trying to piece memories together.

"Yes, your grace," Mabley approached his master and added softly, "You remembered it all again, your grace."

There was no need for him to explain further.

"It would appear, Mabley, that someone had taken me into profound dislike. I recall very little of it. Has the culprit been caught?"

Mabley shook his head. "No, your grace. A Mr. Trevor, the Scottish magistrate, is looking into the matter. I will send Mr. Giles to you, if you wish. I have not been with the family."

"Yes, I would speak with Giles. Damn, but I'm hungry and much in need of a shave and a bath. See to that first, before you send up Giles, will you, Mabley?' He paused a moment and gazed intently at his old retainer. "You're looking a trifle peaked. I trust my nursing did not all fall on your shoulders."

"No, your grace. Miss Brandy took care of you during the nights. Now don't get yourself into a pelter, you must know that Miss Brandy is a very strong-willed young lady! You just rest easy, your grace, and I'll be back shortly." He continued at the uncertain look on his master's face, "The bell cord is broken, your grace. I'll fetch Wee Albie."

"It appears that there are a lot of wee people about! I seem to recall vaguely someone named Wee Robert."

"The Scots doctor. He'll be here to see you this morning, no doubt."

After Mabley closed the door quietly behind him, the duke slowly swung his legs over the side of the bed and tried to rise. He hated the feeling of helplessness, and cursed silently as his legs refused to hold his weight. He sank back down, rubbing the growth of beard on his face. Damn if I'm going to be an invalid, he muttered, and flung back the covers.

Two splotches of dried blood stood out starkly on the white sheet. His movements froze as jagged pieces of memory began to fit themselves together in his mind. He gazed down at himself and saw more blood, as well as his own seed. He dashed his hand across his brow and muttered aloud, "Dear God! Brandy!"

He felt a nagging soreness and raised his hand to touch his neck. He could feel the slight indentation of two rows of teeth. He touched his fingers to his cheek, remembering her tears of pain as he had thrust deep into her.

Mabley returned shortly to find the duke sitting up, staring vacantly ahead of him. He looked at him compassionately, thinking that he must be in pain. "Your grace," he said softly, "Mr. Giles wanted to speak to you. Perhaps you would wish to eat this broth whilst you see him?"

Ian nodded silently. "Yes, Mabley, the bath can wait. Give me the soup and send in Giles."

"Ian, old fellow! If you've got your appetite, you must be on the mend!" Giles crossed to the bed and looked closely at his cousin. "You are feeling better?"

"Yes, Giles, much better. Do sit down while I eat this wretched pap."

Giles lowered himself gracefully into the leather chair at the bedside, and began to tap his fingertips together in a thoughtful way.

"Do you remember anything, Ian?"

"I remember far too much," the duke replied slowly, "but unfortunately none of it concerns the identity of my would-be killer. Mabley tells me there's a fellow by the name of Trevor poking about."

"Yes, an old fool, Lady Adella tells us. He is, I think, a well-meaning fellow, but there are woefully few facts to aid him . . . or any of us, for that matter. As you can well imagine, all the Robertsons are at each other's throats. Accusations and suspicions are rife in the air! I mean to get you away from this place, Ian, as soon as you are well enough to travel."

The duke lowered his soup spoon, silent for some moments. He said finally, "No, I think not, Giles. It is not that I am much concerned about appearing the coward by returning to England . . . it is just that there is much for me to do here. Ranking high amongst them is finding the bastard who shot me."

Giles gave his cousin a rather twisted grin. "Do you refer to Percy?"

"If he is a bastard in character as he was in name, then yes. What does Lady Adella have to say about the matter?"

"She made a cryptic comment about disliking scoundrels and mysteries. Other than that, she has joined in the fray with the rest of the family. Felicity, as you can imagine, has been somewhat of a trial."

The duke said abruptly, "Did you know, Giles, that Brandy has stood guard over me at night? A beef-witted thing to do!"

"No, I did not know. Methinks that would not please dear Felicity over much, though. Brandy is a very unusual girl."

"Indeed, I would have to agree with you, cousin."

"After you were shot, she demanded of Claude exactly where *he* had been! I say, Ian," Giles continued after a moment, a pucker of concern on his brow, "it cannot set right with me, your wanting to remain here. I tell you, no one, including myself, can venture other than suspicious guesses as to the identity of your assassin. Can you not see how foolhardy it is for you to remain, possibly giving the fellow another chance at you?"

"I assure you, Giles, that I shall be very much on my guard! And, if I keep myself surrounded by Robertsons, what chance would the scoundrel have?"

Giles did not appear to be content with the duke's decision, but kept further arguments to himself.

"You know, old boy, Felicity is certain not to be pleased with your decision," he said after a moment. "She has spared no pains in telling everyone what a detestable, horrid place this is and how she plans to see us all gone from here the moment you are better."

"It would appear that I must speak to her. After I have shaved and enjoyed a bath, send her to me, will you, Giles?"

"How very *brave* you are, cousin!" Giles patted the duke's arm and took himself from the room.

The duke tried to concentrate upon the possible identity of his would-be assassin, but found that his thoughts continually veered back to Brandy. "What a damned tangle," he muttered under his breath.

"What did your grace say?" Mabley inquired politely.

"Nothing, Mabley, I was merely thinking aloud."

Giles discovered Felicity sitting alone in the drawing room downstairs. She said in a voice sharp with boredom, "Well, Giles, what of his grace? Is he coming down today?"

Giles eyed the petulant set of Felicity's mouth and the furrow of evident displeasure on her white forehead. There was a glimmer of amusement in his voice as he said, "I found Ian much improved, my dear. Indeed, I left him in Mabley's capable hands, getting a shave if you must know."

"Yes, he is so terribly dark," Felicity said vaguely, looking away.

Giles ignored this reference to his cousin's hirsute body. "Ian has asked to speak to you, my dear, after he has had his bath. I will take you up in a while. You must not act shocked, for the fever and pain from the wound have left him a bit pulled."

"I wish we knew which one of these ghastly men is responsible! No one will say anything, you know! Even while they insult each other in the most vulgar manner imaginable, they are protecting each other, I am certain of it! And that boorish doctor—you saw how he insulted me, Giles!"

Giles vaguely recalled that Wee Robert had not shown what Felicity undoubtedly considered due concern for the upset of her nerves. "He was, most understandably, I thought, very worried about the duke, my dear," he said dryly. He pulled out a small elegant snuff box, flipped it expertly open with one finger and helped himself to a generous pinch. He sneezed delicately and removed a fleck of snuff from his sleeve. "Poor old Mabley, rather worn to a frazzle he is, what with taking care of Ian during the day. Thank God, it is Brandy who——"

"He's another one who shows no proper respect for his betters. I shall see that shriveled old turnip is soon out of my house! What do you mean, he's taken care of the duke during the day? What about Brandy? What has that rude child have to say to anything?"

"Oh, nothing really, my dear," he said, and turned away to gaze a moment at the dusty bagpipes hanging limply over the huge mantelpiece. Beside them hung the crested Robertson coat of arms.

"You of all people mustn't try to bamboozle me! It is *she* who has been with him at night, isn't that true, Giles?"

"Yes," he replied in a calm voice, "but I can see no reason for you to fly into the boughs. Undoubtedly she did a fine job of nursing him."

"Hah! I can just imagine how well the little slut *nursed* him!"

"Really, Felicity, I believe that Ian would take it much

amiss to hear such an unflattering term applied to his ward. Ah, look at the time! I must warn you, my dear, that Ian is set upon staying here. I tried to convince him to leave, but he has no intention of doing so."

Felicity jumped to her feet. "Surely he is in no fit state to make such a decision!"

"I assure you that his mind is quite set on it. You must have learned by now that your betrothed is a most determined, stubborn man."

"Determined is he!" Felicity raged, taking a quick turn about the room. "And just what does he think I am—a weak, simpering little fool like his first wife, Marianne? I will tell him, you may be certain, that I have no intention of being brought to heel by his freakish temper!"

"Oh lord," Giles said, as Felicity, her green eyes fulminating with determination, flung out of the room.

She rapped sharply on the duke's bedchamber door.

"Miss—Miss Trammerley!"

"Pray tell the duke that I wish to see him, Mabley. The corridor is drafty, so do not keep me waiting!"

"His grace is expecting you, miss," Mabley said, and quickly backed out of her way.

"Do come in, Felicity," Ian called from the bed. He said to Mabley under his breath, "Make yourself scarce. Have a mug of ale, then come back."

Mabley nodded with forced politeness to Felicity, and slipped past her out of the room.

Felicity gazed across the room, her eyes flickering briefly toward the mammoth fireplace, then to the huge bed. It was a man's bedchamber, all angular, with no delicate hangings or furnishings to soften its lines. The room was much to her dislike and it suited him, she thought. Ian lay in the center of the bed, his black head in stark relief against the white pillow.

"Giles tells me you are feeling better, your grace," she said, walking stiffly to his bedside.

"Aye," he said in the Scottish vernacular that she loathed. "Thank you for coming, Felicity," he continued, his voice ironic. "I think it important that we talk."

"Giles has already informed me of your idiotish plan! Surely such a decision does not augur well for your health! I would that you tell me that Giles was mistaken and that you will leave this place as soon as you are able!"

"Idiotish plan?" he repeated, his black brows snapping together. "If you wish to hear me repudiate my decision, I fear I must disappoint you! As I explained to Giles, I have still much to do here and have no intention of turning tail and dashing back to England! I am disappointed, Felicity, that you do not appear to understand my reasons."

She drew back at the harshness in his voice, but managed to make a quick recovery. "*I* disappoint *you*, your grace! What about *my* wishes in this matter? Surely you cannot imagine that I view with complaisance being surrounded by vulgar, rude barbarians! And one of them obviously a murderer!"

"I still live, as you see. As to your calling the Robertsons vulgar and rude, madam, it appears to me that you should examine your own behavior. Not one conciliatory word have I heard you utter since you have come to Penderleigh. You pride yourself on being the daughter of an earl, but I will tell you that your manners have given little credence to that fact!"

"How dare you call *my* manners into question, Ian! I suppose you feel that little slut, Brandy, behaves in a manner better to your liking!"

"I hardly think Brandy comes into this conversation, Felicity," he said matter-of-factly.

"Oh, does she not!" Felicity retorted, her tone hard and filled with unsuppressed dislike. "Giles let it slip that your precious Brandy has most obligingly nursed you during the nights! Did you much enjoy her care, your grace?"

"Brandy is most generous, at times overly so," he said in a low voice.

"I suppose you believe I should emulate that little trollop! Or perhaps, you would prefer that I docilely hang my head like your saintly Marianne, and bow to your every ridiculous whim!"

"You go too far, madam!"

"Do I, your grace!" she spat. "Oh yes, you refused to ever discuss her with me, did you not? Did you believe me such a witless fool that I would not quickly discover that I bear a

161

marked resemblance to her? I tell you, Ian, I am not Marianne!"

"You state an irrevocable fact, madam. What is your point?"

The coldness of his tone flung her to further anger. "My point is, your grace, that I shall not play the role of a second Marianne! I once believed that you knew what you owed to me and to your own consequence, but I begin to see that I was sadly mistaken in your character. You behave more in the manner of one of these beastly Scots than an English peer!"

"*Your* behavior, madam, is most enlightening. As to these beastly Scots, I vow I find more in common with them than I do with your gentle, modest presence!"

"There are some, my dear duke, who do not find my presence as repugnant as you seem to do. Indeed, the Marquis of Hardcastle, a most noble, refined gentleman whose suit my father discouraged because of your most assiduous attentions—to think that I spurned him in favor of you!"

"Undoubtedly that estimable gentleman would be most flattered by your opinion! Indeed, I would imagine that you would think him most complaisant until he dared to cross-cut your wishes! I grow weary of arguing with you, Felicity. I have told you my wishes, and I repeat to you, I have no intention of changing my mind."

"I suppose that little fool, Brandy, fairly drips honey about you, pandering to your odious autocratic temperament! That is what you prefer, is it not, your grace? An ignorant, sniveling little——"

"Hold your tongue, madam. You expose your own character more than would be seemly even to the Marquis of Hardcastle!"

"Oh, how very wrong I was about you. To think that I let myself be drawn in just because of your rank and position!"

"Felicity," he said with deadly calm, "you begin to bore me. Perhaps Giles will listen to your ranting, but I tell you I will have no more of it."

She drew up to her full height and squared her shoulders. "You are insulting, and I shall not stand for it!" Her voice became icily formal. "I desire that you return with me to

London as soon as you are able. If you refuse, your grace, I beg to inform you that our engagement is off."

"I refuse," he said softly.

She stared at him in some astonishment, turned away with a withering glance, and marched, head held high, to the door. She said over her shoulder, her voice heavy with sarcasm, "I wish you luck, your grace, with all of your Scottish relatives! You will not object, I am certain, if I send a retraction of our engagement to the *Gazette*."

"Not at all. Say all that is proper to your parents. Felicity," he added, "do not despise a marquis, 'tis but one rank less than a duke."

She slammed the door, not favoring him with a reply.

When Giles entered the duke's bedchamber not many minutes later to see how he had fared in his battle, he drew up short, the look of concern falling ludicrously from his face. "I'll be damned! You've the look of the cat who has swallowed all the cream! What the devil have you done?"

"Congratulate me, Giles, I am no longer a betrothed man! Felicity has most obligingly broken off with me. I believe the estimable Marquis of Hardcastle now stands high in her regard."

Giles sucked in his breath. "I never thought that she would go that far . . . ! What is this! You are laughing!"

"My dear fellow, would you not be profoundly relieved to be rescued from a life of domestic horror? You know, it is strange, I was such a blind ass. One must never try to recreate the past, 'tis folly, particularly. . . ." He paused, a deep smile lighting his eyes.

"Particularly when, Ian?"

"Ah, nothing, Giles! I was but musing aloud, I fear. I think, old fellow, that we would all be best served were you to remove Felicity from Penderleigh Castle and Scotland."

"Very well," Giles said, a reluctant smile tugging at the corners of his mouth.

"Your medicine, your grace."

"Ah, Mabley! See you, Giles, my man refuses to leave my side. As long as I remain abed, I am protected better than the King." He stretched out a large hand toward his cousin, who grasped it firmly. "I thank you, Giles. Do take care. No doubt, I shall see you in London in the not too distant future."

"Very well, Ian," he said slowly. "I shall remove Felicity in the morning, if she is willing."

"I assure you, Giles, if Felicity thought she would have to be in my company again, she would carry you kicking and screaming from Penderleigh this very afternoon!"

Giles gazed intently at his cousin one more time. "You're looking quite blown, Ian. I beg you will rest now. Take good care of your master, Mabley," he added, and took his leave.

The duke turned a wary eye toward his valet. "Damn that vile-tasting pap, Mabley! I am much more in the mood for a celebration! Fetch some claret, man. Surely there must be some in the wine cellars!"

He thought he saw a twinkle in Mabley's rheumy old eyes as he turned to leave the room.

〜❂ 12 ❂〜

The duke caused a good deal of stir when, late the following afternoon, he appeared in the drawing room.

"Good God, Ian!" Bertrand cried, rushing to his side. "Surely, ye should still be in yer bed!"

"I have slept, you know, nearly the entire day, and have grown quite tired of my bedchamber as well as my own company!" He turned from Bertrand and bid the assembled company an easy greeting, though his eyes were wary. His gaze met Brandy's, and though she flushed under his gentle scrutiny, she thrust up her chin.

"Well, lad," Lady Adella said from her high-backed chair by the fireplace, "Bertie told us ye were rather white about the ears this morning. 'Tis nearly fit again ye appear to me."

"Miss Trammerley left this morning with Giles," Constance blurted out. She received a sharp look from Lady Adella, and promptly fell into embarrassed silence.

"Yes, I know," the duke replied, his eyes again going to Brandy's face.

"Ye don't appear too terribly cast down to me, your grace," Claude said.

"All wounds heal, sir," Ian said, a touch of irony in his voice.

"I beg ye to sit down," Percy said, making room for the duke on the sofa. "I have no wish to bear yer weight again. 'Tis powerful heavy ye are!"

Ian had no time to comply with Percy's suggestion, for Crabbe appeared in the doorway to announce dinner. He turned to Brandy and held out his arm. "May I escort you, Brandy?"

165

She gave a quick little nod and placed her hand on his proffered arm.

Amid the usual confusion that attended Lady Adella's preparation to quit the drawing room, Ian leaned down and said softly to Brandy, "You know, do you not, that Miss Trammerley has broken off our engagement?"

"Aye, I know. She was most pleased, I think, to tell us all what she thought of us."

"I would speak to you, Brandy."

She glanced up at him fleetingly, but said nothing.

He did not push her for a response, but merely smiled down at her gently.

If the duke thought that his eyes would detect some sign of guilt on a Robertson face during the course of the evening, he was doomed to be disappointed. Although each Robertson, with the exception of Claude, had paid a short visit to his sick room, full of clucking outrage and concern, none had in any way betrayed himself. And if he had believed that dinner would be a subdued affair, with the pall of mystery hanging heavy in the air, he had to grin to himself, for the Robertsons showed no hesitation in discussing the affair.

"I tell ye, my boy," Lady Adella said over a fork of boiled salmon, " 'tis still convinced I am that it was a worthless tinker who shot ye."

"In which case, lady," the duke said lightly, "the fellow would be long away from Penderleigh. We must trust that he was not also eyeing our sheep!"

"I see ye've still yer sense of humor about ye," Claude said, smacking his lips over a mouthful of bannocks.

"What would ye, Claude," Percy said with a slight sneer, "that the duke accused ye of being a bloody killer, albeit a poor shot?"

Claude choked on his bannocks and Bertrand thwacked him soundly on the back. "Ye'll hold yer wicked tongue, Percy," he cried, purple in the face. " 'Tis sore tired I am of yer barbs!"

"It's all a piece of nonsense, Percy," Constance said. "Poor Uncle Claude can scarce get about with his gouty foot!"

"Ye see what a good lass she is, Bertie?" Claude said to his son, recovering his humor.

"I see," Bertrand said, gazing briefly at Constance's sud-

166

denly lowered face. He turned toward Ian. "Ye must know that Trevor is leaving no stone unturned, Ian."

"Aye," Lady Adella said, "save the one that hides the scoundrel."

"I know, Bertrand," the duke said.

"What do ye intend to do, yer grace?" Percy asked, his voice, for once, sounding perfectly serious.

Ian paused a moment, then said, "That depends upon . . . many things. It will not be long before I can tell you exactly what my plans are."

"At least ye're free of that whining little chit! Good riddance, I say!" Lady Adella added somewhat wistfully, "Though I don't conscience to tell ye that I shall sorely miss Mr. Giles Braidston. A dandy lad that one is!"

It was with some relief that Ian greeted the end of the meal, for his wound was beginning to pain him. "Ye're not looking at all the thing, Ian," Bertrand said, when they rose to follow the ladies to the drawing room. Ian nodded briefly, and Bertrand continued in a low voice, "I know this is a nasty business and that there is no one that ye feel ye can really trust. For so long as ye remain here at Penderleigh, I think it wise to let everyone be told that ye will never be alone."

Ian interrupted, "Really, Bertrand, your concern does you honor, but I have Mabley——"

"A tired old man, Ian," Bertrand said, not mincing matters. "I want to take no chances, nor should ye! When ye leave the castle, I want at least two of us to be near ye all the time. 'Tis a wise precaution, ye must agree."

"Aye," Ian said with a tired smile. "If you fancy to be Saint George, I'll not quibble with you. It would appear that, like Trevor, I will also fail to discover the identity of the fellow. No, Bertrand, say no more. Like you, I also have my suspicions, but they are only suppositions, not tangible proof."

As they entered the drawing room, Ian searched about for Brandy, but she was not there. He bid brief good nights to the family and walked thoughtfully to his room.

The duke rose early the following morning and made his way to the breakfast room, turning a deaf ear to Mabley's protestations. He did not see Brandy. Nor was she in the drawing room or in the nursery with Fiona. Little coward, he thought, and walked from the castle toward the beach, aware that Bertrand and Mabley, his protectors, were trailing not far behind him. He saw her standing on the beach, staring out over the water. He was relieved that Fiona was some distance away, squatting on her haunches, playing with some driftwood.

He made his way quietly down the cliff path. "At last I have run you aground, Brandy! I was beginning to wonder if you were avoiding me. Is it not fortunate that I am acquainted with your favorite haunts?"

She whirled about and saw the duke standing before her, gazing at her intently.

She took a jerking step backward. "Yer grace! Surely ye should not be up so early!"

"If you try to run away from me, I shall catch you and tie you down, if necessary," he said, disregarding. "Now, come here, Brandy."

"Ye shan't give me orders!" she cried, and tentatively took several sideways steps away from him. As he did not move, she whirled about and ran toward the rocky path.

She had gotten no more than three jerky steps when she suddenly felt a strong arm encircle her waist, and was lifted bodily and tucked like some sort of package under the duke's right arm.

"How dare ye!" she gasped, but he only tightened his arm about her waist.

He dropped her unceremoniously on the beach, very near to the lapping waves. "Do you wish me to tie you down, Brandy?"

She gulped in deep breaths of air and gazed up at him dumbly. "Ye'll hurt yer back," she said inconsequentially.

"If I do, it will be your fault. I am not at all used to chasing down girls who climb about like damned mountaingoats!" He gazed down at her flushed face, framed by her thick blond braids. A memory stirred of masses of soft hair swirling over his face, and he wished he had not been so feverish as to forget so much of that night.

He said gently, "You see, I am now quite all right. Both Mabley and Wee Robert were full of your praises. I could throttle you for being so foolhardy, Brandy, but I must thank you for saving my life."

She focused her eyes upon her scuffed sandals and nodded, silently.

"Mabley also informed me that you were my guardian for two nights." He saw that he had embarrassed her and turned to gaze out over the smooth sea.

"I kept my bedroom door open last night and the night before, and a lighted candle just outside in the corridor!"

"You what?"

"To . . . protect ye."

"I see." He looked at her closely, noting the dark smudges under her eyes.

"Brandy, look at me. You know, of course, that I am no longer betrothed to Miss Trammerley."

"Aye, I know. Ye are, of course, upset——"

"Hardly! It has been quite some time now that I realized my mistake, Brandy. I thank providence that Miss Trammerley finally came to the same conclusion."

"Oh."

"Dammit, Brandy, I wish that you would cease this nonsense. I have no intention of allowing you to run away from me, as it appears to me that you would like to do. We really must talk, you know."

She nodded and sat down on a large rock, tucking her legs beneath her and smoothing her skirts over her scuffed sandals. He watched her pull her skirts over her legs and remembered vividly the feel of her soft hips and slender thighs. He felt a stab of desire for her and abruptly turned his eyes away.

As he sat down beside her, Brandy searched frantically for something to say. "Fiona has been quite worried about ye," she managed finally, her voice ridiculously breathless.

He reached out and grasped one of her hands. He felt her trembling in his hold, but did not release her.

"Brandy, attend me. I am sorry for many things . . . but mainly, I am sorry that I hurt you."

"Ye did not hurt me," she cried, flushing at the memory of the tenderness between her thighs.

He gazed at her a moment, puzzled, and released her hand.

She watched him warily as he slowly untied his cravat and bared his neck. "Then why did you do this, Brandy?"

She gazed dumbly at her teeth marks, pale against his skin, but still distinct.

"I cannot show you the tears you left on my cheek. As to the blood stains on the sheets, I only hope that Morag's mental perceptions are as lacking as her physical appearance."

"Stop it!" She tried to scramble away from him, but his right hand shot out and grabbed her arm in a firm hold.

"No, Brandy, no more cowardice and no more evading the issue. I mean to understand you and will not let you go until I do."

"There . . . there is nothing to understand, yer grace. What happened was my choice . . . ye had naught to do with it!"

" 'Twas hardly *all* your choice, my dear. After all——"

"I seduced ye, Ian," she interrupted him baldly, "and I'll not allow ye to feel . . . guilty."

He said with some exasperation, "Come, Brandy, how would you that I feel? I am not in the habit, you know, of bedding young virgins, particularly when they are ladies of quality and related to me to boot!"

"Ye will forget soon enough," she said stubbornly, though she could not meet his eyes.

"But I have no wish to forget, little one. I am now freed of any entanglements and thus in a position for you to make an honest man out of me. Will you be my duchess, Brandy?"

"Nay, Ian."

"What did you say?"

"I will not marry ye," she repeated, her voice low.

"Really, my dear, I do not see that you have much choice in the matter."

"Why, Ian, why have I no choice? Is it because I am no longer a virgin and thus . . . damaged goods?"

"Good God, what a ridiculous thing to say! We shall both do what is right and appropriate. Now, no more nonsense, is that clear?"

For an instant, she felt a tug of amusement at his display of autocratic temper. Just as he had not responded to her question, she chose to ignore his. "Ian, would ye have still wished to be released from Miss Trammerley if what happened between us had not happened?"

He frowned down at her, disliking even to be reminded of the lady in question, since his escape was such a very narrow one. "Certainly," he snapped, "you know quite well that we would never have suited."

Brandy gazed down at a broken fingernail, examining, it seemed, the ragged edges with singular concentration. The words lay flat on her tongue, but she forced herself to say them. "If I hadn't come to yer bed, would ye have ever thought to ask me to be yer wife?"

He gentled his voice. "Brandy, attend to me. I have never thought that my mental powers were overly lacking and, indeed, continue to believe myself a rather acceptable judge of character. I know that you are not indifferent to me—indeed, that fact was fairly obvious from the first evening when you burst into my room. I cannot deny that I tried to ignore you, treat you as a child, but it was because I was still betrothed to Miss Trammerley. You entered my bed of your own volition, Brandy. As it is obvious that you are not now nor ever will be a wanton woman, I am forced to conclude that your heart—as well as your body—belong to me. Of course, I care for you, how could I not? Forgive me if I am obtuse, but it would appear to me that you are inclined strongly to wed me rather than not."

She stared at him mutely, knowing that she could not gainsay him. She pulled her ragged thoughts together and said finally, her voice barely above a whisper, "It is not *my* feelings that I question, yer grace."

"Ian," he said sharply.

"Very well . . . Ian. I—I am young and rather inexperienced, but I am not a fool. I will not wed where there is no love . . . or if the love is all on one side. Nay, don't interrupt me, for I would say what I feel. To be an *English* duchess would require much patience . . . and tolerance, for I am ignorant in yer ways." She floundered a moment, then said in a rush, "Don't ye understand, Ian, ye don't love *me*, ye love *her!* I cannot marry ye, knowing that."

"Dammit, Brandy, it is perfectly clear to me that I never loved Miss Trammerley. You yourself saw how very poorly we suited."

"Aye, I know that."

"Then what——" As if answering his own query, he stiffened almost imperceptibly.

She quickly pressed her point, suppressing for the moment the pain it brought her. "Aye, ye cannot say ye don't love . . . Marianne. Of course ye didn't really care for Miss Trammerley, for she was naught but a blurred copy of yer first wife. Oh, Ian, I cannot win ye from a woman eight years dead! Whenever ye would look at me and see my gracelessness, ye'd but think of *her*, and hate me for it! Love her if ye will . . . but don't force me into rivalry with a ghost!"

He suddenly uncoiled his long legs and in an instant towered over her, his eyes dark and narrowed. "Why are you playing this game with me? Do you wish me to feel more the bounder than I already do? I cannot and will not accept what you have said. Do you not see, Brandy, I must set things aright!"

She rose also, and stood stiff and proud. "Ye are absolved, yer grace, of any dishonor! I refuse to allow ye to sacrifice yerself. Ye need have no concern that anyone will ever know that I shared yer bed, for . . . indeed, I shall never tell anyone!"

"Little fool! You must know that I care mightily for you, that I have long admired you, and yes, desired you."

She said sadly, her amber eyes boring into his, "But ye cannot say that ye love me, can ye, Ian? Not like ye loved Marianne."

She saw that he was very white about the mouth, his body rigid.

"Brandy," he said finally, his voice low and urgent, "I want you to wed me, to come back to England with me. You must realize that it is foolhardy for me to stay, indeed, I can no longer be blind to the fact that the man who shot me will continue to evade me as he is everyone else. There is really naught to hold me here . . . save you."

"I—I am truly sorry, Ian, I cannot." She forced herself to turn away from him. "As for the villain, whoever he is . . . aye, I think ye should return to England, 'tis for the best. Good-bye, Ian."

Without another word, she walked away from him down the beach, toward Fiona.

❧ 13 ❧

Ian and Bertrand stood on the front steps of Penderleigh in quiet conversation, whilst Crabbe and Mabley directed the loading of the carriage. The duke's curricle stood just beyond, Wee Albie holding nervously onto Hercules's reins. It was very early, scarce past seven in the morning.

"As much as I dislike yer leaving, Ian, I can't but admit that it makes me easier in the mind. I will write ye, of course, to tell ye how we progress with the Cheviot sheep."

"See that you do, Bertrand. I am much interested to know how all the family gets along." As he had when he bid his farewells the previous evening at the dinner table, he wondered yet again which one of them wished him dead. Brandy had excused herself shortly after dinner, so that he had had no opportunity to speak privately with her.

"Do not doubt that I shall continue to press Trevor. There must be something more the fellow can do."

"Excuse me, yer grace. May I speak with ye before ye leave?"

Ian turned from Bertrand to see Brandy standing some feet away from him. Her amber eyes looked widely at him and her hands were nervously plucking at her skirt pockets. He took a quick step toward her.

"I'll see how Mabley and Crabbe are faring," Bertrand said, and walked to the carriage.

"I—I did not know ye meant to leave so very early, yer grace. But a moment of yer time, please?"

He nodded and followed her back into the castle, to the drawing room.

173

She saw that he wanted to speak, and forestalled him. "I need money," she said baldly.

"You what?" He gazed at her blankly.

"Perhaps a hundred pounds, if 'tis possible." She saw his dark eyes narrow and rushed on. "Ye said that ye meant to dower both Fiona and me. I need the money now . . . could ye not simply deduct it from my dowry?"

"A most unusual request, and ingenuously put forward. Would it be too bold of me to inquire why you need the funds?" His voice sounded harsh and cold even to his own ears, but he could not help himself.

"I need it for . . . clothes, yer grace."

It was on the tip of his tongue to tell her that such an obvious, bold-faced lie would not serve, but he saw the pleading look in her eyes. Her slender fingers, with their short blunt nails, were plucking at the fringe on her shawl.

"Very well," he said finally, and she breathed a jagged sigh of relief. "Fetch me paper and ink." At her hesitance, he said sharply, " 'Twould be foolishness to give you a hundred pound note. I shall write you a draft and MacPherson will handle the transfer of funds for you."

As if she expected him to change his mind, Brandy turned quickly and raced from the room. When she returned but a few minutes later, he still could not think of a likely reason why she should want the money.

He took the paper and ink from her outstretched hand and betook himself to writing out the instructions. He paused a moment before writing in the amount. He thought she could have very little idea of the value of one hundred pounds. Whatever her reasons for wishing the money, he wanted her to have enough. He entered the sum of two hundred pounds, signed his name, and handed her the paper.

She gasped when she saw the amount.

He said smoothly, "I believe that you will find that . . . clothes are far more dear than you imagine."

"I thank ye, yer grace," she said in a muffled voice. "Ye'll take care, will ye not?"

"Brandy. . . ." He took a step toward her.

She quickly splayed her hands in front of her and backed away from him.

His voice hardened. "Very well. Since I am returning to

London, it is doubtful that you will need to worry about my taking care. I wish you good-bye, Brandy. I trust you will achieve what it is you're after."

He bowed curtly and strode from the room, not looking back.

She turned woodenly and walked to the window. She saw Ian and Bertrand shake hands. Just behind the closed carriage, burdened with luggage strapped firmly to the boot, Mabley stuck his head out of the window to speak to Crabbe. In but a few moments, Ian stepped gracefully into the curricle and, with a final wave to Bertrand, flicked Hercules's reins. The small entourage jerked into motion and was soon lost to sight among the thick rhododendron bushes.

Brandy detested tears, but in this instance, she was not even aware that they were streaking unchecked down her cheeks until she tasted a salty drop. She dashed her hand across her mouth. At least for the moment there was much for her to do. MacPherson lived in Berwick and it would take her at least two hours to walk there. She straightened her shoulders and walked purposefully back up the stairs to her room to change her sandals for a pair of stout walking boots.

Some five days later, the Duke of Portmaine pulled Hercules to a stop in front of the huge columned entrance of the Pontmaine townhouse, a giant edifice that dominated the eastern corner of York Square. It was a bright April afternoon that did not, unfortunately, match his mood.

He dined alone that evening and betook himself to sort through the impressive pile of invitations and correspondence that had accumulated in his absence.

As it was the height of the season, he found that his presence was requested at a seemingly endless number of routs and assemblies. He was on the point of tossing the myriad gilt-edged invitations into the fire when it occurred to him that the last thing he needed was to entomb himself in this barn of a house. He had left Scotland behind and now it was time for him to become an Englishman again.

During the next several weeks, the Duke of Portmaine, jokingly referred to as the Scottish Earl by his friends, was seen to grace countless social functions, dancing with most of the debutantes the season had to offer, even those young ladies who had been unkindly stigmatized as being long in the tooth, squint-eyed, or bracket-faced. If some chose to assume that the duke was trying to mend a broken heart after Miss Trammerley's defection, there were none to gainsay their opinion. The heartless chit, it was noted, had already ensnared the Marquis of Hardcastle, and the couple could be seen cooing at each other in an open landau nearly every afternoon in the park.

The gossips were kept well supplied, as it appeared that the duke passed an equal amount of time in various gaming halls, and with several frail barques of beauty. It seemed also that the duke was becoming fond of opera. Not only was his presence noted in his box several nights a week, but also it was rumored that he was seen upon several occasions leaving the apartment of the voluptuous leading lady.

All in all, it was suspected that the Duke of Portmaine was going to the devil. No one was surprised, when the season drew to a close in the beginning of June, that none of the young ladies who had dared to flirt with his grace had received an offer of marriage. Miss Trammerley's announcement, however, appeared in the *Gazette*. It appeared that she had consented to allow the Marquis of Hardcastle to make her his in the fall.

The duke shook his head when he read the announcement. James, his butler, however, was the only one to see the amused smile that played about his grace's stern mouth. "Poor fellow!" he heard the duke mutter under his breath.

One morning toward the middle of June, the duke did not emerge from his bedchamber until nearly noon, his head throbbing from a surfeit of brandy consumed the night before. He thought of his opera singer, and agreed with his weary body that he had also had a surfeit of that lady's charms.

He was forcing himself to drink a cup of steaming strong coffee, when James soundlessly appeared at his elbow, bearing a silver salver that held his grace's mail.

"Good God, hasn't everyone yet had the good sense to leave town and go to Brighton? More damned invitations!"

James did not bother to reply to this rhetorical question, having no wish to become the butt of his grace's rather ticklish humor. He stood quietly behind his master as the duke leafed listlessly through the various sized envelopes. He saw with some surprise that his grace singled out a letter, one that had come all the way from Scotland, and with a trembling hand, slit it open.

The duke perused the letter, then smiled grimly. "Well, it seems that Percy has achieved at least one of his goals!"

"Yes, your grace?" James ventured.

"One of my Robertson kinsmen, James," the duke said briefly. "He is to wed Miss Joanna MacDonald in two weeks' time. My presence is graciously requested."

"Ah," James said, for want of anything better.

The duke was silent for several minutes. James watched, fascinated, as the duke tapped his fingertips together, his dark eyes seeming to stare at a delicate Dresden figure atop the buhl cabinet in the corner.

"Will your grace be returning to Scotland?" James asked finally, trying to hide his curiosity.

The duke turned slowly in his chair, and James was astounded to see that the grim lines had disappeared and a wide smile was on his master's lips.

"Methinks, James, that there is nothing more worthless than a stupid man! Scotland must be beautiful in the summer with all the heather in bloom. Fetch me writing materials, I must write to Giles and cancel our evening."

"Yes, your grace."

"And James, inform Mabley that we will be leaving within the hour. I wish the carriage and my curricle brought around and ready for a journey by one o'clock."

"Will your grace be gone long?" James asked.

"Well, there is to be a wedding, you know!" the duke replied with what James considered overabundant enthusiasm. "I will keep you informed, never fear!"

Not many minutes later, the duke was shrugging himself into a light tan riding coat. He looked quickly at the clock on the mantel, then consulted his own watch. He turned to leave his bedchamber when his eyes fell upon the small painted miniature of Marianne that sat in its place of honor atop his dresser. He gazed into the leaf-green eyes rendered so lifelike by the artist.

He clasped the miniature in his hand and strode downstairs. "James," he said to his butler, "while I am gone, see to the placement of this painting in the picture gallery, where it belongs." He tossed the miniature into James's outstretched hands, pulled on his gloves, and walked away, his stride firm.

Brandy lay on her back, her arms pillowing her head, staring up at the cloud-strewn sky. Darkening clouds were jostling for dominance, swept in by a building squall from the sea. A sharp wind tugged tendrils of hair loose from her braids and whipped them into her eyes.

She sat up listlessly and brushed away the tangles with the back of her hand. She gazed toward the castle, its aged gray stone etched in stark relief against the dying afternoon light. She rose slowly to her feet and smoothed her gown, knowing that she must return and force her lips to smile. Percy and Joanna MacDonald were due to arrive on the morrow and even Morag had bathed in honor of the pending wedding.

How strange it was, she thought, moving slowly along the cliff path, that the pain had not lessened over the past two months. She had not been so foolish as to believe that she could forget him. She wondered if he occasionally thought of her, and if so, what his thoughts were.

She heard the rumble of wheels in the distance and reckoned disinterestedly that they had mistaken the day that Percy was coming. She looked up to see a mud-spattered curricle pull gracefully around the bend and draw to a halt on the graveled drive in front of the castle.

"Here we are, Hercules, we have arrived before the storm!" Ian jumped down to the ground and patted his stallion's steaming neck. He gazed toward the castle and wondered for perhaps the twentieth time how he would approach Brandy. After rehearsing many possible scenes in his mind, he had decided that if she proved to be difficult, he would merely throw her over his shoulder and elope with her. He smiled even now at the thought.

Perhaps it was the streaking dark clouds whirling in over the sea that made him turn for a moment toward the cliff, or simply the clean smell of the sea air. He saw Brandy standing not far from him, her skirts billowing about her in the rising wind, standing so still that he would not have seen her otherwise.

All the practiced eloquent phrases disappeared from his mind as though they had never existed. He called her name aloud and took a step toward her, his arms outstretched.

Brandy only saw his mouth form her name, for the wind whipped away the sound. She grasped her skirts and ran full tilt toward him. She flew into his open arms and would have toppled them both had not Ian leaned forward to catch her. She wrapped her arms tightly around his neck and buried her face against his cheek.

He felt her thick lashes against his face and held her more tightly against him, one arm across her back and the other curved beneath her hips. He felt a tremendous shudder pass through her body, and he gave a shaking laugh. "Come, my little love, you'll strangle me," he whispered into her ear. He felt an intense desire to let his fingers caress her soft hips, and quickly eased her to the ground.

"Will you not look at me, Brandy?" Gently, he cupped her chin with his hand and forced her to gaze up at him. He kissed her deeply, savoring the sweetness of her mouth, the fresh salty smell of her hair. "You'll have me now, Brandy?"

She gazed up at him, her eyes huge and luminous, her expression unfathomable. He answered her unspoken question.

"I am a stupid man, my dear. It took me much too long to come to my senses. My only concern now is that I shall be the one with the surfeit of love in our marriage."

"Marianne?" she whispered.

"In a bitter-sweet past, Brandy, where she belongs. 'Tis no longer Marianne or someone like her that I desire—'tis a stubborn Scottish lass with thick blond hair and amber eyes. Answer me now, will you have me?"

"Ye're a dreadful bully, Ian, and so odiously autocratic."

"I'll gladly submit to being reformed."

"Are ye certain? Ye know that I cannot even speak English."

"Aye, but seeing that I cannot live without ye, I'll have to learn tolerance."

Hercules chose that moment to nudge his master in the back. "You see, even my horse agrees with me. You must say yes before he tramples us both."

"Aye—yes."

He leaned over and kissed her again, lightly this time.

"Come, Brandy, I want to tell Lady Adella, Bertrand . . . even scratchy Morag!"

Her expressive face fell into lines of consternation.

He frowned down at her. "Whatever is the matter? You're ashamed of me already?"

"Oh no, Ian, 'tis not that! Please, let us say nothing this evening. I would wish to wait until tomorrow." She saw his jaw tighten and hastened to say, "Please, Ian, trust me. Tomorrow ye can tell my family . . . if it is still yer wish."

"What do you mean, if it is still my wish? What game is it you're playing, my girl?"

"No game, Ian. . . . Please, yer grace, allow me this." She tugged at his hand, her eyes pleading.

"Very well," he said slowly. "But if I dislike your reasons, Brandy, I think I shall beat you."

She gave a glimmer of a smile. "It will be as ye wish, yer grace."

As no stable boy emerged, Ian and Brandy led Hercules to the stables. She watched him silently as he removed the harness and rubbed down his horse with handfuls of fresh hay. He looked up at her and a frown furrowed his forehead. "You've grown thin."

"Aye, I've not been terribly hungry."

"And there are dark circles under your eyes."

"I—I haven't slept well."

"I shall give you two months to put meat back on your bones, little one. If you don't, I shall surely suspect you of playing me false."

"We shall see," was all that she said.

Brandy excused herself the moment Crabbe, with a wide grin on his cadaverous face, ushered the duke into the drawing room. She ordered Morag to tell Wee Albie to bring the tub that didn't leak to her room.

Some two hours later, her hair still damp from its washing, Brandy smiled shyly at Ian from across the expanse of dining table, but his attention was claimed by a chattering Constance.

"Fancy yer coming back for Percy's wedding! Grandmama didn't really think ye'd return, what with Percy acting the way he did . . . and probably trying to shoot——!"

"Hold yer runaway tongue, girl!" Lady Adella said sharply.

"There's not a mite of proof, and I'll thank ye not to mention the dreadful business! It has been two months, yer grace, and it is to be hoped that ye've no more bloodletting to fear."

There was a moment of strained silence, each member at the table thinking his own thoughts.

Lady Adella broke the silence with a crude laugh. " 'Tis poor Joanna MacDonald who'll have the bloodletting!"

Brandy choked on her wine and Constance leaned over to thump her on the back.

Lady Adella snorted. "Ye're such a prude, child! At yer age, even ye must know what happens between a man and a woman!"

Brandy looked up, mortified, to see a wolfish grin on Ian's face. To relieve her embarrassment, he turned to Bertrand. "Tell me, how are the crofters faring with the Cheviot sheep?"

"There are smiles on their faces, for they can foresee more food on their tables."

"Those damned sheep eat everything in sight," Claude grunted.

"And they do smell so!" Constance said.

"Aye, Bertie," Lady Adella said in a crafty voice, "ye need to take care, else Constance won't have ye and ye'll be fit only for Morag."

"Oh, Grandmama!" Constance cried, her green eyes flying to Bertrand's face. He seemed not at all put out, she thought, embarrassed herself to her toes. He said, with a hint of amusement, "I assure you, Lady Adella, that Fraser has the most sensitive nose of all of us! Never does he allow me into the dining room until he's sniffed about me at least twice! As to Constance," he added cautiously, smiling toward her, "I trust she has noticed naught amiss since the sheep have arrived."

"I vow she scarce sees ye anymore, Bertie," Claude said, "what with ye spending all yer time with yer account books or in the enclosures!"

Brandy looked up. "But I thought ye took Bertrand his lunch sometimes, Connie."

Constance shifted uncomfortably in her chair. Ian smiled to himself, for it appeared that Bertrand had made some headway with the girl during the past two months. He certainly seemed more certain of himself. He gazed fondly down the table at Brandy, wondering if she realized that she had put her sister to the blush.

Lady Adella seemed unusually mellow to him, but then again, he thought wryly, money had continued to flow freely up to Penderleigh. He could well imagine that the old lady would keep her ire in check so long as he made it worth her while.

"How is yer cousin, Mr. Braidston?" Lady Adella asked, a fond glint in her eyes.

"Giles? He goes along very well, I think, lady. As my decision to come up to Scotland was rather sudden, I was forced to write him a note. Of a certainty, he would have wished you a fond greeting."

"Too much of a dapper dog for my tastes," Claude said.

Ian found that his eyes rested hungrily upon Brandy throughout the rest of the meal. He decided that he would personally burn the muslin gown she was wearing, along with the tartan shawl. In the middle of a bite of fish, he was suddenly reminded of the two hundred pounds, for clothes, she had told him. What a clanker! Undoubtedly she would tell him soon enough what she had really done with the money. He looked up as Lady Adella said, "Ye look burned to a socket, my boy! I think I'll spare ye the torture of the girls' singing! Crabb, ye old sot, pour all of us a glass of port. Then the duke can take himself off to bed."

"An admirable suggestion, my lady," the duke agreed.

Shortly thereafter, Lady Adella led Constance and Brandy from the dining room, exhorting Bertrand not to bore Ian on his first evening back with estate affairs. "He'll have plenty of time to poke around yer sheep, after all."

But Bertrand's enthusiasm was difficult to stem and it was a good twenty minutes before Claude thwacked his cane on the floor and demanded to join the ladies.

As Brandy was not in the drawing room, Ian soon made good his escape, pleading the weariness Lady Adella so kindly bestowed upon him. He made his way up the winding staircase, down the long dim corridor toward the earl's bedchamber. He paused momentarily outside Brandy's room, repressing the urge to see her before he retired.

The summer storm had blown in and pounding rain

streaked down the window panes in the earl's bedchamber. Ian pulled the faded curtains and moved toward the sputtering fire. He added more clumps of peat and stirred the crackling embers with the toe of his boot. As with his first visit to Penderleigh, he was without the assistance of Mabley, whose carriage rumbled along a good day behind him.

He slipped a small pistol from his portmanteau and laid it atop the table beside his bed before he stripped off his clothes and changed into a dressing gown. He poured himself a glass of claret and sank down into a deep leather armchair, stretching his feet toward the fire.

The claret had a soporific effect, and soon the flames were dancing in blurred patterns before his eyes. He was suddenly jerked awake by a soft, insistent knocking on the door. He quickly rose, grasped the small pistol, and called, "Enter."

"Brandy!"

She stepped tentatively into the room, closing the door quietly behind her. She was dressed from neck to toe in a flowing white cotton nightgown that made her look absurdly young. He caught his breath at her hair. It hung in long silken waves to her waist, one thick tress falling forward over her shoulder. Her amber eyes were huge in her pale face.

He took a step forward. "Love, you know that you shouldn't come to my room."

He saw that her hands were twisting nervously in the folds of her nightgown and promptly forgot the ridiculous codes of propriety. He hastened to her. "What is it, Brandy?" He touched his hands to her shoulders and found that she was trembling. He laid the pistol down and took her hands in his. "Come to the fire and warm yourself."

She gazed up at him fleetingly and did as he bid her.

"Sit here."

He pulled up a chair near to the fire and placed his own across from her.

She drew a deep breath and plowed forward, knowing what she must do. "Ye wondered why I did not wish to announce our engagement this evening. It's just that. . . ."

"That what?" he demanded, an impatient edge to his voice.

"Please, Ian, don't send me away! Ye must realize that I . . . Ian, 'twas Marianne who shared yer passion that first time! I must be certain, do not ye see? I must know that it is me ye love, for myself—that it is me ye desire now, not Marianne."

"So you wish to stay with me tonight? Share my bed? Do I take it that on the morrow you will tell me if I have passed muster? Really, Brandy, you are such a chuckle-headed little fool!"

She gazed back at him defiantly. "Mayhap *that* part of marriage is not important to ye, Ian, but it is to me. That is, 'tis important that I know! Don't ye dare grin at me like that, ye odious man. I am perfectly serious. Please, Ian, let me stay with ye tonight."

"I do hope that I do not fail your test, Brandy! Lord, what a comedown for me were you to refuse to marry me because you think me a poor lover! Very well, my dear, I will consider myself irrevocably compromised."

She wanted to protest his mocking her, and his ridiculous twisting of her reasons, but the opportunity slipped by her, unnoticed. He came to her and pulled her to her feet, all the while smiling down at her in a most disturbing way. "Little idiot," he whispered, and lowered his mouth to hers. He pulled her tightly against him, winding one hand through the masses of silky hair and allowing the other hand to sweep down her back to her hips.

He released her after a moment, grinning down at her.

"That is so very . . . pleasant!" she gasped.

"If you will remember, little one, there is much more, and hopefully you will find that equally as pleasant." He kissed her and stroked her until she sighed with pleasure. He delighted in the openness of her response, in her naturalness. Gently, he eased his hands to the tie-string at the neck of her nightgown and began to draw it open. To his surprise, he felt her stiffen and draw away slightly from him.

"What is this, my love? How can you seduce me, if you will not let me remove this ridiculous nightgown?"

She shook her head, mute, and looked distressed.

"Brandy?"

"Nay," she choked, "please, Ian." She stared doggedly up at him, and then with a deep breath of resolution, joined her fingers to his and pulled open her nightgown. In a quick movement, she slipped her arms from the sleeves and let it fall to her waist. She gazed up at him, watching him closely.

He sucked in his breath in amazement. To think he had believed her a slender, almost thin young girl, still immature. He gazed at the most glorious breasts he had ever beheld in his life. They were incredibly white and rounded, the nipples a soft, pale pink, blending with an artist's touch into the creamy ivory.

"*Good God!*"

The color fled her face and with a low sob, she turned her face away.

"Brandy," he said, baffled.

"I—I understand, Ian, truly I do. I have hidden my ugliness from ye, and 'twas unfair."

"*What* ugliness?" He searched for some sort of disfiguring mole.

"I'm like a : . . . cow! I would not stop growing and had to bind myself so as not to draw attention to myself." She clutched her nightgown against her breasts.

He could only shake his head. "Are you telling me that you think your breasts ugly?" he demanded, unable to keep a bubble of laughter from entering his voice.

"Aye, but I'll not have ye mock me!"

"I do not mock you, little one. Tell me, Brandy, wherever did you get this notion? Did someone tell you that you were ugly?"

"Aye, Morag. 'Twas when I was fourteen and my dresses wouldn't button. She laughed at me and said I was in a fair way of growing two fine melons for the market! She said it would never do for an earl's granddaughter to hang out of all her clothes."

"I'll kill the woman!"

"But she was right! I tried as best I could to bind myself, but Percy knew, even though I always wore my shawl. He was always so odious . . . like I was some sort of freak!"

"Brandy, do you recall when we were alone in the crofter's hut? I wanted you then and you pulled away from me."

She looked up at him, puzzled. "I thought it was ye who pulled away from me! But, aye, it is true. I didn't want ye to see me. I was ashamed."

"I think," he said slowly, "that we have spent much of our time together being confused as to the other's motives. And the blue velvet gown I brought for you from Edinburgh? It was quite low cut if I remember correctly."

"It is a beautiful gown," she said wistfully, "but I looked like naught but bosom!"

He smiled at her tenderly. "Brandy, have I ever lied to you, or done anything to make you mistrust my words?"

"Nay."

"Give me both of your hands and drop the nightgown."

She started at his request and for an instant did not move.

"Give me your hands."

She stretched out one hand toward him, still clutching the nightgown with the other.

"Both hands, if you please."

She closed her eyes tightly and blindly thrust out her other hand. The nightgown rested an instant on her hips, then fell with a soft rustle to the floor.

He swallowed another exclamation at her beauty. The fullness of her breasts was emphasized by a tiny waist that curved out into supple, slim hips. Her belly was flat, her creamy skin covered lower down by a triangle of curling dark blond hair. Her legs were long and slim, but beautifully curved down to slender ankles.

"Open your eyes, Brandy. Now, come with me."

He helped her step out of the nightgown and led her by the hand to a long, narrow mirror that hung next to an old armoire. He stationed her in front of the mirror. "You are a beautiful woman. Look at yourself and tell me if you can possibly doubt my words."

She felt his hands grip her shoulders more tightly, and forced her eyes to rest upon her image. Her breasts stared back at her and she gasped in embarrassment and tried to pull away from him.

"I will not have your husband-to-be called a liar! Dammit, Brandy, look!"

She opened her eyes and looked again at herself in the mirror. She saw that he was standing behind her, his hands on her bare shoulders. His eyes met hers in the mirror, and very slowly, he pulled her hair back from her face and shoulders. He brought his hand around and cupped her chin. "Do you have any dislike for your face? No? Excellent. Let us continue."

He drew a deep breath to control his desire for her and gently let his hands move downward, his fingers caressing her, until each hand cupped a breast.

He saw her eyelashes flutter and her lips part. He leaned down and planted a light kiss on her temple. "Your breasts are exquisite. Contrive to remember that Morag is quite scrawny. Jealousy and sheer stupidity made her say what she did."

He forced his hands to leave her breasts and move down to encircle her waist. As his fingers roved to her belly, he felt her shudder with desire. Her breathing quickened and he felt his own control near to breaking.

"Remember you once told me that I was the beautiful one? Such a fool you are, Brandy."

She turned in his arms and wrapped her own about his neck. "Ye promise, Ian?" she whispered.

"Aye, I promise."

She pulled open the sash of his dressing gown and he felt her hand move from his bare chest downward to his belly.

"You're a witch," he moaned, and flung off the dressing gown.

He swung her up into his arms and carried her to the bed. "I swear I'll not hurt you this time."

She wanted to tell him how very magnificent he was, but his lips closed over her breast and she gasped at the delicious sensation that crashed through her body. He wound his hands in the thick masses of blond hair and sought out her mouth, teasing her with his tongue until she opened her lips to him. She felt his hands sweep down her back to caress her hips and stroke the softness between her thighs.

"Please, Ian," she moaned softly, her hands upon him, caressing him, urging him into her.

Her body shuddered as he entered her, and she pressed her hands against his back, drawing him deeper into her. She waited for the pain, for she felt herself stretching to hold him, but there was no pain, only an insistent throbbing that was building inside her. She moved beneath him naturally, and clutched him tightly to her. She groaned his name into his mouth and let the exquisite pleasure engulf her. He gasped aloud and she felt him release his seed deep within her.

Brandy felt a lazy feeling of contentment that made her wonder if anything could exist outside this room, outside of them.

"Well, Brandy," he said presently, shifting his weight off of her, "do you think my desire for you sufficient? Will you accept me both as your husband and your lover?"

She gazed up at him, her eyes smoky, and nodded, unable to find the words to tell him how she felt.

He laughed, a deep rumbling sound, full of pleasure. "I wasted two months, Brandy. But never again will I willingly let you out of my sight."

"Or yer bed, Ian?"

"That too, love." He squeezed her so tightly that she yelped for breath.

"Ian, may I ask ye something?"

At the seriousness in her voice, he drew back slightly so that he could see her full face. "Aye?"

"Do ye truly want children? I remember ye joked about having a half a dozen little Fionas."

"Indeed I do, Brandy." He thought of Felicity's scathing talk of being a brood mare and hastily added, "But only as many as you desire."

She sighed with contentment. "That is good."

He tweaked her ear and gazed at her, his smile a half question.

"When do ye wish to marry, Ian?"

"Soon, my love. When it suits you, but I do not wish to wait too long."

"I do not think it would be wise."

"What would not be wise?"

"Waiting too long to wed."

"Are we again talking at cross-purposes?"

She gave him a very disturbing smile and said softly, "Nay, 'tis just that I would like to be slender when we wed."

"Slender? You're like a reed now, my love. Are you planning to gorge yourself on Cook's haggis?"

"Nay, in fact, it makes me quite ill."

"Brandy," he threatened, "cease speaking in circles!"

"Very well, yer grace," she said in a docile voice. "I am most pleased that ye want children, for in truth, we shall have a wee bairn by Christmas."

He was ominously quiet for many moments. "Do you mean to tell me that you're pregnant?"

"Aye."

"And you did not tell me?"

"But I am telling ye now, Ian."

He gripped her by the shoulders and shook her. "Dammit, you little wretch! What if I had not come back?"

"I—I don't know," she said, lowering her head from his glaring eyes. "I have only been certain for about two weeks."

He groaned in exasperation and turned on his back, focusing his eyes on the length of wooden beam above his head. He thought of the vagaries of fate. Dear God, what if he had not come to his senses? At the same time, he admitted to a deep sense of masculine accomplishment. So what if the child was born two months early? It could hardly matter, for he would remove her soon to Carmichael Hall.

He turned and pulled her roughly into his arms. "God, but you're a stubborn wench! If you ever keep anything from me again, Brandy, I swear that I'll thrash you."

"Not until after Christmas, I pray!"

He spoke with sudden decision, "No big wedding in Hanover Square for you, my girl! You will not mind foregoing all that wedding finery and folderol?"

"Bah, 'tis nothing!"

"Excellent. I shall have Bertrand help with the arrangements. Will you wed me on Saturday, Brandy?"

"Aye, Ian, but mind, only because I want to be slender!"

"At least I shall not have to worry about your care. Edward Mulhouse, a doctor and an excellent friend of mine in Suffolk, will attend you."

"Surely, Ian," she said in some alarm, "we needn't concern ourselves about that until the fall."

"Don't be a goose. Edward is young, but a finer doctor you'll not find anywhere."

"He's young?" she said, her voice low with embarrassment.

"Good God, Brandy, you seduce me without a 'by your leave'——"

"Wretched man, 'twas not like that at all."

"And then you show this ridiculous maidenly shyness at being examined by a doctor. I most assuredly will drub some sense into your head. No more of this nonsensical prattle, and that, madam, is an order!"

"I will not suffer your displays of autocratic temper, yer grace," she cried, torn between amusement and mortification at the thought of another man, albeit a doctor, touching her.

"We shall see, my dear," he said with a grin, and gently kissed her lips.

He let his hands rove over her flat belly. It seemed incredible that his child nestled there, deep within her womb. He felt her slender body tremble at his touch. He let his fingers continue to explore her, until, in frustration, she pounded her fists on his chest.

He smiled at her tenderly in the soft candlelight and brought them both again to aching pleasure.

He remembered to ask her before she fell contentedly asleep, her cheek against his chest, "Brandy, whatever did you want the two hundred pounds for?"

She was silent for some moments, and he felt her breasts quicken their upward and downward movement against him.

"I told ye, Ian," she managed finally, " 'twas for clothes."

"Come, my girl, that's a clanker, and well you know it."

"I cannot imagine that a mere two hundred pounds could matter a whit to ye!"

"Stop trying to turn the tables. You know very well that I am not a miser or the least bit clutch-fisted!"

She buried her face against his shoulder and said in a muffled voice, "I beg ye, Ian, do not ask me for a reckoning, for I cannot—nay, I will not tell ye."

"You *refuse* to tell me?" he said in a voice of ominous quiet.

"Aye, I must refuse," she said stoutly. In an attempt to cajole him out of his temper, she added with a teasing smile, "I'll thank ye to remember yer promise—not to thrash me until after Christmas!"

He slapped her lightly on her hips, and smiled reluctantly. "We will speak more of this later, Brandy."

Thankful that he did not push her further, Brandy curled up close to him and burrowed her face against his chest.

Ian awoke near dawn the next morning, betook himself to recall the necessities of propriety, and not without some difficulty managed to slip Brandy back into her nightgown. He disliked disturbing her peaceful sleep almost as much as covering her lovely body.

He carried her quietly to her room, on the watch for any early-rising servants. He kissed her gently on the forehead and returned to his bed for several more hours' sleep.

Brandy was not present the next morning at breakfast and Ian smiled to himself, picturing her languid and deliciously exhausted from their lovemaking. Bertrand, though, was soon shown into the breakfast room by Crabbe, and Ian grimaced slightly at the sight of the heavy account ledger he carried under his arm.

"Good morning, Ian. I trust ye slept well last night," Bertrand said with his usual smile, and sat himself down at the table.

The duke repressed a grin of amusement. "Tolerably well, Bertrand, tolerably well. Good lord, man, do you intend to addle my wits with all of your numbers even before I've had my porridge?"

"Nay, I'm not so rag-mannered as all that! I merely thought to . . . summarize all that we've accomplished in the last two months."

"I had thought you had done that last evening!"

"Oh no," Bertrand replied cheerfully, "that was only a prelude, ye know, but a tantalizing beginning to whet yer curiosity!"

"Devil seize you, Bertrand! Very well, lead on MacDuff!"

If Bertrand thought the duke's attention to be wandering during his recital, he made no mention of the fact until, at the end of a half hour, he paused, seeing that Ian was gazing thoughtfully out the window. "I daresay that Napoleon will much appreciate my services!"

"Napoleon? What the devil are you talking about, Bertrand?"

"Nonsense, I assure ye! I just wanted to assure myself that yer thoughts were indeed many miles away from here!"

The duke grinned ruefully. "I do beg your pardon. If you must know, I have much on my mind at the moment."

"Ye are worried that yer attacker still awaits ye here?"

"Perhaps, in part."

"Then what are ye plotting, Ian?"

"That, my friend," the duke said, smiling suddenly, "you

will discover soon enough! It appears to me, my dear fellow, after observing you and Constance at the dinner table last evening, that you've made rather impressive headway since I last saw you."

Bertrand appeared to be in rapt concentration of his knuckles for several moments. "Dammit," he blurted out, "she is so very young, and skittish! Ye must know that Lady Adella and my father are forever twitting the both of us." He sighed and said somewhat in the matter of a stoic, "I really have not all that much to offer her. Although Percy is no longer a problem—thank God!—she naturally dreams of fine clothes, carriages, servants of her own, and the like. Not to mention rubbing shoulders in fine society."

"Methinks that may prove to be less of a problem than you believe," Ian said quietly. "I'll tell you what I think," he said abruptly. "That is, if you do not mind my meddling in your affairs."

"I do not see why I would mind," Bertrand said gruffly. "Lady Adella and my father show no hesitation at all!"

"What I think," the duke continued, "is that your hands are much too light on the reins. It is quite clear to me, after last evening, that Constance is not at all indifferent to you. Quite the contrary, in fact," he continued, seeing that Bertrand would likely disclaim this notion. "She needs but a firm hand—your firm hand—to ring down the curtain. You must know that Constance is endowed with the most romantic nature and would be susceptible to a rather, er, *masterful* approach. If you haven't recognized that, Bertrand, I must think you the greatest clothhead imaginable."

Bertrand ran his fingers through the shock of red hair on his forehead. Though he was silent, it appeared to the duke that he was much struck by his words. He suddenly drew a resolute breath, and struck the palm of his hand against his knee. "Damned if ye're not right! Ye really think it requires naught but a firm push to topple her over the edge?"

"Precisely. And if you have not the wherewithall to carry that off, I will wash my hands of you!"

Bertrand rose, his ledger book forgotten. "Aye," he said softly, more to himself than to the duke, " 'twill be the very thing. I must think about it, though. Aye, I must think about it."

"I wish you luck, Gallahad," the duke said gaily, as Bertrand strode purposefully from the breakfast room.

Bertrand rehearsed many such masterful scenes in his mind as he went about his duties during the day, grunting when he found one not to his liking, and grinning broadly at another that caught his fancy. He was on the point of returning to the dower house to scrub himself down when he saw Constance approaching him. A gentle breeze had ruffled her soft black curls and he thought she appeared utterly delectable. He squared his shoulders and waited for her to draw near.

"Och! Ye smell like a sheep, Bertie!" she exclaimed, her nostrils quivering.

Undaunted, he said, "Aye, Connie. I fear though that it's not to be helped . . . at least during the day."

Her green eyes widened. "What do ye mean, at least during the day?"

"What I mean, Connie, is that at night, ye'll ne'er have cause to take me into dislike!"

"Oh!" She studied the toe of her shoe.

"Would ye like to walk with me?" He asked, realizing that they were standing opposite each other like two statues.

"Aye," she said, and when he put out his hand, she did not hesitate to lace her fingers into his.

He said abruptly, "Connie, when will ye be sixteen?"

"In August, Bertie."

"Aye," he admitted, "I should have remembered. After all, I've known ye all yer life."

Constance thought of the plump, wild-haired little girl that she had once been, and blanched. Then a memory of Bertrand when he was all of fourteen years old popped into her mind, and she giggled. "Ye were so tall and . . . gangly! And all that red hair!"

"Do ye think that our children would have my mop of red hair or lovely silk black hair like yers, Connie?"

Her fingers tightened spasmodically in his. "What a question, Bertie! I fear ye've been in the sun too long!" She peeped up at him from beneath her lashes.

"Nay, it's ye who I've let rove about in the sun over long! And ye can forget all yer childish nonsense about Percy, or any other man for that matter!"

She tossed her black curls. "And what if I don't, Master Bertrand?"

"I'll beat ye," he said, grasping her shoulders and forcing her to look up at him.

"Ye—ye would?" she asked, suddenly breathless.

"Aye, black and blue, if ever ye dare look at another man!"

"But surely, I'd not look . . . pretty, if ye beat me."

It was borne upon him forcibly that he had long mishandled her, and he sent a silent prayer of thanks to the duke. He maintained a fierce look and at the same time lowered his voice to a husky tone. "Ne'er would I harm yer beauty, Connie, but I would, mayhap, take my hand to yer . . . lovely hips."

He congratulated himself, for she turned a delicious pink and her moist lips parted.

"I think, my dear, that ye'll wed with me—in August, when ye turn sixteen. I have no intention of waiting for ye longer, Constance."

She eyed him a moment, doubtfully, then smiled shyly. She nodded.

He promptly pulled her tight against his chest and searched out her soft mouth.

The duke gazed about the crowded drawing room, wondering where the devil Brandy was. He had not seen her all day and was beginning to grow anxious. His frown vanished when Bertrand entered, his face wreathed in smiles.

"My dear fellow," he asked quietly, "can I assume from the blissful expression on your face that your suit has prospered?"

"Aye, that ye can, Ian, that ye can! I beg ye not to say anything, for I would announce our engagement right and proper at the dinner table."

Ian realized suddenly that Bertrand was looking past him, toward the door, his mouth agape. "Good God!" he exclaimed.

Ian turned about to see Brandy gracefully entering the drawing room. Though he did not exclaim as did Bertrand, he sucked in his breath. She wore the blue velvet gown he had bought for her in Edinburgh and she walked straight and tall, her shoulders back. Her glorious breasts blossomed above the bodice. She had fashioned her hair high atop her head, threaded with a matching blue velvet ribbon, and two long curls rested provocatively over her bare shoulders. He was delighted at her transformation.

He saw, with some amusement, that like Bertrand, the rest of the family were held for a moment in speechless silence.

Brandy searched out his eyes and drew herself up even straighter at the warm approval she read there.

Constance found her tongue and blurted out, "Brandy, what have ye done to yerself? How did ye manage to arrange yer hair like that? I thought ye knew only how to plait braids! And yer. . . ." She halted in embarrased confusion, her eyes on Brandy's bosom.

Brandy was spared the necessity of replying, for Lady Adella gave a sudden roar of laughter. "Shut your mouth, Connie, yer tongue runs on wheels! Well, child, 'tis no longer a scraggily weed ye are! Come here, girl, let me get a closer look at ye!"

Bertrand, who had long held the belief that his Constance was, at least in the physical sense, far more mature than Brandy, managed to contain further surprise, and said warmly, "Ye look lovely, Brandy. The dress Ian bought ye becomes ye most well."

"It's damned remarkable, that's what it is," Claude sputtered, groping for his eyeglass.

"I thank ye all," Brandy said calmly, and sat down in a most stately manner next to Lady Adella, trying as best she could to appear unconcerned at the stir she had created.

"Now if ye'll only stop chewing at yer fingernails, miss," Lady Adella said severely. "Lord, I begin to think ye look like me, child, when I was yer age!"

"I question that even Brandy could achieve such distinction," the duke said with a pronounced twinkle in his eyes.

Only Crabbe displayed no outward emotion upon seeing Brandy, when he shortly entered. "Dinner, yer grace!"

The duke rose and crossed to Brandy. "May I have the honor, Miss Robertson, of escorting you to dinner?"

"Since ye've asked me with proper respect and deference, yer grace, I suppose it would be very small of me to say nay to ye."

"Never *small*," he whispered close to her ear, "and I'll thank you never to say nay to me, either."

She grinned up at him impishly and pinched his arm.

He said pensively as they walked across the entrance hall toward the dining room, "Did you think me so unwilling last night, my dear, that you must needs take special pains with your appearance? Not, of course, that I disapprove that lovely gown and your attributes that complement it. I am most fortunate to be able to observe you both in your glorious plumage and in your equally enticing natural state."

"And what shall I say about ye, yer grace? I've told ye often enough that I think ye beautiful . . . and especially, of course, in yer natural state."

"Baggage!"

"Heh! What is this about states and baggage? I thought yer man arrived today with yer luggage."

Ian replied with aplomb, "Indeed, Lady Adella, Mabley did arrive this afternoon. As to 'states,' I also find myself considerably confused as to their meaning."

Ian seated Brandy, then walked to the head of the table. He said in a low voice to Crabbe, who stood at his elbow, "Be so good as to unearth several bottles of champagne, will you, Crabbe?"

Bertrand found that he could contain himself only until Morag and Crabbe took themselves out of the dining room. At a wink from the duke, he cleared his throat and sent Constance a quick reassuring smile.

"I would like to say, Father, Lady Adella, that in spite of yer infernal meddling and yer crass attempts at matchmaking, Constance has finally convinced me that it is my filial duty to comply with yer wishes and wed with her!"

"Bertie!" Constance cried. "Ye know 'twas not at all like that!"

"Oh, Connie, it's marvelous! I'm so happy for ye!" Brandy said, and despite her exquisite coiffeur, pulled her sister to her in a quick hug.

"I told ye, Claude," Lady Adella said with a huge grin, "that 'twas more likely that our Connie would seduce Bertie!"

"Bless my bones, Bertie, now it's to be hoped that the lass can keep ye from that trollop in the village!"

Bertrand gazed uncertainly toward Constance at this outrageous remark from his sire, but saw that she appeared rather pleased about this prospect.

"He'll nay look at another woman, Uncle Claude, I promise ye!"

"When is the portentous event to take place, Bertrand?" the duke asked.

"In August, when Constance turns sixteen."

Lady Adella primly folded her lips together and remarked with her natural perversity, "I think Claude, that the child is much too young for marriage. What with Bertie's pleasures in the village, believe ye not that he can wait to wed with her for two or three years?"

"Grandmama, I am not a child!"

"Lady Adella," Bertrand said smoothly, "was not Constance's mother but sixteen when she wedded yer son?"

"Hoisted on your own petard, lady!" the duke said.

Claude looked with some confusion at Lady Adella. "What is this, lady, ye want to butter yer bread on both sides?"

"Aye, and in the middle too," Brandy murmured.

"Ye can shut yer mouth, my fine little lady! At least our Constance has secured herself a husband, while ye, ye silly child, will probably hang on my sleeve till ye've got gray hair!" As her words did not at all appear to discomfit Brandy, she turned a glowering eye upon Bertrand. "So, my bucky lad, ye've tied up everything right and tight! May I ask why ye didn't ask my permission or yer father's afore ye approached my little Connie?"

The duke interposed smoothly, "Surely, Lady Adella, you could not think Bertrand so remiss. Let me hasten to assure you that Bertrand most properly sought my permission, as Constance's guardian, before securing her agreement."

"Yer permission!" Lady Adella fairly roared. "Look ye, duke or no duke, ye're an impertinent jackanapes!" She drew up, her expression suddenly wily. "As her guardian, my dear duke, may I ask what ye intend to do for her? I'll nay let her go empty-handed to her husband!"

"No," the duke said, his voice maddeningly calm, "I, of course, have no intention of doing so. However could you think that I would be so ramshackle! No, do not, I pray, give me your opinion of that question!" He paused and looked first at Claude, then at Bertrand. "I would that you all attend me. You will recall, undoubtedly, that someone was most desirous of securing my demise. Indeed, that person may still nourish hopes in that regard. However, I am as certain in my own mind as I can be that you, Bertrand, were in no way responsible." He was silent for a moment, regarding the sea of questioning faces around the table.

"I am of the further belief that an Englishman, despite the fact that he holds circuitous blood ties to Scotland, should not hold a Scottish estate or title. I think that I have come to better understand Scotland, its people, and its traditions. A Scottish earldom must have a Scottish master, 'tis only right and just. Therefore, as soon as Claude and Bertrand have been reinherited under Scottish law, I intend that both the earldom and Penderleigh revert to them, just as it would have if the old earl had not cut Douglass out of what was rightfully his. That, Lady Adella, is, I suppose, in part my dowry to Constance. She will, someday, become the Countess of Penderleigh."

"That was what ye were so intent upon this morning when I tried to talk to ye," Bertrand said, so startled that he could think of nothing else to say.

"Yes, in part."

"I'll be damned!" Claude muttered, unable to believe his ears.

"Explain yerself, yer grace!" Lady Adella commanded.

The duke raised a quieting hand to still the babble of voices. "There is really nothing more to explain, lady, save that, as I said, a Scottish earldom belongs to the Scots, just as it is appropriate, that as an Englishman I hold English lands."

"But ye've poured *English* money into Penderleigh!" Bertrand exclaimed.

"Aye, 'twas needed. Now with the proper raw materials, so to speak, Penderleigh will turn a fine profit, particularly, Bertrand, under your fine management."

"I will be the Earl of Penderleigh," Claude announced suddenly.

"And ye, Connie," Bertrand said with a quiet smile, "will some day soon have yer fine clothes and carriages and mayhap even a house in Edinburgh."

"I shall be a countess," Constance breathed, still unable to believe her good fortune.

"Aye, sister, and a more lovely countess I could not imagine," Brandy said. " 'Tis most kind of ye, Ian."

"It is only just, my dear," he said.

"Yer mother must have played yer father false, Ian," Lady Adella suddenly announced, "for never could ye have gotten such an idea from that little creeper she married!"

Ian said rather stiffly, "The Fourth Duke of Portmaine, Lord Charles, was many things, lady, but numbering amongst them was not the nature of a little creeper."

"And what if," Lady Adella continued slyly, "the Scottish courts do not choose to reverse the disinheritance?"

"I have the utmost confidence in your abilities, Lady Adella. But, of course, if there is any delay whatsoever, I will be forced to step in and see that the thing is done." He found himself somewhat amused by the old lady's antics. His plucking the power from her hands had to be quite an uncomfortable shock to her. He was on the point of concluding that she had thrown in her hand, when she said acidly, "And just what, my fine *English* duke, do ye intend to do about my Brandy and Fiona? Now that ye've broken with Miss Trammerley, ye've quite ruined Brandy's chances!"

"Grandmama!" Brandy cried.

"Hush yer mouth, child! Well, yer grace, what brilliant scheme have ye concocted for them?"

"I think," the duke said slowly, studiously avoiding Brandy's eyes, "that there is only one thing for me to do."

"What is it?" Lady Adella snapped.

"I suppose," the duke continued imperturbably, "that I simply must marry Brandy. As her guardian, of course, I most humbly secured my permission."

"Marry Brandy!" she screeched.

"I say, Ian——" Bertrand began.

"Oh, Brandy, ye a duchess! And I—a countess!"

"I'll be damned!" Claude muttered.

"As to Fiona," the duke continued calmly, "I think we will give her a few years yet before we find her a husband. Ah, here is Crabbe with the champagne!"

"We shall all be drunk as wheelbarrows, what with so many congratulations!" Constance exclaimed.

Although Lady Adella dutifully toasted the repeated announcement of each happy event, it was obvious that she was in the throes of some powerful emotion. When Claude chanced to mutter again, "I shall be the Earl of Penderleigh," she turned on him, setting down her champagne glass with a decided snap.

"Crow as much as ye please, ye old fool! Ye're just like old Angus, forever boasting that *he* was the lord of the castle, when naught could be further from the truth! Ye know well that I was always both master and mistress, and will continue to be so after the duke has left us. I'll continue to play the bagpipes, and ye'll dance to my tune!"

Claude drew back his shoulders in an assumption of dignity that Ian had never before observed in him.

He said with devastating calm, "Ye've always been a power-mongering old witch, lady! Aye, Old Angus allowed ye to play off yer tricks, holding us all on a tight rein, making us dance or cower as the mood struck ye! Ye are naught now but the *dowager* countess of Penderleigh, and as such, 'tis likely ye belong in the dower house. However, lady, if ye make a push to mind yer tongue and grant me the proper respect and deference due to the Earl of Penderleigh and the head of the household, I suppose that I'll let ye stay in the castle."

Lady Adella's face was purple with rage, and Ian thought she would expire on the spot.

"Ye said to me yerself, lady," Claude continued in a low voice, "that it was time for ye to make retribution. The duke has done yer work for ye."

Bertrand sat forward in his chair, his eyes on Lady Adella. "Will ye tell us now about my Grandfather Douglass, why it was that the old earl suddenly disinherited him?"

"Aye, lady, 'tis time ye made a clean breast of it," Claude said. "Go ahead, for if ye don't, I shall. After all, if it hadn't been for ye and yer hot-blooded ways——"

"Shut yer mouth, Claude!" Lady Adella sank down into her chair and slumped forward in defeat. "Ye impudent whiner. Douglass should never have told ye!"

"For God's sake, told him what?" Bertrand demanded.

Lady Adella clutched her wine glass and stared down into the red liquid. "Very well. As ye know, being the eldest son, Douglass should have inherited the title and ye, Claude, should have followed neatly after him. I was much younger then, ye know, and Douglass was a man, unlike that weak, rutting Angus. It's lovers we were, with none the wiser for it, until the old earl caught us. A terrible temper the old earl had, and he beat Douglass until he was nearly senseless. He severed the line on that day, disinherited his firstborn son and all his descendants. Angus never knew the reason, the gloating prig!"

"My father, Douglass, told me the true reason for his banishment on his deathbed," Claude added softly.

"I wonder," the duke said thoughtfully, turning toward Brandy, "if I should more closely inquire into your antecedents." This bald comment achieved the result he had hoped it would. Lady Adella whipped up her head and glared at him. "I'll thank ye to watch yer tongue, my fine duke. 'Tis possible that there's dirty linen somewhere in yer closet!"

"I'll thank ye not to say anything about dirty linen, lady!" Claude said sharply. "Douglass married and I was born in wedlock!"

"I think," Brandy said somewhat shakily, "that enough is enough. Do ye not think, yer grace, that we should repair to the drawing room for perhaps some quiet music?"

"To soothe all the savage breasts? Admirable suggestion, my dear."

If the soft Scottish ballads did not have this effect, they did at least prevent further raised voices.

The duke, guessing aright that Lady Adella could not for long be kept in a repressive spirit, was not at all surprised to hear her say as he escorted Brandy from the drawing room, seemingly much pleased with herself, "A countess and a duchess. Aye, I've done well by the both of the girls."

"If I may congratulate yer grace," Fraser said, after saluting the duke in his usual manner with his garden trowel, his round face touched with a smile.

"I thank you, Fraser. Is Bertrand about?"

"Aye, yer grace, in the parlor he is, having his lunch. As to Master Claude—well, yer grace, ye can well imagine that he slept very little last night! Master Bertrand said that all he could do was sit in front of the fireplace, mutter to himself that he was going to be the Earl of Penderleigh, and slap his hand on his knee."

Such verbosity from a usually laconic man made the duke smile to himself as he followed Fraser to the parlor.

"Ian! Come in, come in! Fraser, bring his grace some of yer excellent scones and strawberry jam. Like me, his grace must keep up his strength—trying times ahead for the both of us!"

The duke sat himself across from Bertrand at the small circular table and said, after Fraser had left the parlor, "More trying than you imagine, Bertrand! And that is why I am here. Just how does one procure a special license in Scotland?"

Bertrand raised a startled eyebrow. "I had no idea that ye wished to move forward so quickly!"

"I don't wish to give Brandy any time to change her mind," the duke replied smoothly, "There is also the matter of a parson."

"Yer scones, yer grace," Fraser said, moving quietly to his elbow. The duke nodded and said no more until Fraser had once again taken his leave.

"Well, ye know that Percy and Joanna are to arrive in the next day or two. Do ye wish to avail yerself of their parson?" He shook his head. "Lord, I can't wait to see the look on Percy's face!"

"Hopefully, he will cloak his ire and leash his barbs."

"Aye? What is it, Fraser!" Bertrand asked, turning in his chair.

A deep frown furrowed Fraser's brow. "I don't rightly know, Master Bertrand. 'Tis Wee Albie come with a message fer his grace." He extended a folded sheet of paper toward the duke.

"What the devil?" Ian took the paper from Fraser and spread it out on the table before him. He read the large, scrawled words once, then yet again, unable to believe what he was seeing. ". . . if ye wish to see Brandy alive again, ye will come unarmed and *alone* to the abandoned wooden barn that lies just to the west of the high cliff road. . . ."

"Fetch me Wee Albie! At once, Fraser!"

"Aye, yer grace!"

"Good God, Ian, what is the matter? What is that letter?"

Ian shook his head as Wee Albie, his elbow firmly held by Fraser, shuffled his huge feet into the room.

The duke raised the folded paper. "Where did you get this?"

Wee Albie blanched at the harshness of the duke's voice and looked wildly toward Bertrand.

"Quickly man! Who gave you this?"

"A man what were muffled to his ears, yer grace. He said it were the matter of greatest urgency."

"Ian, for God's sake!"

"Excuse me, Bertrand," the duke said, striding quickly to the parlor door, "I pray you not to tell anyone of this. Hopefully, I will be with you again soon."

The duke slammed out of the dower house and broke into a run back to the castle. When he gained his bedchamber, he ignored Mabley's startled countenance, grabbed his small, ivory-handled pistol, and slipped it into the top of his hessian.

He forced himself to be calm as the scrawled words flashed again and again into his mind. ". . . *if ye wish to see Brandy alive again . . .*" It was a madman, a Scottish madman. He quickly jerked the bridle over Hercules's head and pulled the saddle girth tight. He swung up into the saddle and dug his heels into Hercules's stomach. Unused to such indelicate treatment, Hercules snorted, whipped up upon his hind legs, and crashed down, only to find his master's heels kicking again against his tender belly. He hurtled forward, barely checking his long stride as Ian veered him off of the graveled drive toward the cliff road.

Brandy became aware of something sharp digging into her cheek and slowly opened her eyes. She groaned as a jagged pain pounded in her temple, unable for the moment to bring her mind soundly into her body. As the pain receded, she gingerly placed her fingers against the side of her head. The discomfort against her cheek, she discovered, was from loose straws of hay.

"I thought perhaps that I had killed you."

She forced her blurred vision in the direction of that calm voice. She saw Giles Braidston sitting across from her on a bale of hay, a pistol in his hand.

"Giles!"

"As you see, Brandy."

She stared at him, willing her wits to form a logical fabric of thought. She said slowly, "I was standing at the cliff edge, watching Fiona on the beach. . . ." She rubbed her hand against her temple. "I heard something . . . then there was nothing."

"I had to strike you with the butt of my pistol."

She gazed at him, as slowly the significance of events took shape in her mind, drawing her to the inevitable conclusion. "How very stupid we have all been," she said finally, surprised at the detached calm of her own voice.

"Perhaps, Brandy, but I prefer to think that my plan is rather brilliant. As you say, no one in Scotland thought to suspect an Englishman, an Englishman, I might add, who is also the duke's own first cousin."

"On the beach . . . 'twas ye, Giles, 'twas ye!"

"Yes, and had it not been for your interference, I should now be the Duke of Portmaine."

She gazed about her, realizing almost at once where she was. "I am . . . yer bait?"

"Yes, I could hit upon no other way. I doubt not that Ian at this very moment is riding *ventre à terre* to save you. He must fail. Indeed, your duke has finally come to the end of his charmed existence."

Giles suddenly rose and cocked his ear toward the barn door. "If I mistake not, that is Ian now."

Brandy twisted about, pulling herself to a sitting position, and looked wildly toward the barn door. She screamed, "Ian! Go back!"

Brandy gazed in mute misery as Ian kicked in the rickety wooden door and hurtled into the barn. He blinked rapidly to accustom his eyes to the dim interior, then drew in his breath in disbelief. Brandy lay propped up against a moldering pile of hay. Giles was standing near to her, a pistol held in his outstretched hand.

"Giles! What the devil!" He strode forward.

"Hold right there, if you please, cousin!"

"What is the meaning of this, Giles?" The question was an absurd one, for as with Brandy, the truth of the matter burst upon him in an instant. "Brandy, are you all right?"

"Aye. Oh, Ian, ye should not have come!"

"Don't be a fool, Brandy. Clever of you, Giles, with your

Scottish spelling—you had me quite convinced that I would find Percy here."

"Yes," Giles concurred with a brief bow, "It was rather a good touch. You would have saved me much trouble, Ian, had you succumbed that first time."

"Why, Giles?"

"I do so dislike that blunt manner of yours, duke, but since you will know the truth, I must plead guilty of greed. A plain *Mister* Giles Braidston has never been to my liking, you know."

Ian said slowly, instinctively sparring for time, "But two years separate us in age, Giles. You have known all your life that I was to hold the title. As to your income, 'tis hardly to be despised."

"Paltry, Ian, paltry. I cannot remember the day when I was not heavily in debt. Being your nominal heir has, indeed, been the only bar to my more pressing creditors. No, Ian, 'tis the Duke of Portmaine that I must be, and after today, all of your vast wealth will be in my hands."

Ian forced himself to keep his voice steady, not to show incredulity or anger. "You made no attempts on my life when I married Marianne, Giles. There could quite easily have been an heir born within another year, had she not died."

Giles said, his voice almost gentle, "My dear cousin, do you not recall how very much time I spent with your young wife? We were much the same age, you know, and it required little effort on my part to gain her confidence, for she held you in tremendous awe. You always wondered, did you not, what prompted her to be so bold as to take herself off to France, supposedly to save her parents? You cursed yourself because you did not gain her trust, because you failed to save her from the guillotine. One afternoon whilst you were off at your club, I paid her a visit and found to my surprise that Sir William Dacre had just affirmed that she was pregnant. Within hours, cousin, I presented her with a letter, again supposedly written in great haste, from her esteemed parents, the Comte and Comtesse de Vaux, begging her to come to France and plead their case before Robespierre's tribunal. I was most eloquent, I assure you, and finally convinced her that if you knew she was carrying your precious heir, you would never let her journey to France. She pleaded with me to help her. I had got her to Paris when she tearfully told me that she had left you a letter. I thought myself quite done in until she told me that she had dared not mention my name for fear that you would blame *me!* I did then what I had to do. I sent Marianne's direction to the citizen's committee, and was on a packet back to London within the hour. I only discovered later that her parents had fallen under the guillotine nearly a week before."

Ian's jaw worked frantically. "You swine! You filthy bastard swine!"

"Don't move, Ian, or I swear I'll kill Brandy! Surely you must realize that there was naught else I could do. If she had borne you a son, I could have no longer nourished hope of becoming the Duke of Portmaine!"

Brandy cried, "But Miss Trammerley—Felicity!—she was to marry Ian, yet ye did not kill her, 'twas Ian who was yer target!"

Giles turned his gaze toward her for but an instant. "As I told you, Brandy, Scotland was a blessed opportunity and one I could not afford to pass by. Everyone was sure to suspect one of the Robertsons. And I must admit that Felicity was a very different kettle of fish from Marianne! Such a greedy, cold lady, Ian. How lucky you were to be rid of her. I must admit that she taxed my ingenuity, for her mind was so much set upon being the Duchess of Portmaine."

The duke said slowly, "All those barbs to her as well as to me . . . I thought it merely your way of warning me, protecting me."

"Yes, indeed, cousin. I had nearly given up hope of routing the lady when your autocratic, stubborn temper combined with her hatred of the Robertsons and Scotland finally won the day."

"You encouraged her in her jealousy, did you not, Giles? 'Twas you who pushed her to come to Scotland, you who made her question my honor."

"Your reasoning, as usual, cousin, is acute. Of course I did not realize until the letter you wrote me on the day you left London that your regard had fallen in quite another direction. How did it feel, Ian, to have your betrothed and your mistress under the same roof?"

"Ian! Don't, I pray ye!" Brandy cried at the duke's sudden furious step forward.

Giles took a hasty step backward, only a few feet in front of Brandy. Brandy found herself growing almost morbidly calm, for she knew that Giles would kill them both when he had finished his bragging. She barely heard Giles's voice as she frantically searched about for something, anything she could use as a weapon. She had almost decided to hurl herself at him, when she espied a long wooden-handled haying fork, half buried under clumps of moldering hay. She inched toward it until the toe of her shoe reached the fork.

"Surely you must realize, Ian," Giles said, "that I cannot allow you to wed Brandy. I, of course, regret what I must do, but there is simply no other way. My plan is distasteful, I admit, for I do not wish to kill Brandy. But there is no hope for it."

Ian felt the butt of the pistol resting against his leg. It was but seconds away from his tensed hand. He saw Brandy moving slowing behind Giles. If only somehow she could distract him, if but for an instant.

"I regret, Ian, that I must conclude our conversation. I have a long ride ahead of me and wish to be well ensconced in London when the news of your tragic death at the hand of a Scottish Robertson comes to my ears."

From the corner of his eye, Ian saw that Brandy was easing the haying fork into her hands. If Giles saw her movement, all would be lost. He rushed into speech.

"I had never guessed that you so despised me, Giles. Did you conceive your plan when you first heard of my Scottish inheritance?"

"No, not at first. But enough, Ian. I am not without feeling and assume that you would wish to die first. I am truly sorry, cousin, but I must now bid you a final adieu."

"No!" Brandy shrieked as she heaved up the haying fork and, with all her strength, swung it against Giles's back.

More startled than hurt, Giles whirled on her, striking the side of her face with the butt of his pistol, sending her sprawling to the ground.

Ian hurled himself toward Giles, grabbing furiously at his arm. They grappled in panting silence, Giles struggling to turn the pistol inward to the duke's chest. He felt himself weakening in his cousin's powerful grasp and tried desperately to pull himself free. He stumbled backward, jerking the duke with him. Ian stepped on the pronged blades of the haying fork, and the wooden handle whipped up, striking his arm. Giles drove his fist into Ian's stomach and leaped back, shakily aiming the pistol at the duke's head.

"Hold, Mr. Braidston!"

Giles only dimly heard the sharp command. As he tightened his finger on the trigger, he heard a crashing report explode in his ears.

Ian watched in amazement as Giles, his face distorted in ghastly surprise, weaved above him, then fell heavily to the ground.

"Are you all right, y'grace?"

Ian gazed up into the leathery face above him, for an instant too stunned to speak. "You saved our lives, man! Who the devil are you?"

"Me name's Scroggins, y'grace," he said, and dropped the smoking pistol to help Ian to his feet. "The young lady hired me two months ago to protect you. You've led me a fine chase, y'grace, what with all your gallivanting about in London, then your trip to Scotland. Always fancied visiting Scotland, I did."

The two hundred pounds. "Brandy!"

Brandy was struggling up on her elbows, her vision blurred from the blow Giles had given her. "I am all right, Ian. Aye, I am all right."

Ian dropped to his knees beside her and cupped her chin in his hand. Gently his fingers explored the line of her jaw. He smiled at her tenderly. "Your jaw isn't broken, thank God." He turned briefly toward Giles's fallen body. "He's dead?"

"Yes, indeed, y'grace. I couldn't take the chance of only winging 'im, for he still might have shot you."

"My thanks, Scroggins."

Scroggins chuckled. "I don't mind telling you, y'grace, I was beginning to wonder if the young lady weren't a bit screwy in her thinking! But an assignment is as you finds it, even though you have to trek all over the countryside." He frowned down at Giles's still form. "Mighty wily cove, your cousin was. Very nearly fooled I was! But I knowed something was in the wind when you flew off on that mighty brute's back, your eyes blazing murder."

Ian gazed a final time at Giles's prone figure. Brandy placed her hand upon his arm. "Let us leave this place, yer grace."

"I'll take care of 'im, y'grace, you take care of the young lady."

Ian nodded and, cupping Brandy's elbow with his hand for support, walked beside her from the barn. The bright afternoon sun blazed down from a cloudless blue sky. Ian drew a deep breath. Never had life seemed more precious and, at the same time, more fragile.

"I owe you much, Brandy, including my life. I cannot remember when the expenditure of two hundred pounds bought me so very much."

"I never knew who the man was. You see, Mr. MacPherson arranged it all. He proudly informed me that he had hired the services of a former Bow Street Runner." She paused a moment, gazing up at his profile. "I am sorry for deceiving ye, Ian, but I thought if I told ye the truth about the money, ye would be extraordinarily angry, mayhap even send MacPherson and the man I hired packing."

He thought grimly that this might very likely have been the case. "Perhaps," he said. "How do you feel, my love?" He gently laid his fingers against her cheek.

"Like I've been knocked in the head too many times."

"I fear that you will be black and blue at your wedding. Everyone will think that I am a cruel man, not at all worthy of you," he added with only a glimmer of a smile.

"Ian . . . I am so sorry about Marianne."

For a moment, he could not bring himself to speak. "Thank you, Brandy," he said and, scooping her up in his arms, swung up upon Hercules's back. "Let us go home."

～ 14 ～

Davers, the Carmichael butler for more than thirty-five summers, a fact that he unhesitatingly employed to dampen pretensions amongst the junior members of the duke's staff, gazed out on the front lawn from the long parlor windows at two loudly squawking peacocks that had just proudly emerged, tail feathers spread in riotous color, from behind the stalwart trunks of the line of elm trees that bordered the perimeter of the home wood.

"Grabble-tongued creatures," he muttered to Mrs. Osmington, the duke's briskly efficient housekeeper. "Wouldn't surprise me one mite if Dr. Mulhouse, jokester that he is, presented them as a wedding present only because her grace said that England lacked the color of Scotland. It's my belief that the scraggly bleaters will scare away the deer!"

"Well, you must know, Davers," said Mrs. Osmington, her fingers unconsciously fiddling with the huge circle of keys at her waist, "I heard her grace laugh in that good-natured way of hers and say that what she had been thinking of was purple heather, not peacocks."

Davers grunted and turned away from the windows. He withdrew a large round watch from his black coat pocket. "Dr. Mulhouse has been upstairs for over an hour with her grace. It is hoped that all is well with the heir."

Mrs. Osmington nodded her head in a peculiarly birdlike movement. "At least her grace, most sensibly in my opinion, is very conscious of her delicate condition, not galloping about the countryside like Lady Dorrington, who I am convinced, suffered complications because——" She drew to a disconcerted halt. "How right you are! Such a long time it has been and nearly lunchtime it is. I must inform Cook that it's likely we'll have another place at the table."

Dr. Edward Mulhouse was at that moment gently admonishing his flushed and embarrassed patient. "Come, Brandy, relax your stomach muscles. There, that is much better. Ah, the babe kicked me." He smiled as his hand carefully pressed against her growing belly. " 'Tis a lively child you'll have, Brandy."

"The babe's a little brute," Ian said, trying his best to distract Brandy. "In that respect, he will be just like his mother."

"I don't know about that," Edward said, rising. "From the way he kicks, I venture to think that he will be toplofty and full of his own consequence, like his father!"

The two men laughed, like those conceited crowing peacocks, Brandy thought resentfully, glaring at the both of them as she hastily pulled down her nightgown.

Edward did not turn back to her until she had completed this operation. "You're the picture of health, Brandy, and so is the babe. You've nothing to worry about, save, of course, Ian's fidgets, which must, I am certain, drive you quite distracted! I swear if he demands one more detail of the birthing process, I shall think him questioning my abilities and be forced to give him a sharp setdown!"

"Don't be impertinent, Edward! My love, I will send Lucy to you, though it is likely that your little pug of a maid is at this moment pacing the corridor like a clucking mother hen. Come downstairs with me, Edward, whilst Brandy dresses. You'll have luncheon with us, of course." Ian patted Brandy's hand and accompanied Edward from the bedchamber.

Edward said ruefully as they walked down the great staircase, past the second footman, into the hunting room, "If you hadn't been present, I believe she would have refused even to admit me."

"Perhaps, but in spite of her grumbling, she did keep to the bargain. You know, she promised when the babe kicked that she would let you examine her. Now, Edward, is everything truly as excellent as you told Brandy?"

"Indeed yes," Edward said, accepting a glass of sherry. "The babe is smaller than I expected and that is good. I think the less weight she gains the better. 'Twill make the birthing

211

easier for her. At least that is the modern view of many of your top-o'-the trees accoucheurs in London." Edward's blue eyes twinkled. "She is also carrying the babe very high, which in my experience, indicates a boy. But I refuse to lay a wager with you!"

"I believe Brandy is thinking wistfully of a daughter—a pert, redheaded little girl like her sister, Fiona. The child will come to live with us after the birth of the baby."

"Good lord, Ian, what a staid, virtuous family man you're becoming! Within a year of your marriage, you'll have two children hanging on your coattails. What is this Brandy was telling me the other day—you've struck some sort of Proserpine arrangement?"

"Nothing quite so mythological or as formal as all that. I assure you that I do not equate Hades with Scotland, and indeed look forward to spending the spring months at Penderleigh. I would never ask Brandy to become completely uprooted from what she has held dear for her entire life."

Edward moved closer to the fire. "You almost convince me to beg a place in your party. Lord, but the cold weather is upon us early this year."

"I only hope that your peacocks take a chill and fold down their feathers!"

"Unkind, Ian, unkind! What is one to bestow upon a duke at his marriage?" He gazed a moment about the large, dark-paneled chamber, the gun collections sufficient, he thought wryly, to outfit an entire regiment. "I do trust that the peacocks don't keep you awake at night with their squawking."

"Much you would care, my needle-witted friend. Speaking of needle-witted, I've a letter from Scotland, from Lady Adella. Its contents are certain to divert Brandy's mind from her trying experience with you. I only hope that she will not go into convulsions at what the old lady terms 'the earl's blockish, repulsive behavior'! Poor Claude, he's only held the title for little more than a month now. I dread to hear how he will be stigmatized when we go to Penderleigh in April."

Although Brandy did not fall into convulsions at the rather lengthy recital of Lady Adella's woes, she did choke over her soup with laughter, causing her husband to pat her on the back and adjure her to behave with more dignity, as befitted her station.

"Poor Grandmama! She sounds dreadfully out of curl. To think," she added in an awed voice, "that Uncle Claude would have the temerity to order her to turn over the keys of the castle to Constance! Not, of course, that Grandmama ever much concerned herself with housekeeping matters, but to call her naught but 'a meddlesome, interfering old woman and *only* the dowager countess'—I vow she must have been near to apoplexy."

"She sounds like a regular old Tartar," Edward said.

"That she is, but I fancy she will come about. Ah, Brandy, listen to this: Lady Adella says that Percy has been hot off the mark and 'planted a bairn in Joanna's belly.' It appears that Percy is showing himself quite the model husband, a circumstance, she adds, that will last only as long as Joanna's extreme strength of character."

"We must write," Brandy interposed, "and say all that is proper. I think if anyone can curb Percy's more undesirable tendencies, it is Joanna."

"I doubt that not," the duke said dryly. "It is she who holds the purse strings. Her last scrawling line, if I can make it out—ah, yes, it appears that Fiona begs her to tell you that she has nearly tamed the porridge, no papou——"

"Porpoise, Ian, porpoise! How delightful for her."

"And I thought you were the only mermaid, my love. Although a pregnant mermaid is almost more than I care to contemplate."

"Odious man," Brandy retorted, flinging her napkin at him. "Do tell him, Edward, that we are to have twins. That would give him his just deserts, to have a mountainously gross and lumpy wife."

Edward laughed. "I cannot, Brandy. You must find another way to give him his comeuppance."

Ian grinned at her, refusing to be drawn. He looked down again at Lady Adella's letter. "Your esteemed grandmother appears to have spent all her excess bile, it would seem. Well, Edward, now that you are in possession of the bulk of our family skeletons, I trust that you will not resort to blackmail."

"Nothing so exciting, I fear. Indeed," he added with a slight grimace, consulting his watch, "I must leave your amiable company and pay a visit to Rigby Hall. Lady Eleanor, you know, is breeding again."

As they rose from the table, Ian said, "Poor Edward, if the gentlemen of your acquaintance continue the way they are going, you will find yourself boot-deep in babes."

"Ye are odiously vulgar, yer grace," Brandy said, as she smoothed the pale yellow muslin gown over her rounded belly.

They stood on the front steps and waved Edward on his way. Brandy turned her face up to her husband. "Ye know," she said in great seriousness, "that England simply does not have the *smell* of Scotland."

"No, there are no sheep within many miles of here."

"*That* is not what I meant!"

"I know, love," he said, tucking her hand in the crook of his arm. "But to recompense you for the sea and the heather, we do boast two terribly smart peacocks."

About the Author

Catherine Coulter was born and raised on a ranch in Texas and educated at the University of Texas and Boston College, a background which has left her equally fond of horseback riding, Baroque music, and European history. She has traveled widely and settled for a time in England and France, where she developed a special interest in Regency England and the Napoleonic era.

Today, Catherine Coulter is both a writer and a businesswoman, living in San Francisco. She is also the author of several other Regency Romances—THE AUTUMN COUNTESS, THE REBEL BRIDE, LORD DEVERILL'S HEIR, and LORD HARRY'S FOLLY—available in Signet editions.

Recommended Regency Romances from SIGNET